"You'll never trust me, will you?"

Sam shook his head and continued. "You can't get beyond the fact that I was an ass way back when. Well, I've got a news flash for you, sweetheart." He stood and leaned toward her, eyes glittering. "People can change! But you're so stubborn—or so terrified of really living—that you won't take people out of the little compartments you've put them in. Face it, Beth, you're afraid of change. You can't handle it."

She started to protest, but he interrupted her, saying, "I'm glad I know now that I'm unable to live with your opinion of me. If we ever got married—heaven forbid—you'd always be expecting me to fail you. With every mistake I made, you'd say, 'That's the real Sam coming out,' instead of, 'Sam, who's a pretty terrific guy, made a mistake.'" He looked at her coldly, tremendously disappointed.

"I think you'd better leave," Beth whispered....

ABOUT THE AUTHOR

After working in the publishing field for
several years, Beverley Bryan makes her debut
as author with the publication of her first
Superromance novel, *What Friends Are For*. The
book's setting of Orillia, Ontario, is special to
Bev because it was there, while working at a
summer camp, that she met her husband. The
couple, along with their dog, Casper, make
their home in Toronto.

What Friends are For

BEVERLEY BRYAN

Harlequin Books

TORONTO • NEW YORK • LONDON
AMSTERDAM • PARIS • SYDNEY • HAMBURG
STOCKHOLM • ATHENS • TOKYO • MILAN

Published September 1991

ISBN 0-373-70469-0

WHAT FRIENDS ARE FOR

To Brian Rosenbaum,
for his love and support,
and to Norman and Lorraine Katz,
for encouraging creativity and independence.

Special thanks to Paula Ruch,
my big sister and personal dietitian,
for her assistance.

PROLOGUE

DR. ROBERT GEFFEN slowly lifted his gaze from the charts on his desk to Sam Sarnoff's serious face. Solemnly he said, "I'm afraid my news isn't good, Sam."

Sam shut his eyes and felt his heartbeat accelerate. So this was what it had come to—all the late nights of desperate studying to get that scholarship to business school, all the long days of excruciatingly hard work once he'd entered the business world—all down the tubes.

An image of his dead father sprang suddenly and unexpectedly into his mind. The humble immigrant from Kiev, Russia, had worked as a common laborer for most of his days in Canada, and it had pained Sam that his kind, selfless father, who was so deserving of the finer things in life, had never been able to afford them. Sam had vowed to make good, and had grown up with a vision of buying a new and luxurious house for his beloved Ma and Pa, even though his father had gently admonished him for valuing material over spiritual success.

So here he was, a successful entrepreneur—well on his way to becoming a millionaire—with a gorgeous, if slightly sterile condominium and plenty of cash, stocks and bonds, but little else to show for his life of thirty years. His long-gone parents were, no doubt, looking down at him from heaven and shaking their heads sadly at the horrible lesson their sweet but misguided son had learned.

He wondered vaguely how much time he had and what it was he had contracted. He had felt lousy enough to finally agree to undergo a complete physical examination, but he hadn't dreamed he'd been suffering from anything life-threatening. It was probably some form of cancer; both his parents had been cursed with it. It occurred to him that he should have been glad there were no children to watch him suffer, but he only felt a sharp pang at the realization that he hadn't shared his good fortune with anyone or influenced anyone's life to any great extent.

He opened his eyes. "What is it?" he croaked, barely able to get the words out.

Bob, whom Sam had known since grade school, spoke firmly but gently. "I'm going to make a phone call that will explain everything. Listen carefully, all right?"

As if in a trance, Sam watched his old friend pick up the phone and dial. It struck him that there were too many digits for a local call. Some kind of experimental treatment center? he wondered dimly, his senses working at half speed.

"Hello, may I please speak to Dr. Joel Green?"

Suddenly a wave of sheer panic washed over Sam. *This can't be happening,* he thought, stricken, and for the first time since his mother had died, he composed a short, to-the-point prayer. *Please God, if you only spare me, I'll do whatever you want. I'll give all my money to charity, I'll be good to my fellowman, and I'll take care of myself. Just please let me have another chance—*

"Hiya, good buddy, it's Bob.... Not a whole heck of a lot. How about yourself...? No, I don't believe it!"

Just tell me what I've got, Sam thought irritably, annoyed at Bob's back-slapping tone.

"Oh, is that right...? You don't say... Heh-heh, well, those of us practising *real* medicine, away from your country-club atmosphere, would disagree!"

Now Sam was positively fuming at Bob's jocularity. How dare he make light of the situation, and how dare he ridicule the treatment centers that were doing so much good! Was that actually a twinkle in his eye? *Insensitive so-and-so,* Sam thought furiously. *Where the hell is your bedside manner?*

"Hey, listen, Joel. I've got a patient here—an old friend, actually—who's desperately in need of some spa-type pampering. He's well on the way to high blood pressure, high cholesterol, obesity, alcoholism—take your pick. Do you think you can fit him in for, oh, two weeks, starting on Saturday?"

Spa-type pampering... on the way to high blood pressure...

Sam's despondency promptly vanished. "You low-life!" he yelled, trying to yank the phone away from Bob. "What are you trying to do? Kill me by shock?"

Bob held on firmly to the phone and said, "Great. I'll call you later with more details." He hung up and held a warning hand out to Sam, who was about to grab his collar. "Now, just hold on a second, buddy. All I said was my news wasn't good. You did the rest."

Sam's hand stopped in midair, and his brown eyes narrowed to slits. Slowly lowering his hands, he said accusingly, "You knew damn well what you were doing."

Bob leaned back in his chair. "Okay, so maybe I did try to scare you a little bit."

Sam began to pace like a caged animal. He quickly ran his hands through his thick, chestnut-colored but prematurely graying hair. "Why? Jeez, Bob, you know my parents both died of cancer. You scared the living daylights out of me."

Bob sat forward in his chair and looked directly into Sam's eyes. Bluntly he said, "Some people need to be scared."

Sam looked at him warily for a long moment, then sat back down in the chair across from Bob's desk. "Okay, I'm listening."

"Good." Once again, Bob tilted his chair back. After a long pause he said carefully, "You told me you were having trouble sleeping and concentrating. You also told me you drank a fair bit and ate on the run most of the time. And you work like the devil and have little time for leisure. All of those things point to a fairly high level of stress that's not being combated by exercise—"

"I exercised enough for a lifetime in high school, didn't I?" Sam shot back, feeling the need to defend himself.

Bob shook his head. "Sorry, pal. It doesn't work that way. Your present fitness level is quite low—remember the caliper and treadmill tests we did?—and your dietary habits are atrocious, based on what you told me. You're about thirty pounds overweight right now. Sam, although your parents ultimately died of cancer, remember your father also suffered from heart disease and your mother had high blood pressure. Heredity is not on your side, friend, and unless you change your ways and live a healthier life, you'll end up with a whole host of medical problems, too. And most likely, you'll die an early death." He looked at Sam intently and added, "I'm being hard on you because I care about you. I don't like watching people I care about throw their lives away."

Sam lifted his head slightly to stare beyond Bob's head, out the window behind him. Only a few moments ago he'd been sure he was dying. Now he was being given a second chance. Did he want it?

The question had popped into his head quickly, shocking him. Of course he wanted it. Who wouldn't? Immediately an answering voice piped up, *Well, you don't have much to live for, do you?*

Another shocker.

He took a moment to try to think of something—anything—that made his life worth living. There was his job. It had satisfied him at one point, had made him feel as if he were keeping part of his heritage alive.

His mother had been so pleased when he'd expressed interest in marketing her "secret" Russian-style recipes for mustards, sauces and salad dressings. She hadn't lived to see the product line become the huge success it was, in demand not only in all the finest stores in Toronto, but all across North America. Now he didn't so much enjoy his work as throw himself into it with an almost religious zeal. In many ways it had become a memorial to his parents. It suddenly occurred to him that it was also something more: a means of staving off the incredible emptiness of the rest of his life....

"Tell me about this spa thing," he finally asked Bob.

Bob grinned. "I knew you'd listen to reason. My powers of persuasion are phenomenal."

"Your powers of persuasion stink. I could have croaked from heart failure right here on your beautiful pearl-gray carpet."

Bob's hands flew up. "All right, all right!" He reached into a file drawer in his desk, pulled out a handful of brochures and handed them to Sam. "It's a great place. I went to medical school with the resident physician—the guy I just spoke to. Also on the premises are a dietitian, a psychologist, exercise instructors, and great facilities. There are more luxurious spas you could go to—at incredibly inflated prices—but as far as I'm concerned, this place has more than enough. And the food there is fabulous."

Sam looked suspicious. "Don't they starve you at these places?"

Bob shook his head. "Uh-uh. This place believes in teaching people good habits for life. No crash dieting here. I'm telling you, Sam, after a couple of weeks at Couchiching Spa, you'll want to live healthily for the rest of your life. You'll feel relaxed and in tune with your body. Oh, and there's gorgeous scenery, too."

It had been a long time since he'd had a holiday, Sam mused. Or any fun, for that matter. And Bob was making the place sound like a regular resort. *Who knows,* he thought, *maybe I'll even meet someone....*

Now where had that thought come from, he wondered with a start. Was that what his inner voice had been trying to tell him? That he needed a mate? He *had* been somewhat of a hermit in the past couple of years, only occasionally attending dinner parties or going out on blind dates set up by well-meaning friends. He'd had plenty of casual sexual encounters in his college days—most of which he regretted—and forgettable one-night stands were not what he was looking for now. But he didn't have the time to invest in searching for a woman he could spend the rest of his life with.

Maybe you should make the time, a little voice whispered in his ear. And out of nowhere a vision of a pretty, plump brunette from long ago flashed into his mind—someone he might have been happy with. All at once he made a decision.

"Okay, Bob. Call your friend back. Tell him he can expect me this Saturday."

CHAPTER ONE

"GEE," BETH FINLAYSON said dryly as she looked around Jill Sanders's close-to-empty living room. "You've done a great job with the place."

Jill sighed dramatically. "There's no need for sarcasm. You're supposed to be my best friend—tell me whatever I do is okay and all that." She plopped down on a floor cushion. "I know I promised I'd have it finished by the first of June, but I just couldn't seem to scrape up the cash." Her eyes lit up. "Say, what if I tell people it's *supposed* to look like this? Isn't minimalism in style?"

Beth had to laugh at the sight of the petite but energetic blonde sprawled on the floor, looking at her with eager eyes. "You know, it just might work," she said. More seriously, she added, "I know what you mean about the money. My place is sort of on hold, too—" she glanced around briefly "—though I must admit I'm ahead of you by leaps and bounds."

That was what they got for being partners in a successful spa, she mused. Just when they had begun to accumulate some money, they had invested in personal property, putting themselves in a house-rich, cash-poor situation.

Jill got up and headed toward the kitchen. On the way, she called, "I'd love to be able to tell you to put your feet up, but... Say, what do you want, anyway? I don't have much—peach cooler, beer, diet cola..."

"Do you have any food? I'm starving."

"Didn't you eat dinner?"

"No, I worked through it."

Jill sounded shocked. "Miss Three-balanced-meals-a-day *worked through dinner?* For shame!"

"Oh, stuff it," Beth said amiably. "I'm only human. And besides, some of Jane's more esoteric experiments simply do not agree with me. There were three choices, as usual, but only one entrée didn't have flowers in it. That was the steak teriyaki, and I've just about overdosed on it. I think Jane's resorting to repetition just to make us try the artsy stuff."

Jane Bunting was the spa's ultracompetent, ultraimaginative, and sometimes ultratemperamental cook. Though Jane had a free hand in the kitchen—Beth concentrated on counseling clients while Jane handled all purchasing and cooking for the dining room—Beth still had to work fairly closely with Jane on a consulting level, which sometimes took its toll. Fortunately she had managed to talk Jane into serving at least one simple entrée at each meal, and no one could touch her skinless chicken dishes or her mouth-watering vegetarian lasagna. All foods served in the dining room were low in calories, sodium and fat content—Beth approved all recipes. Generally she enjoyed the eccentric cook's cuisine, but at times even she secretly longed for regular old meat loaf, or macaroni and cheese.

Jill, on the other hand, made no secret of her preferences. "Believe me, you have my sympathy," she said. "I drove to Dairy Queen. But I don't have anything you would want, my dear—unless dietitians are into nachos and ice-cream bars these days." After a pause she added, "There's an unidentifiable green object on the middle shelf of my fridge, but I'm not sure if that means it's healthy or just moldy."

"I think I'll pass. I will have that diet cola, though."

A moment later, Jill came back into the living room with a wine cooler and a diet cola—and two straws.

Beth rolled her eyes. "Minimalism in utensils, too?"

Jill grinned. "Right on. Glasses are passé, didn't you know?"

They sank onto the floor, with their backs to a wall.

"Ahh." Beth sighed after taking a long, slow sip of the drink. "It's been a tough day."

"Tell me about it! Have you met with the new-age architect yet?"

Beth nearly choked on their drinks. "Did I ever! Is he for real? He told me people should garnish their dinner plates with amethyst crystals and consider the building of a house a Zen-like experience."

Jill giggled. "He had a whole entourage of groupies with him at stretch-and-strength class. He insisted on giving me his reaction to each exercise—along with the reactions of the various spirits that inhabit his body.''

''You're kidding!''

''I wish I were. And don't think the rest of them didn't get into the act. He turned my exercise class into a regular encounter group! I'm eternally grateful that he's only here for the weekend, though I'm sure there'll be a handful of crackpots to take his place.''

Now it was Beth's turn to giggle. Then, glancing at her watch, she said, ''Speaking of encounter groups, shouldn't we head over to the meeting? Mike called it for eight.''

Jill turned doleful eyes on her friend. ''Can't we play hooky?''

Beth shot Jill a concerned look. ''He's not still giving you trouble, is he?'' Mike Petrie was the business manager in the three-year-old venture and another partner, along with Dr. Joel Green, the resident physician, and Dr. Selma White, the spa's behavioral psychologist.

The five partners had been friends all through university, having originally met as undergraduates at the University of Guelph in Guelph, Ontario. They had all lived in the same residence building, and though their personalities were quite different, they had soon found themselves fast friends due to their shared values— each of them possessed a fiercely independent spirit and a desire to get the most out of life. Jill and Beth, who roomed together, had become particularly close, the lively and popular Jill drawing out the quieter

Beth, and Beth, in turn, getting Jill to become more attuned to her sensitive, analytical side.

The bunch had kept in touch even after some had gone on to different graduate schools. After a few years in the business world, during which they had experienced a collective depression, they had realized their talents could be pooled if they opened a spa together. The idea had been born after they'd consumed a few liters of cheap wine one evening, and rather remarkably, it had still seemed feasible in daylight. They'd given it their best shot, and within two years, all debts had been paid off and a healthy profit margin had begun to show itself.

So far, their personal relationships hadn't threatened their business relationships, but Beth knew Mike could make life miserable for Jill if he wanted to. Beth had suspected for a while that the slick financial wizard was carrying a torch for the perky fitness director. He was a smooth operator who would make subtle passes at virtually any attractive female he came in contact with, but he'd bombarded Jill even more than most lately. This was strange, considering that he'd known her for years, and until recently, had never indicated any romantic interest. He'd changed rather suddenly and was getting more and more aggressive. It was almost as if he couldn't believe that someone he was attracted to could resist him. Mike was a man who usually got what he wanted. Beth was grateful that she wasn't his type: he liked his women vivacious and bubbly.

Jill nodded and sighed. "Unfortunately I must answer in the affirmative. That's the price I have to pay for being nice to him, I guess. The guy's a genius when it comes to making money—I admire him for that particular talent—and he's fun to go out with on occasion, especially since he looks so great in tight jeans, but it was obviously a mistake to play the pal with him. I just don't know what's gotten into him lately."

She shook her head. "Recently he's taken to presenting me with 'small' tokens of his affection: gold pins, sterling-silver earrings, personalized stationery and very expensive perfume. When I try to tell him I can't accept them, he gets mad." She shook her head again. "I should have kept a respectable distance, like you."

"Oh, I don't know about that," Beth mused. "I think underneath all the attitude, Mike's a pretty sensitive guy." She paused for a moment and sipped at her cola. "He was really sweet when I had my appendix out, remember? I have seen him in reflective moods. Unfortunately they're few and far between." She hesitated again, then shrugged and said, "I've just never known how to deal with superslick people like Mike."

Jill looked at her friend and said, "Oh, come on. You're not nearly as shy now as you were in university. You were just a late bloomer." At that, Beth jabbed her friend playfully on the arm, but Jill continued. "You fairly radiate confidence and sophistication now. What's more, you're a thousand times better looking than me, and since Mike seems to have a thing for tall, long-haired brunettes, I'm really baffled. You even have blue eyes.'' She sighed. "Why me?"

Beth grinned. "For the same reason all the men flocked to you in college. Your sparkling personality." She got up and said, "Well, shall we go?"

"Yeah, yeah," Jill grumbled, getting up, too. "Here, give me your can. Just let me have five minutes to freshen up, okay?"

Soon they were walking along a woodsy path to Mike's bungalow. Mike had been the first to build a home on the spa property—Beth had always thought cynically that he'd welcomed the opportunity to romance the guests—and he'd quickly been followed by Selma and Joel when more land had become available. Beth and Jill had been the holdouts, not sure whether they wanted to give up the considerable benefits of living in a cosmopolitan city like Toronto for the relatively slow pace of life in Orillia, Ontario, population 24,000.

Before living at the spa, they had shared a room there on weekdays, and on weekends had gone back to the apartment they shared in Toronto; Beth's receptionist scheduled only weekday appointments, and Jill's assistant took over her exercise classes when she was gone. But the spa had begun to demand more and more of their time, and soon, the commute, which took an hour and a half each way, simply became too much of a burden. When their friends and co-workers began moving to the spa, and new and interesting guests began to arrive every day, it no longer seemed such a bad idea to leave the city they'd grown up in. Not to mention the fact that the cost of living was far more manageable in Orillia than Toronto. Moreover, the spa grounds were simply stunning, set off by the natural beauty of Lake Couchiching.

The spa's glass-and-cedar main building, where the majority of guest rooms were located—there were a few luxurious bungalows for the well-heeled—blended beautifully with the surrounding landscape. A spacious living-dining area with floor-to-ceiling windows overlooked the lake, rolling hills and lovely gardens. Also in the main building were the partners' offices, an indoor swimming pool—for those who disliked the lake—a lounge, a library and a music room.

Special evening programs for the guests were carefully planned by an energetic young woman named Polly Palmer who lived in town. Sometimes, the partners participated. But most nights they would go into town, where they might stroll along Mississaga Street, Orillia's "main drag," or eat a leisurely dinner at The Ossawippi Express, a restored historic railway train in which fine French food was served. Sometimes they would walk in lovely Centennial Park, on the shore of the lake, or ride in Mike's luxury passenger boat, which was docked in the marina there. Of course, one could always just curl up with a book at home. All in all, it was a peaceful life, and Beth was quite satisfied.

She sighed contentedly.

"Whatcha thinkin' about?" Jill asked.

"Just that I'm happy here."

Jill smiled. "Yeah, me, too. It's a nice life." When they arrived at Mike's door, she added, "Although it does have its drawbacks."

Beth slapped her friend on the back playfully. "Not to worry, friend. I'll protect you."

Jill rolled her eyes and said, "Now why doesn't that comfort me?"

They stepped inside, and as always, Beth found herself admiring Mike's impressive home. The walls were a cool white, and the open-concept living-dining area contained a minimum of furniture, but every piece was gorgeous—and expensive looking. Leather couches and ultramodern paintings in pastel colors dominated the room. The dining table was made of pickled pine, and a beautiful flower-patterned dhurrie rug was spread over the bleached hardwood floor. A fire was crackling behind the grate of the white-painted brick fireplace, and the track lights above the couches were set down low. Beth wondered, as she always did, how Mike had managed to put the place together so quickly, and as always, she came to the conclusion that a business manager had to know things about saving money that ordinary mortals didn't.

She waved cheerfully to Mike, Selma and Joel, who were standing in front of the fireplace, but before she could say anything, Jill grumbled, "For God's sake, Mike, give us some light or we'll all fall asleep." With that, she walked over to join the group, Beth following.

Mike, who was a bit too tall, too dark and too handsome for Beth's taste—he just missed sleazy, in her judgment—grinned lasciviously and said, "A little romantic atmosphere never hurt anybody."

Beth and Jill exchanged a quick look, but Jill was spared having to reply when Joel grabbed Mike by the shoulders and cried, "Mike, I never knew you cared! So many wasted years! So much—"

"Can it, Green," Mike said darkly as he watched the women saunter over to the sofa.

Joel, the lighthearted doctor who Beth always thought looked like a leprechaun due to his short, thick stature and reddish hair and beard, replied jovially, "Okay, okay. Let's just get this show on the road. This is not my idea of a swell time, Mike, my man. Some of us do have better things to do." The other partners knew that Joel had started to date an attractive divorcée who lived in town. Beth was pleased for the good doctor; he had an abundance of warmth and love to share with a woman. Mike on the other hand, seemed merely jealous of his friend's good fortune.

At Mike's hard look, Joel put up his hands. "Okay, no more hassling, I promise. But puh-leeze, let's get this over with!"

"I'm not sure it's that simple," Mike said, a bit melodramatically, Beth thought. At Mike's words, she, Jill and Selma turned their attention to the men.

"Sounds ominous," Selma commented. "Why don't you sit down and tell us more?"

Mike promptly lowered himself onto the love seat across from the sofa, and bowed his head for a moment before lifting it again and looking slowly around the circle of now-curious faces. He took a deep breath before he began talking.

"I guess the only way to do this is just to come right out and state the problem, which is, basically, that overhead costs have risen substantially in the past few months, but incoming revenues haven't." He paused for a moment, appearing to choose his words carefully. "We can't do much about the basic overhead costs. We've made some improvements here, and thus have brought on some of the extra costs ourselves. But apart from that, utility costs have been raised across the board. What we have to do—and soon—is figure out ways we can increase business. We've been doing well, but the numbers are telling us we have to have a full house much of the time if we're to have a hope of really making it big." Once again he looked around the circle. This time the faces registered surprise, even mild shock.

"Just how bad is it?" Joel asked, quite serious now.

"Bad enough to make us want to pull up our socks and not rest on our laurels. We've accomplished a lot in the past three years, but it's time to enter a new phase. Instead of concentrating on building the business, we now have to streamline, make it one-hundred percent cost-effective. Which brings me to another thing we have to do, and that is, figure out which special touches we've added, or were planning to add, that we can do without.''

Beth broke in. ''Mike, why can't we just raise our prices in proportion to the added costs?''

Mike brought his fingers together in a pyramid shape and replied, a tad patronizingly in Beth's opinion, ''It doesn't always work that way, Beth. Don't forget, we're still a pretty small-potatoes operation compared to the really cushy spas. There's a ceiling to the prices we can charge. If we go above that ceiling, potential customers might take their business elsewhere, figuring that for a couple of hundred bucks extra, they could go to one of the more luxurious places.''

At that, Selma, the most practical of the bunch— Beth thought of her as a surrogate mother, though she was the same age as the rest of them—said bracingly, ''Okay, we understand the problem. What, exactly, are we supposed to do?''

''Well, like I said, we should all try to come up with ways we can cut costs in our individual departments. Secondly, we should all think of ways we can increase business without incurring extra costs. We don't have to do that tonight. We can think about it and meet again in a few days.''

''I'm for that,'' Jill announced. ''I don't know about the rest of you, but this is really upsetting to me. I doubt I could even talk about it rationally now.'' She turned an accusing look on Mike. "Why didn't you tell us sooner?"

In a hurt tone, Mike responded, "That's not fair, Jill. I'm telling you now. We're not sunk yet. There are lots of things we can do. I'm being up-front with you."

"He's right, Jill," Beth said decisively. "If you all recall, we played a much more active role in the business management of the spa in the beginning, but it was obvious the rest of us were complete dunces at that sort of thing. We agreed to let Mike take over, and only give our input when we looked at the annual reports. I, for one, still trust Mike to do what's best. I expect he's done just that until now and will continue to do so in the future."

"I agree," Selma said, turning a comforting smile on Mike.

"I guess I do, too," Joel agreed, shrugging.

"Same here," Jill admitted, jumping up and beginning to pace nervously. "It just makes me so mad. We work so hard and we still have to worry about going under. It's so unfair."

"Hey," Beth said excitedly. "I just remembered something. That reporter from *City Life* is coming to do an article on us soon—on June 15, I think." *City Life* was a weekly newspaper that dealt with arts and leisure in and around Toronto. The group had been thrilled when a reporter had contacted them about doing a piece on the spa.

"That's right," Selma said approvingly. "He's sure to be positive about us. And *City Life* has a huge circulation. If a piece in there doesn't do the trick, nothing will.''

"Great," Joel said with enthusiasm, turning to Mike. "So everything's fine and we can leave now, right?''

Mike shook his head. "I'm afraid we'll have to institute measures before then. June 15 is less than two weeks away. This is a crisis situation. I suggest we meet again in a week to discuss what we're going to do, and we'll take it from there. I really don't think the changes we'll be making will influence the article, so don't worry about that." He rose. "So, back here next Friday, okay?''

Joel headed for the door at a rapid pace, and the rest of the group shuffled out dispiritedly. When Jill reached the door, she called out, "Wait, didn't anybody get ahold of this week's reservation list?''

Mike snapped his fingers. "Yeah, I did. Hang on a minute—I'll get it." As he walked to his study he said loudly, "Karen was in a really foul mood today, so you guys better appreciate this." Karen Blondell, the reservations manager and customer service representative, was a middle-aged local woman who lived with her mother and had few friends. Her prim-and-proper approach was great for efficiency, but lousy for employee relations. She treated the front desk as if it were her private domain, and often made her bosses feel like wayward children poking into the cookie jar for wanting to see the reservation list for the following week. It had become a Friday evening tradition, gloating over capturing the elusive list and accompanying application forms from Karen.

Mike returned to the living room waving the sheaf of papers gleefully. "Gather 'round, kiddies. I've already had a preview—there are some real cases coming."

"Mike," Selma chided him, "we're supposed to be sympathetic and helpful—we want to solve people's problems, not contribute to them."

"I just crunch numbers, Selma. You can be as helpful and sympathetic as you like."

As Selma clucked her disapproval, Jill and Beth exchanged a what-do-you-expect look, and Joel grabbed the papers out of Mike's hand.

"Hey!"

Joel flashed Mike his best impish grin. "Sorry, buddy. Fastest hands win."

Mike pouted, and Joel cleared his throat dramatically. After glancing briefly at the list, he hooted. "A fine bunch we have here, ladies and germs. A fine bunch!"

Jill rolled her eyes. "Cut it out, Joel. Just give us the lowdown."

"Well, we have a Mr. Andy Erdrich, who has written a fairly lengthy autobiography on his application, the gist of which seems to be that he's coming here to lose weight. He claims he's recently learned to live a spiritually fulfilling life by breathing in the essence of animal figurines."

"You're making that up!" Beth said accusingly while the others howled—except Selma, but even she was unable to withhold a smile.

Joel held out the form he was reading. "Am not— I swear on my stethoscope."

Beth laughed. "Okay, okay, I believe you." She shook her head. "What is happening to the world? And why on earth do all these people come to our spa?"

"Something about the very word attracts weirdos," Jill muttered.

"People in need of help," Selma corrected her.

"Yes, ma'am." Jill smiled and turned back to Joel. "Do go on. This is fascinating, as usual."

"Next we have a Mrs. Marshall Fairfield III, a Rosedale matron who has chosen to come to our humble little spa basically because it's the only one her tony friends *don't* patronize. She says she's been to spas before, but to relax, not to work. She actually wants to sweat this time, but she doesn't want anyone—anyone who is anybody, that is—to see her sweat."

"Great," Jill muttered, "a weirdo and a prima donna. Who's next?"

Joel's eyes skimmed the list and the application forms further. "Actually everybody else looks depressingly conventional. There are your regulation workaholics and unable-to-cope-anymores and I-feel-so-ugly-and-I'm-so-down-I-hate-myself types. Oh, I did get a call a couple of days ago from a doctor buddy of mine who's sending up a friend of his—some hotshot in the food business. Actually he called twice. The first time, the guy was in the office, so Bob couldn't say too much. When he called back, he said the fellow wasn't particularly excited about coming, so he could give us a bit of a hard time. Apparently he's been written up in *Maclean's* and *Canadian Business*. He's some sort of marketing genius. Name's Sam Sarnoff."

At the name, Beth's stomach promptly lifted and fell back down again with an alarming thud. She was certain everyone had heard. *It can't be,* she thought, panicking. *There must be dozens of them in Toronto.* She racked her brains for a seemingly innocuous question to pose to Joel that would let her know if this was the same Sam Sarnoff. After a moment she asked, as calmly as she could manage, "How old is he?"

"Same as you, darlin'." Joel shook his head. "Scary, isn't it? The guy's only thirty and he's already headed toward a thousand and one medical problems. According to my buddy, Bob, he's an overweight insomniac, completely stressed out—no wife, no social life, no fun, no nothing—just work, work, work, twelve to fifteen hours a day."

"The guy's crazy," Mike pronounced. "A new age has dawned. Work is supposed to be fun, and the quicker you can retire, the better. What the hell is a guy like that beating his brains out for? He's got everything he could possibly want—and more—and it's still not enough. I'll tell you this much, if that was me,

I'd have hightailed it to the Bahamas after making my first million.''

"You know what, Mike?" Jill asked. "We believe you. But I, for one, am tiring of this discussion, so if we're all done talking business, I'm going to drag myself back to my humble home and tuck myself in." She glanced over at Beth, who was frowning and appeared lost in thought. "You coming, kid?"

Beth shook herself out of her reverie and said in a subdued voice, "Yeah, I'm coming." She stood up slowly and Jill peered at her.

"Are you okay, hon?"

"I'm fine," Beth said quickly. "Just a little tired, that's all. I didn't realize how exhausted I was until about a minute ago."

"Hold on, ladies, I'll join you." Selma rose from the couch and gathered her handbag. "Good night, gentlemen. It's been illuminating, as always."

Joel lifted a brow. "Is that a hint of sarcasm from our esteemed psychologist? Aren't you people of the opinion that sarcasm is the very basest form of humor—an unsuitable, undeniably hostile response to stress?"

"Good night, Joel."

"Good night, Selma."

BETH LET OUT a grateful sigh after closing her door on Jill and Selma, who had insisted on coming in and "cheering Beth up." Her thoughts still in turmoil, she wandered into the kitchen, and, like an automaton, poured water into the copper kettle. She sat herself down at the oak table and thought back—way back—to the time when she was an unattractive, overweight bookworm and Sam Sarnoff was the consummate jock—captain of the football team, no less.

She smiled wistfully, still able to conjure up the memories of those bittersweet days. She hadn't so much been rejected by the "cool" crowd, as tolerated. Neither had she blended in with the noncreative academic types. She had always been on the fringe—an observer and not a participant. How she'd envied Sam and his crowd with their easy smiles and their teasing chatter.

Sam had had another side to him, though: a thoughtful, intelligent, articulate side that was revealed in school newspaper articles and in his private conversations with Beth after story meetings. The two gung-ho reporters had struck up quite a friendship as a result of those talks, which were about school, people and life in general. Beth was madly attracted to Sam right off the bat, and in time, Sam, too, had admitted he wanted to be more than just friends.

It was late in their final year of high school when they'd finally gone out on a couple of real dates, but Beth had learned soon enough that Sam was loath to reveal the nature of their relationship to the general public. Upon speaking to his best friend Todd one day, she'd deduced that Sam hadn't even told him they were officially "going out." The final straw was the prom, which Beth just assumed they'd be attending together. Not so Sam. When she brought it up, he wouldn't even look at her, just mumbled that he didn't feel like going this year. Beth knew the real reason: he couldn't handle having other people see them together as a real couple. She'd told him what a rat he was, and the funny thing was, he hadn't even argued.

In time, her heartbreak had been replaced with anger, and then, sheer disappointment. At a certain point, she'd all but forgotten him. New developments in her life had occurred in astonishingly rapid succession, and had managed to obliterate the painful memories of high school.

As Jill had said earlier that evening, she'd been a late bloomer. But once she'd gotten into the business environment, she had blossomed on a personal level as well as a professional one. The social pressures of school were finally off her; she didn't have to spend time with any people except those she truly liked. Thanks to that, and her success at work, her shyness was soon a thing of the past. On top of that, she'd managed to lose forty pounds. She'd started seriously dieting in the second year of university, knowing that if she was overweight, people would never take her seriously as a nutritionist, and she had come to passionately believe in the benefits of healthy living.

Dates came slowly at first, then in droves. Only two relationships since then had been fairly serious. The first man with whom she'd contemplated a future was Jim Coulter, a slick, sexy co-worker at a fitness club where she'd worked as a consultant. Jim introduced her to sex, then deceit. She realized later that he'd looked too much like Sam for her own good. So she started looking for the very opposite of Jim and ended up with Alex Marsden, an extremely sensitive caterer who initially made an impression on her when he cried about the death of his cat. At last, here was a sensitive eighties man, a man in touch with his feelings! It took her a few months to clue in to the fact that he couldn't have cared less about *her* feelings. . . .

And now, after all these years, she was going to see Sam again. She grimaced and shook her head, wondering why it was that people never did completely forget high school, with all its pettiness and exaggerated emotional turmoil. A few short words, and it all came to the fore with crystal clarity. She recalled Joel's description of the present-day Sam. Obviously he was no longer involved in sports. Joel had made it sound as if he'd let himself go completely to seed. And there had been something about him being single and having no social life. That was odd, she mused, considering how popular he'd been in high school. She smiled again, thinking that perhaps their relationship had at least made him see he didn't belong with the cheerleader types.

If that were the case, they'd have more in common now. Despite her newfound confidence and popularity, Beth still didn't feel as if she fit in with the rest of the world. She still suffered from the odd acute attack of low self-esteem. Selma had informed her that it took the mind quite a few years to catch up with the body after a radical change. After all this time, Beth still tended to withdraw from overly attractive men, fearful of the "inevitable" rejection.

Apparently Sam was no longer so attractive. Would he pursue a relationship with her now? Beth wondered. The thought was intriguing, and after she finished her tea, she went to bed with enticing visions of the high-school-aged Sam Sarnoff dancing in her head.

CHAPTER TWO

HE WAS ALREADY CRAVING a burger. Not just any burger—and especially not a healthy, flame-broiled burger with only lettuce, tomatoes and sprouts on it, complete with a crunchy whole-wheat roll. That was what he'd been served at lunch. He supposed it had been sporting of the spa people to offer something that vaguely resembled fast food, but the burger, though admittedly tasty, had only sparked a desire for a *real* burger: a half pounder—fried, of course—with great gobs of "special sauce"—he didn't know what was in that and didn't particularly care—enclosed in a thick, fluffy cloud of a white bun, just full to bursting with refined white flour.

The advertisements hadn't been joking, apparently: burger "attacks" were obviously a very real phenomenon. Sam's need for the elusive burger was so acute, he actually felt pains shooting up and down his stomach—or was that simple hunger? It could also be exhaustion, he thought grimly as he walked—staggered, actually—from his private bungalow to the main building, on his way to an appointment with the spa's dietitian. He only hoped his stomach wouldn't growl embarrassingly in her office.

Or was it a him? he wondered. He hadn't bothered reading the spa's brochures—he hadn't had time, having been in too much of a panic completing last-minute tasks at work. And he'd been active since arriving at the spa early in the morning. There had been a brief introductory lecture and tour for the new arrivals, and they'd promptly been given a schedule of all the services and activities offered by the spa. He had thought low-impact aerobics sounded the least painful, but his muscles were letting him know he'd been quite wrong. He'd missed the bit on the brochure about the dietitian, but another new guest—a snooty, older woman who seemed to have sensed that he, too, had money to burn—had mentioned that she was going to make an appointment after class. He'd asked her to make one for him, too. The less he had to do himself, the better. He'd brought a pile of work with him, and he intended to devote every spare moment to his business.

He almost regretted that the place was so exquisite. The scenery *was* sensational, as Bob had promised, and Sam had felt the difference in the air immediately upon arriving. As the burger attack bore out, his appetite had already improved considerably. Despite his recent weight gain, he'd never had an overly active appetite; the increase was due to eating junk instead of nutritious foods when he did eat. For the first time in a long time, he actually wanted to taste his food, really enjoy it.

Too bad there was little he could do about it. Actually, there was something, he realized on second thought. He could drive into town for a burger at the Dairy Queen he'd taken note of on the way in. But first he had to take care of that damn appointment....

At last he arrived at the main building, and he checked the directory in the hall for the location of the dietitian's office.

"Sam! I've been looking all over for you!"

He groaned inwardly at the sound of Andy Erdrich's booming voice, and grimaced at the hearty slap that was ostensibly an indication of the man's happiness at seeing him.

"What do you think about this fresh air, eh?" Andy breathed in deeply and pounded his fists on his chest in satisfaction. "Nothin' like it, I tell ya."

"You're so right, Andy. Listen, I wish I could stay and chat, but I've got an appointment with the dietitian right now—"

Andy held up a hand. "Say no more. All I wanted to tell you was I'm getting some people together in my room during the free hour before dinner to learn about animal figurine energy. We'd love to have you join us—"

"Gee whiz, I'd love to—it sounds fascinating—but you see, I brought along all this work, and—"

"Work!" Andy looked horrified. "You're not supposed to do any work here! You're supposed to free your spirit, get in touch with nature, learn to unleash your creative and spiritual powers—"

"I'll try, Andy, I really will, but I'm also going to try to keep my business afloat." He could barely contain his impatience. "In the meantime, I've got an appointment with the dietitian." He decided he was justified in being out-and-out rude to Andy—the man's active proselytizing had been exceptionally annoying, especially in light of his crazy beliefs. Sam turned back to the board to look for the dietitian's office.

Another slap on the back made him grit his teeth.

"Sure thing, pal. Hey, no hard feelings, okay? It's just that I want to share all my wonderful discoveries with my fellow man. I'll catch you later—and Sam, even if you don't want to learn about animal figurine energy, I really recommend trying to loosen up a bit while you're here. You might even find you enjoy it." He turned to go, to Sam's relief. "By the way," he added over his shoulder, "you want room 222."

Sam turned. "Thanks," he mumbled, thoroughly annoyed at the man's holier-than-thou attitude. He stalked through the lobby and up the stairs and didn't stop until he was at the reception desk in room 222. Still angry, at first he barely noticed the sign listing the names of the resident physician, the behavioral psychologist and the dietitian. Suddenly his eyes widened.

The name jumped out at him. *Beth Finlayson, R.P.Dt.*

Could it possibly be the same Beth Finlayson? he wondered frantically. If so, he certainly didn't want to go through with his appointment, but neither could he cancel now—she undoubtedly knew he'd made an appointment with her. If he backed out, he'd look stupid.

He cursed himself for not having read the brochures. Wasn't the first rule of business to always read the fine print? He was just about to hightail it out the door and go back to his room to try to come up with a plan when the perky-looking receptionist looked up and smiled at him.

"You must be Mr. Sarnoff," she said pleasantly. "Ms. Finlayson is expecting you. Please have a seat. She shouldn't be long now."

Trapped. Sam sighed as he sank onto a comfortable leather sofa, and he began to prepare himself for the inevitable....

BETH DIDN'T WANT her appointment with Mrs. Marshall Fairfield III to end, even if the woman *was* one of the most obnoxious clients she had ever had. Somehow she'd weathered the exceptionally silly questions the woman had peppered the hour with, and now Beth found that far from wanting to get rid of the woman, she wanted to keep her there all afternoon. Better silliness than angst. And her next appointment was bound to be fraught with plenty of angst.

But Beth hadn't done too many things in her life that were daring, or even slightly irresponsible, so al-

though it was tempting to buzz Cheryl, the receptionist, and tell her she had to cancel the next
appointment—she was feeling terribly ill—she simply
couldn't do it. There was nothing left but to take a
deep breath, tell Mrs. Marshall Fairfield III that her
hour was up and ask Cheryl to send Sam Sarnoff in.

Which was exactly what she did before she could
talk herself out of it. She had to blink when he walked
in to make sure her eyes weren't playing tricks on her.
The features were the same, but there the resem-
blance ended between the man in her office and the
Sam Sarnoff she'd known in high school. Where the
latter had sported a healthy, ruddy complexion and a
firm, toned body, this man's face was pale, with bluish
rings under his big brown eyes, and he was decidedly
overweight. His thick head of brown hair had turned
prematurely gray, and he was visibly nervous, fidget-
ing and already turning to the clock.

Beth recognized the symptoms of unhealthy living
when she saw them. But still evident under all the surface signs of decay was an undeniable handsomeness
and a nobility of bearing—something that indicated
real class.

Aware that she had stared slightly too long, Beth
sternly told herself to get her heartbeat under control,
and she rose out of her chair to walk around the front
of her desk. Holding out her hand, she said as
warmly—but still professionally—as she could, "Sam,
it's been ages. It's so nice to see you again."

"Likewise," Sam returned, his face reddening slightly. Beth knew instinctively that he was uncomfortable seeing her under the circumstances. But why had he come to the spa if he'd wanted to avoid her? she wondered. She was an integral part of the program. Her question was answered when Sam continued in a rush, "Actually I had no idea that you worked here. My doctor seems to think I could use some coaching in the area of healthy living—" he gave an embarrassed laugh "—and he sent me here. But I have to be honest, I didn't even glance at the brochures. Someone else made this appointment for me...." He trailed off, but after a second, added, "That's not to say I'm not delighted to see you. I am—it's a pleasure. You look . . . wonderful, and—"

"Thank you." Beth smiled, grateful for the opportunity to end his awkward monologue. Walking back to her chair, she said, "Please, have a seat." When she was safely seated herself, she continued, "So, before we get down to the matter of 'healthy living' I want to congratulate you. I hear you've become quite a success in the food industry, though I must confess I don't know exactly what it is that you do." She felt her smile soften a bit, and despite her better instincts, she said quietly, "I always knew you would do great."

Sam looked at her quickly and directly for a moment, then lowered his eyes. "Yes, well, I've been lucky. I've also worked hard—too hard, my doctor seems to think. But it's paid off." He looked at her again and smiled. "I'm the proud owner of The Great

Canadian Condiment Company, which manufactures some fabulous gourmet salad oils and condiments." In a more serious tone, he added, "Actually this is the first time I've been away from the business for a substantial length of time, and I must say, I'm a little nervous about it."

Beth had picked up on that the instant he'd come in. She'd seen a lot like him before—workaholics whose doctors had virtually ordered them to come to Couchiching Spa, but whose vacations ultimately made not a whit of a difference because they were so addicted to life in the fast lane.

Beth could see quite clearly how this session was going to go. He would listen to her opening spiel about good habits for life a little impatiently, and his eyes would glaze over when she explained the fine points of the controlled energy diet that had been created by the Ontario Dietetic Association and approved by the Ontario Medical Association. The weight control diet, which was really more of a training program by which people learned to eat a mix of low fat foods from various food groups, would seem like too much work for him. He'd see it as an endeavor that was neither time nor cost-efficient. And on top of the weight control diet, he'd have to learn to watch his sodium level, too. No, there was no way he'd be interested. After all, how could he know whether the result would be worth the effort? Beth had worked with enough big businessmen to know that they needed results they could see. It was the bottom line that counted.

She couldn't stifle a grin. Once upon a time, Sam's bottom line had been very attractive, indeed....

SAM FELT HIS EYES glaze over. Beth was explaining that foods were divided into groups—proteins, starches, milk, fruits, vegetables and fats. She had already asked him assorted questions about his eating habits and had made up a chart showing him how many servings he could eat out of each group at every meal. She'd also prepared a sample menu for him.

On the one hand, her approach seemed straightforward and sensible but on the other, it was going to take an awful lot of discipline to learn such radically new habits. He wasn't sure it was worth his while. After all, a diet wasn't like a production line. In the manufacturing world, if you changed your methods, you could see results almost instantly, see your output increase daily. Sam didn't know if a mere one or two pounds a week would be enough to spur him on to greater—or lesser, as it were—things. And as for feeling better, he didn't buy it. Virtually nothing made him feel as good as a half pounder, a chocolate shake and a large order of fries. That wasn't to say he didn't appreciate more sophisticated food—he was, after all, in the food business—but unfortunately his taste ran more to calorie-laden French cuisine.

But it was more than the prospect of dieting that was causing his attention to wander. Seeing Beth after all these years had been a shock, especially since he'd only recently caught himself thinking about her for no apparent reason. He'd told her she looked wonderful, but that word didn't begin to describe what he was really thinking. The truth was, she looked devastatingly sexy, undeniably alluring. And that, combined with the sweet nature and sassy smarts he knew she possessed, was almost enough to undo him.

Was some strange cosmic joke being played on him? In high school, he—the jock, the hero, the guy with the year-round tan and the whiter-than-white smile—hadn't had the courage to reveal his real feelings about her to his friends. He wouldn't have been able to endure the ribbing—and there would have been plenty of that, though Beth had been pretty well liked for an overweight wallflower.

Not only did he feel awkward now because of the way their relationship had ended, but he felt just a teeny bit peeved at the subtle shift in the balance of power between them. In what seemed like a lifetime before, Sam had been the one to call the shots. Now he was in Beth's hands.

He looked at her, making sure he nodded and made some appropriate comment when she asked, "Do you see?" and he wondered how the transformation from ugly duckling to swan had come about. There was even a change in her manner of speaking: she was less hesitant, more confident now—thoroughly in control. And yet, there was a softness in her voice; the same warm, feminine tone that he'd always loved. But was that a hint of pity he detected in her words? A touch of patronization, too?

And was that how he had sounded to her in high school? He was appalled at the thought.

He suddenly needed to get out of there, gather his thoughts together. He was infinitely relieved when she handed him the sheets she'd been pointing to, plus some relevant brochures, and indicated that their session was up. He mumbled something in return and left the office quickly.

And then he did the hardest physical work he'd done in a long, long time. He ran downstairs, out the door and straight to the nature trail he'd seen on the tour in the morning.

He needed a good long walk.

BETH YANKED her long brown hair into a ponytail. *Stupid, stupid, stupid,* she berated herself. She'd been completely unable to get a grip on herself during Sam's session and had handled the awkward meeting with all the finesse of a cow. She sighed when she was finally able to trap the unwieldy mass in an elastic band.

She was obviously still very much attracted to Sam Sarnoff, even though he looked atrocious—for him— and quite clearly didn't care two bits about healthy living. He had come to the spa under duress and apparently couldn't wait to get home to his precious round-the-clock business and his barbecued potato chips. He was not for her. He'd proved that way back in high school.

She couldn't help a small feeling of satisfaction from surfacing. Today *she'd* been the one in control. *She'd* had the upper hand. It was shameful to be happy about that, but Lord, revenge felt sweet! There had been far more to his awkwardness today than the normal embarrassment overweight patients felt in their first session. He'd felt the shift in the balance of power, too—she was sure of it. And she sensed instinctively that he also felt lousy about the way he'd ended their relationship.

She felt a twinge of regret. He'd looked so uncomfortable, squirming in his chair—like a bird trapped in a cage.

"Silly girl, you can't gloat for five minutes straight," she muttered as she tugged on a white leather skirt. The fact was, she'd hated seeing him in that position. And it probably *was* just simple embarrassment. No doubt she'd fantasized the shift in the balance of power, as well.

Still, she hated seeing him backed against a wall. She knew he'd have to work through all the psychological ramifications of his weight gain—if he even realized there *were* psychological ramifications. She had the feeling that his lackluster social life at present had a lot to do with diminished self-esteem. When he regained it, he'd likely be his old social self again.

"Which is why you can't afford to get soft," she ordered herself as she stared at her reflection after throwing on an oversize black-and-white cotton knit pullover.

"Soft as in flabby?" Jill called. Entering Beth's bedroom, she said, "Sorry for barging in, but you left your door unlocked." Peering at her friend critically, she added, "I wouldn't worry about getting soft. You look fabulous. Great sweater."

Beth sighed. "Thanks. It's a different kind of soft I'm worried about."

Jill stretched out on Beth's antique brass bed. "Sounds intriguing. Do tell."

"There's not much to tell. Remember Mike mentioned a Sam Sarnoff at our meeting?"

"The biz whiz?"

"Right. Well, I knew him in high school. We worked on the school newspaper together."

Jill sat up. "How interesting that you didn't mention this earlier. And how utterly fascinating that you turned kelly green when his name was mentioned yesterday."

Beth glared at her friend as she scooped up a series of shirts and skirts she had rejected before settling on the black-and-white ensemble. Left over from her high school days—and exacerbated by Sam's arrival—was a silly paranoia about being dressed inappropriately. As she hung her clothes on their hangers she said, "I was surprised, that's all."

"Uh-huh."

"Okay, so I was shocked. You want the dirt, I'll give you the dirt. He was the jock, I was the wallflower. We went out on a couple of dates, but he didn't have the courage to tell his friends about us. Now the tables are turned. I'm in the driver's seat and I'm still attracted to him, but I can't give in to that attraction. As soon as he gets in control again—if he manages to do that— he'll be on the lookout for a glamorous social type.'' She sighed again as she flopped down onto her bed next to Jill.

Jill only shrugged. ''Have a fling. Get him out of your system.''

''Jill!''

''All right, all right! Somehow, I knew you wouldn't go for that.'' She lay back down and stared up at the ceiling. ''God, why is it that people carry high school with them the rest of their lives. All that—emotion!'' She shivered.

Beth grinned. ''I was thinking that very same thing just last night.''

''So what are you going to do?''

''Put it out of my mind and have the most fatten- ing dinner on the menu, of course.''

''Brava,'' Jill said approvingly.

On the way to the dining room they picked up Selma, and soon, she, too, was apprised of the situa- tion. Beth asked her advice.

''Why do you have to do anything?'' Selma asked in her typically sensible manner. ''Why not let things happen naturally, take their own course?''

''Oh, Selma—'' Beth couldn't help laughing ''—how I wish I were you sometimes. How is it that you're our age and so wise? Don't you ever have any problems?''

"Everybody has problems, honey. Don't you think that they don't."

"But some people have more problems than others," Jill said grimly, and Beth followed her line of vision to Mike, who had seen the women arrive at the dining hall entrance and was making a beeline toward his prey.

"Uh, ladies, excuse me, but I have to run. Suddenly I've developed a splitting headache—clichéd, I know, but it's all I can think of. Toodle-loo!" With that, Jill pivoted and tore off.

"Where'd she go?" Mike asked in an aggrieved tone as he reached Beth and Selma.

"Headache," Beth said,

"Headache, huh? Hmm, she's been sick a lot lately. I haven't been able to spend one minute with her. Maybe she's not eating right, Beth."

"Mike, she's never eaten right and she never will. But somehow, I don't think that's her problem these days."

"No?" He shrugged. "Well, if she refuses to talk about it, there's no helping her, is there? Listen, I've been talking up the gal from Rosedale. She could bring in a lot of money—"

Just then, Andy Erdrich came up to Selma and boomed, "Selma, wonderful to see you again." He took her by the elbow and began guiding her away. "I've been meaning to talk to you about incorporating animal figurine energy sessions into your program…."

As his voice trailed off, Beth shrugged at Selma, who was sending her an I'm-sorry-I'll-have-to-set-him-straight look. Mike, too, took off—still in pursuit of Jill, she presumed.

It seemed she was on her own tonight. She glanced around the room and realized with surprise that it was full. Apparently she'd taken an exceptionally long time getting ready. With increasing dismay, she saw there were no empty seats.

No, there was one—next to Sam Sarnoff.

Beth took a deep breath. It was going to be a long night.

CHAPTER THREE

BETH STOPPED just before she reached the table. He hadn't seen her, and she wanted to make sure the phony smile she'd pasted on her face was still in place. After a moment she said, "Hi there" in a sickeningly bright tone.

He turned quickly and stood. "Oh! Hello yourself."

Since he looked so horrifyingly ill at ease, Beth took the initiative and ensconced herself in the empty seat next to him. He looked relieved that she'd done something, and he sat back down.

"Well," she continued in the same sunny tone she'd never used before, "it looks as if you're settled right in."

The relief was gone suddenly, and the ill-at-ease quality was back. "Yeah, well, I guess I'm more comfortable in a dining room than in a dietitian's office."

Beth immediately recognized her gaffe. *Great,* she thought glumly. She had to marvel that he could still be witty when he was obviously wishing that he was anywhere else in the galaxy. She, on the other hand, felt like a dud contestant at a beauty contest—the kind that was embarrassingly overenthusiastic.

She plowed ahead anyway. Turning on the bright smile again, she replied smoothly, "Oh, come on now, you'd fit in just about anywhere, I imagine."

"Flattery will get you everywhere," he said, smiling and adding, "I may even follow your diet for that."

It actually worked! Maybe this wouldn't be so bad, after all....

"So tell me," he asked, seemingly more relaxed now. "Does your cook always work such wonders with so few calories? This lemon chicken is marvelous."

"Oh, yes. Jane's fabulous. Be sure to try the vegetarian lasagna and the grilled salmon before you go." *But nothing else,* she added silently.

"She's a real artist. Even the salad was top-notch. I've always had the gourmet's scorn for low-calorie dressings, but I may just have a chat with your Jane before I leave." He smiled again, and in the blink of an eye, became the eighteen-year-old football star again. "Who knows? I may even have to give you credit when I create a new line of dressings...."

"That would be nice," Beth said woodenly, unsure how to respond all of a sudden. She was thankful when Ann, a part-time waitress, caught her eye and came over.

"Hi, Beth! Did you just come in? Can I get you something?"

"I'll just have the lemon chicken, Ann. Skip the salad. I'm already behind everyone else."

"Sure thing." Ann turned to Sam and smiled demurely. "Is everything all right, Mr. Sarnoff?"

Did he have that effect on all women? Beth wondered grumpily. And with graying hair and a gut, to boot. It was truly unbelievable!

He smiled back, a warm but slightly self-contained smile, designed, Beth guessed, to be polite yet romantically discouraging. He was a genius. "Everything's fine, Ann. My compliments to the chef." Beth noted the astute use of the waitress's first name. Slightly cheeky from a stranger, but it worked for Sam. People never guessed that he had a habit of cultivating favor—a habit she was sure was completely unconscious by now. He'd been a public relations whiz even in high school. Without ever expending any energy, he'd been able to get anyone and everyone to love him. It just wasn't fair!

When Ann had gone, Sam touched Beth's arm lightly and said, "Beth, I'd like to introduce you to some people I don't believe you've had a chance to meet." With that irritatingly smooth tone, he introduced her to the others at the table—all of whom were delighted to be seated with the resident dietitian and proceeded to tell their food-related woes to her in minute detail. She didn't have much of a chance to talk to Sam—which should have been a relief, she told herself. She did notice that he only picked at the remainder of his meal. Either he was lying through his teeth about enjoying his food, or he was afraid of eating it in front of her.

When people were finishing their second and third cups of decaffeinated coffee, Sam politely excused himself, and though he held Beth's eyes for a moment or two longer than he held anyone else's, she realized once again that he was making a great effort to remain carefully distant. She sighed as she watched him exit and hardly heard the tale of food misadventures being relayed by a plump, sad-looking woman from Toronto. Overwhelmed by guilt after a while, she ended up urging the woman to come see her in her office first thing in the morning, and then she, too, beat a hasty retreat.

Unfortunately for the sad-looking woman from Toronto, Beth didn't do too much better the next day. She found herself unable to concentrate, drifting off at the most inappropriate moments. When she wasn't thinking about Sam, she was thinking about the fact that the spa was in trouble. It couldn't fail, not now, not when they'd all come so far and accomplished so much.... Resolutely she forced her mind away from business concerns. Mike had given them a warning, that was all. Surely if they were in real trouble, he would have told them long ago....

Still, she couldn't focus. Thankfully she could recite the details related to the controlled energy diet by rote. All that was missing was her usual supersensitive manner. Luckily her client didn't seem to notice.

When she had a spare couple of hours, she attended a high-energy aerobics class led by Jill, and afterward, the two went for a swim in the indoor pool.

"Okay, let's take stock," Jill said when she came up for air after a graceful dive. Beth was already treading water, and Jill joined her. "What's happening with your man?"

Beth shot her friend a dark look and said, "He's not my man." With that, she did an energetic butterfly stroke to one side of the pool. Jill followed.

"Okay," she said when she got there. "He's not your man. I'll rephrase the question. What's happening?"

"*Nothing* is happening." She did the crawl to the other side.

"You don't seem too happy about that," Jill called after her.

Beth called back, "Are you trying to take Selma's job away from her?"

Jill sputtered as she swallowed some water, but continued her dogged pursuit. "How come I'm in better shape than you but you're a better swimmer than me?" she complained when she'd caught up to Beth.

Beth grinned. "Swimming is one form of exercise I don't have to talk myself in to doing."

"Aha! The woman smiles!"

"Very funny."

"It's not funny at all. It's very sad, actually. This guy is having quite the effect on you."

"He is not," Beth denied hotly, kicking her feet violently, but remaining propped up against the side wall of the pool, her arms resting on the ledge.

"Oh, no?"

"No!"

"Fine!" She paused. "Then why are you so upset?"

Beth was tiring of the conversation. She already regretted having told Jill about Sam. After all, nothing was going to happen. He would leave and she'd think about him for another dozen years. . . .

"Look," she said, "I'll admit I'm attracted to Sam—I always have been—but I know he's not for me. And anyway, he's totally freaked out by the fact that I'm a dietitian. He can't even eat when he's with me."

"You ate together?"

Beth sighed in exasperation. "Yes, we ate together—after *you* left me alone last night. Selma was lassooed by that animal-figurine energy kook, and there was only one other empty seat in the dining room—and it was next to Sam."

"Hmm. This gets interestinger and interestinger."

Beth rolled her eyes. "No, it doesn't. Believe me, it doesn't." Cocking her head mischievously, she said, "Okay, Miss Matchmaker, it's your turn. Tell me what's happening with our intrepid financial wizard."

"Nothing, I hope. Unlike yourself, I harbor no secret fantasies about my pursuer."

"I *don't* harbor secret fantasies, and he's *not*—"

"Oh, please, Beth. Spare me. Anyway, I haven't seen Mike since last night."

"Uh-oh."

"Uh-oh what?"

"I'm sorry, Jill. I think I jinxed you. Guess who just walked in?"

"I don't *believe* this. Does he have radar or something? And I can't even escape this time!"

"Gee, that's too bad," Beth said in a casual tone as she hoisted herself onto the ledge, then stood up.

"Hey, where are you going?"

Beth smiled beatifically. "Paybacks."

"*Paybacks!* Beth, that is so childish, I can't believe it. After all I've done—"

But Beth only laughed and walked away, cheerfully waving at Mike before exiting the pool area.

Mike waved back at Beth and smiled to himself as he spotted Jill in the pool. He'd known she was going to be here. He kept a close eye on her whenever he could and knew her routine like the back of his hand. He definitely deserved a pat on the back. All was proceeding smoothly, from the plan he'd devised to pay back his "creditors" to "Operation Jill." He'd started to panic a while back when a major investment had gone sour, but he'd come up with the perfect solution, and so far, no one suspected a thing. With Jill on his side, his co-workers would be even less likely to suspect anything. It was sheer genius.

Of course, she was still resisting him, but she'd give in soon enough. He'd gotten everything he wanted in life so far, and a pretty blond wife would be the icing on the cake. He could just see it now: they'd live in the suburbs, join a country club, go up to the cottage on weekends... Yessir, she would be his one day. He'd fought for everything he had—unlike his partners, who'd all had it relatively easy—and he'd fight for Jill, too.

"Hi there," he called out to her as he eased himself to a sitting position on the edge of the pool.

She waved as she swam to the other side. *So, she's going to play it this way,* he thought. *Well, two can play that game.* He swam in her direction, overtook her and passed her without her noticing. When she got to the ledge and came up for air, her eyes widened at the sight of him.

"Surprised you, huh?"

"Uh, yeah. Listen, Mike, I'd love to chat, but this is the only time I get to exercise without twenty-five other people around, and I really have to take advantage, you know?"

"Sure, sure. Hey, I've got tickets for the Stones in Toronto next Saturday. How'd you like to join me? It should be a blast."

"Oh! It sounds terrific, but I—I've got plans already. Thanks anyway."

"Plans? Oh, okay. No sweat. Not too many people would turn down Stones tickets, though. Sure you don't want to change your plans?" *Damn, I should have told her some other people were coming.*

"Mmm. Sorry, I don't think I can. But thanks again for asking. I guess the concert's sold-out, huh? I saw them at the El Mocambo years ago. I figure nothing could top that, so I don't feel too bad about missing this one."

"Well, it wouldn't have been *just* the concert—but never mind."

He was pleased to see her smile. She was relaxing—he could feel it. He plowed ahead, pressing his advantage. "I was planning on taking you to see—are you ready for this—my new racehorse!"

She just stared at him dumbly and said, "Your what?"

He laughed gleefully. "You heard right. You are speaking to the part owner of the sweetest little filly you ever saw. She's gonna be a winner for me—yes-sirree."

"Mike, please tell me if I'm out of line, but how on earth can you afford a racehorse?"

He wiggled his eyebrows. "Trade secrets."

"I guess so. Any chance of sharing them with your terminally poverty-stricken and mathematically incompetent co-workers?"

He laughed. "But of course, my dear—for a price."

"No chance, Petrie." With that, she dived underwater and swam off again. But that was okay. He was getting to her, he could tell. It was just a matter of time, and he could wait. Everything was going—swimmingly!

Feeling very satisfied with himself, he, too, dived underwater and caught up with her once more....

UNBEKNOWNST TO BETH, Sam walked out of the men's change room shortly after she walked into the ladies'. He saw that there were only a few people in the pool, for which he was relieved. It had been a long time since he'd gone swimming, and he was slightly self-conscious about how he looked in his bathing suit. There had been a time when more than a few glances would have come his way, but those days were long gone....

He took a closer look at the people in the pool area. One woman—was it the aerobics instructor?—appeared to be checking him out, but her interest didn't appear to be romantic in nature. She seemed simply... curious. She also appeared to be trying to distance herself from an almost too handsome man, who apparently wasn't aware that the object of his affections was completely indifferent to him.

Sam forced his eyes away from the pair. It was a bad habit he had: staring at people, trying to read them and figure out what made them tick. It was a much-valued business skill, but he was on vacation now. He had a sudden vision of stacks of work waiting for him in his room, but he pushed it away. He just wasn't ready to tackle it yet.

He walked over to the diving board, positioned himself at the end of it, took a deep breath and leaped off. When he rose to the surface, he shook his head and felt himself smile. It actually felt good! He *wanted* to swim! With an energy he hadn't felt for a long, long time, he glided with graceful strokes to the far end of the pool, then back. He stopped at ten lengths, not wanting to run himself too hard. Maybe Bob was right, he mused. Perhaps there was something to this exercise stuff. Maybe he would slowly begin to feel— not to mention look—better.

Feeling refreshed and relaxed at the end of his swim, he took a hot, invigorating shower, and when he was done, he began to walk back toward his cabin. He took deep breaths as he went, feeling better than he had in some time.

Midway, he bumped—quite literally—into Beth, who'd already been to her bungalow and was heading back to the main building.

"Oh, I'm so sorry!" he said contritely.

"It's okay," she replied hastily. "Really!"

"No, it's not. I insist on making it up to you." He grinned. "I'm glad it happened, actually. I wanted to get you alone one of these lovely nights and talk about old times. I'm sorry if I seemed a little gruff last evening—I wasn't in the best of moods." He didn't tell her that he hadn't had the foggiest notion as to how to talk to her, and since then, he'd decided he should just be himself, pretend she wasn't a health professional who'd been disgusted with his life-style, pretend they hadn't known each other way back when. . . .

"Why don't we have dinner together again—try to wrangle a table for two in the dining room?"

Warning bells rang in Beth's head. This was the old Sam—the flirtatious Sam she'd been so attracted to in high school—definitely bad news. She had known he would eventually revert to his old, overconfident self, but she hadn't imagined it would take so little time!

Well, she wasn't going to be the same pushover now that she had been then. She'd show him.

She smiled—a little icily. A fleeting confused expression flitted over his face. *Victory,* Beth thought. He hadn't expected a cool reaction.

"I am sorry, Sam," she said, taking great pains to sound like a ticket reservations clerk with a major airline, "but I'm not available tonight. Maybe some other time. I'm sure I'll see you around, though."

And then she turned on her heel and didn't even look back to see a dumbfounded Sam just standing there, staring after her wonderingly.

She fumbled through her appointments that afternoon, once again unable to devote her full attention to her clients. She wished revenge had tasted sweeter, but she only had a bitter taste in her mouth. She'd acted like a kid. What a way to have shown him she'd blossomed into a mature, confident businesswoman!

She was infinitely relieved when the last of her clients walked out of her office. She'd thought long and hard about the situation, and she knew what she had to do. She'd have to apologize—maybe even explain her feelings, tell him why she'd acted the way she had. That was the mature thing to do.

Then again, if nothing was said, their relationship—or whatever it was—would just fizzle out and they'd never see each other again.

So why was she so anxious to set things right?

She thought about that for a while. To leave him with a good impression of her, definitely. And yes, she sighed—to leave the door open to future communication.

Her head began to spin. Why did she always have to analyze each and every ramification of each and every one of her actions? With a ferocity startling even to her, she slammed her notebook down on her desk and strode out of her office and out of the building into the approaching night.

Half an hour later, while going through the age-old ritual of deciding what to wear to dinner, Beth heard the doorbell ring. It was Jill.

The fitness director looked pointedly at Beth's beautifully styled hair, fresh manicure and silk bathrobe, and said with a grin, "Getting into a mood, are we? I guess all your efforts are not for the benefit of your friends, who are dining in town tonight. I assume you've forgotten."

"Oh, my gosh! I'm sorry, Jill—"

She raised a hand. "Please don't apologize for having a love life. It's in very poor taste."

"I don't—"

"Have a love life. Yeah, yeah. Tell me more."

"It's true! I was rude to Sam today—I turned down his invitation to dinner—and I decided I should apologize and tell him I've changed my mind—"

"Aha!"

"There's nothing to 'Aha' about," Beth said emphatically. Then her tone turned contrite. "I completely forgot about dinner in town. I'm real sorry."

"Say no more. I forgive you—even though you're really striking out between what you did this afternoon at the pool and this. But I have a generous spirit. Good luck tonight."

"You, too. Is Mike going?"

Jill sighed. "Yes. He seems to have stepped up his campaign. Do you know what he told me today?"

"I can't guess."

"No, you can't. You'd never get it in a million years. He's the part owner of a *racehorse!*"

"You're kidding!"

"Nope. I'm pretty sure he was serious. He asked me to the Stones on Saturday and when I turned him down he said he'd also planned to show me the horse."

Beth shook her head. "I can't believe that guy. Where on earth is he getting the money?"

"Exactly what I asked. He just laughed it off." Her expression turned serious. "Can I ask you something?"

"Sure. Why don't you come in for a bit?"

Jill shook her head. "Thanks but no thanks. I've really got to run. Just a quick question—doesn't it seem odd to you that Mike is buying all this lavish stuff at the same time that he's telling everybody the place is in trouble?''

Beth shrugged. ''Not so odd. I'm sure he's got zillions of investments. But I agree that flashing his money around right now is in poor taste, to use your expression.''

Jill nodded. ''Well, it sure is applicable in this case.''

''Taste is a personal matter, dear. To each his own and all that.''

''Yeah, well, I wish he had someone he could call his own. It sure ain't gonna be me. Well, enough of this conversation. I guess you have to get all spiffed up. See you later!''

''Bye, Jill, and sorry again about tonight.''

''No problem,'' Jill called over her shoulder. She was already at the end of the driveway.

Beth shut the door gently, wishing she had gone with Jill. Now, the choice was between sharing the evening with Sam, or spending it alone, with only a pint of ice cream and the television for company.

Telling herself firmly that she was doing the right thing, the mature thing, she whipped a western-cut denim dress out of her closet, and some silver-and-turquoise earrings out of her jewelry box. She was not going to waste one more minute acting like a lovesick adolescent!

In twenty minutes she was ready. Satisfied, she looked at her watch. It was early enough that Sam would still be in his cabin. She'd call and suggest they go to dinner together.

Before she could lose her courage, she dialed the reservations desk.

"Couchiching Spa, reservations."

"Hi, Karen, it's Beth. Listen, I need a phone number—for Sam Sarnoff. He's probably in one of the bungalows."

Silence. Beth knew the woman was trying to make her feel that she'd done something wrong. Apparently she couldn't think of what, though. All she said was "Just a moment" in a stone-cold tone, but Beth regarded that as a won battle.

When she had the number it took every ounce of courage she had to dial it. But she did. She considered hanging up after Sam identified himself, but she didn't do that, either.

Instead, she said, "Hi, Sam. It's Beth. I just wanted to say that I'm sorry I was so rude earlier. If the invitation to eat dinner with you is still open I'd be delighted to take you up on it." She expelled a breath, relieved that it was over with. But in a moment, the lack of response on the other end of the line had her panicking. What if he hated assertive women? What if she'd hurt him so terribly that he'd never forgive her? What if—

"Of course it's still open. I'm surprised but infinitely glad that you called. Tell me where you are and I'll come get you."

"Oh, no," she said quickly, for some reason not wanting him to see her home. Anyway, his cabin was on the way to the dining hall. "I'll come by your place. It's much easier."

"Okay by me. I'm in bungalow number four."

The nicest one, Beth thought automatically. "Great," she said. "Will you be ready in ten minutes?"

"Will do. See you then."

"Bye," she whispered, and placed the phone down, wondering once again why she was so determined to have him think well of her. She sighed. Obviously behind the great clothes and the million-dollar figure, there was still an insecure teenager just waiting to bring her down....

Dinner went extraordinarily well, however. There were no tables for two left by the time they got there, but they managed to find seats at a table with a young couple completely wrapped up in each other—literally as well as figuratively—and a stern-looking old man who had brought along a spy thriller and showed no inclination whatsoever to put it down, save when he had to navigate a particularly large morsel of food to his mouth. Beth and Sam were thus free to talk to each other to their hearts' content.

The food was marvelous. Beth took great pains to convince Sam to try the meatless lasagna, and was relieved when she succeeded. In between bites, they told each other where they'd been and what they'd done since they'd seen each other last.

"And your parents, Sam? How are they?" Beth asked after taking a sip of mineral water.

Sam was silent for a moment. "They've both passed away, Beth. I lost my father when I was in my first year of university, and my mother when the business was just starting out. They both had cancer."

"Oh, Sam, I'm so sorry. How awful for you," Beth said sincerely. Sam had been one of those rare teenagers who had managed to be independent and just slightly rebellious and still maintain terrific relationships with his parents. Beth knew they had to have been very special people. What a loss for him to have sustained, she thought.

"It was pretty awful. I still think about them a lot. But as time goes on, the pain gets easier to bear." He turned away briefly, then went back to attacking his lasagna. "And your parents! How are they doing? And Barb?"

Beth smiled. "Well, my parents have stopped bugging me about my weight, thank goodness. And Barb is doing great." This was a slight exaggeration. Beth's sister—older by four years—was having marital problems, which Beth's parents knew nothing about. Barb had always been the perfect daughter—held up to Beth as all that a daughter should be: beautiful, friendly and popular—not to mention slim. Barb had enjoyed pleasing her parents too much, though. She'd married too young, for all the wrong reasons, and was paying the price. She and her doctor husband had been married fourteen years, and Mark, the 'perfect' husband, had recently pleaded guilty to carrying on a flaming affair with his nurse. Barb had found the telltale receipts in his pants pocket. It was all so clichéd and so incredibly sad. Beth ached for the sister she'd always envied. Barb had admitted all in a rare long phone call to Beth and had pleaded with her not to tell their parents. She was still trying to figure out what to do. Beth was thankful no children were involved— Barb and Mark had been trying for years, to no avail.

To Sam, all she said was "I'm afraid none of them will rest until I'm married."

Sam grinned back. "They only want to make sure you're happy."

"I'm afraid my parents are a tad more concerned with making themselves happy, though they'd never admit that." Beth knew it was time to switch to another topic. Though she loved her folks dearly, and understood them better now that she was an adult, she still had a hard time dealing with them. Consequently she had a hard time talking about them. How could she explain her relationship with them when she didn't even understand it? All her life they had had very set ideas about what they wanted their daughters to accomplish. First on the list for each was marrying well, and second was providing them with a pack of grandkids. Barb had married well—or so her parents thought—but she'd failed in the grandkids department. To their credit, they'd known enough not to blame anyone for that. But the situation had definitely increased the pressure on Beth.

The period of Beth's adolescence had been particularly hard. Beth's mother had constantly urged her to try to lose weight, to try to look more like slender golden girl Barb. If she did lose weight, Mrs. Finlayson's rationale went, she'd get more dates. Beth would point out that she didn't want to go out with anyone who wouldn't go out with her just because she was overweight, but that didn't stop her mother. When Beth did decide to lose the weight—for her own reasons—she had thought her mother would be content. But then she'd begun her campaign to get her precious daughter married off. Reconciled to the possibility that she might not ever marry, Beth had recently tried to involve her mother in her work. But though Lillian sometimes did tell Beth that she was proud of the things she was doing, Beth had the uneasy feeling that her mother thought of her career as a hobby—something to keep her occupied until she got married.

Beth sighed. "I'm sorry, Sam. It's hard for me to talk about my parents—particularly my mother. We haven't had the smoothest of relationships. But I know I'm lucky to have my folks—and I do love them. I also respect a lot of their values." She wrinkled her nose. "Others I have trouble with."

"I think everybody has that problem," Sam said thoughtfully. "You may be thankful for much of what your parents taught you, but you're bound to disagree with them in certain areas. And you can't be expected to live your life according to their expectations. You've got to be you."

"I've got to be me," Beth repeated. "There's a song in that. . . ."

Soon they were on to other subjects. Beth asked about Sam's younger sister, Evelyn, and Sam told her she was married to a wonderful guy and had a beautiful little girl just about to enter the first grade. And after some persuasion on Beth's part, Sam went on to explain the fundamentals of the mustard business.

"First," he intoned, "some background information on mustard." He cleared his throat dramatically and Beth quirked an eyebrow. "Mustard," he continued, pretending to be oblivious to her grimace, "is the common name for the Cruciferae, a large family chiefly of herbs indigenous to northern, temperate regions. These flowers are cultivated for their seeds, which, when ground, are used as the condiment we know and love as mustard. As a dietitian, you'll surely be fascinated by the fact that mustard is rich in sulfur compounds and vitamin C—"

"That's all very nice," she interrupted him, "but I'm afraid I'm not all that interested in the origins of mustard."

"Oh?" he said dryly. "I can't imagine why. . . ."

"Nooo. . . there's a bit more to it than simple boredom, I'm afraid. You see, there's something I haven't told you."

"Oh?" he said again.

She looked down, then up again, sheepishly. "I'm allergic to mustard."

He stared at her for a moment, then burst out laughing. "You're...allergic...to mustard," he squeezed out between loud guffaws. "That's really funny." Shaking his head, he quipped, "I hope you have nothing against salad dressings."

"Nothing at all." She laughed, too, relieved that he'd found her admission amusing. She had tended to think of it as a bad omen. "And while I may not be interested in hearing about all the sterling qualities of the stuff that treats me so badly, I *am* interested in hearing about marketing and distribution. Who do you sell to, Sam? Let's hear the good stuff!"

He laughed. "We're doing very well. I see us as positioned at the high end of the market—we're selling to fine food shops and department stores all across Canada. Best of all, we've recently broken into the American market."

"Sam, that's wonderful! I'm impressed!"

He looked down modestly. "I've worked hard and had good luck, too. I'm pleased." Wistfully, he added, "I only wish my mother was alive to see what a success the business has become. I started out with her mustard and salad dressing recipes, you know."

"No, I didn't know," Beth said quietly. "That's really beautiful, Sam. The business is a way of keeping your parents' memory alive."

He nodded. "Exactly. And that's why I'm so devoted to it—probably too much so."

She couldn't say anything. It was hard to tell someone he was putting too much work into something that was, in effect, a memorial to his parents.

In a lighter tone, Sam said, "Okay, enough of the serious stuff. Dessert is on the way, and we have to talk about something silly, like—" he leaned forward menacingly "—math class!"

Beth groaned. "Please, anything but that!"

"Do you remember Mrs. Pinsky?" With that, they collapsed into a fit of laughter, and they spent the next hour reminiscing, carefully sidestepping the matter of their relationship and its disintegration.

After dinner, they went for a long walk along the lakeshore. When Sam suggested that they sit on the rocks and relax for a while, Beth hesitated for a moment, then agreed. They found a comfortable spot on a large flat rock at the water's edge, and Sam promptly took off his shoes and socks and dangled his feet in the lake. Since he looked so relaxed, Beth decided to follow his example.

They were silent for a couple of minutes, and then Sam said, "It's so peaceful. You must love living here."

Beth smiled. "It has its moments."

"It's so different from the city."

From "the city" Beth knew he meant Toronto, not Orillia. And it certainly was different from Toronto. That place seemed a world away sometimes.

"It's very different," she agreed. "And I'm glad I decided to move here. That's not to say I don't miss

Toronto occasionally. Orillia isn't exactly Canada's cultural hot spot.''

"It must have been hard to make the move.''

"Not as hard as you might think. I had my friends here, and I'd been working here for a while before I moved up permanently.''

There were a couple more minutes of silence, and suddenly Beth realized they were acting like prospective lovers. And though she was having a wonderful time and was incredibly attracted to him—it was all she could do not to bend over and place a tender kiss on his neck—she knew she couldn't let herself succumb to his charms.

So why was she rooted to the spot? It couldn't have been that she was waiting for him to lean over, to run his hands through her hair or put his arm around her and hold her close....

No, of course not!

Yet when he did turn to face her, and cupped her chin gently in his hands, she hardly dared breathe. And when he said softly, "You're a very special woman, Beth Finlayson, and this time, I'm not going to blow it," she could find no words with which to respond.

And when he brought his face toward hers and placed his lips on her mouth with great tenderness, pulling away was the last thing on her mind. The connection was electric. The kiss was soft, but intense, and years of repressed emotion welled up in her.

At that moment, Beth knew she was a lost woman. Her resolve to stay away meant nothing. She'd take what he could give and live with the pain that would inevitably come after the loving.

CHAPTER FOUR

SAM COULD BARELY keep track of the lengths he was swimming—too many thoughts were swimming around in his head. He'd been elated when Beth hadn't pulled away from him the previous night. He had even felt her begin to respond to his kiss. He hadn't meant to do that; after she had put him neatly in his place when he'd asked her to dinner, he had wondered if he'd been too cavalier—repeating past patterns, expecting her to jump when he said so. *She* had the upper hand now, and she had clearly wanted to get him back for the hurt he'd inflicted on her in the past.

So when she'd called to apologize for her coolness, he'd been startled—but not all that surprised. The flip side of being as sensitive as Beth was was being big enough to admit when a mistake had been made. Obviously she'd realized his interest in her was genuine. After her rejection of his invitation, he'd decided to be cooler toward her, but he hadn't been able to help accepting her apology. Nor had he been able to help enjoying her stimulating company.

Or falling under her spell.

Now, in the sobering daylight, he realized he'd let himself get carried away. Because of her ambivalence he'd have to go slowly, keep things light for a while. Besides, he was in a pretty confused state himself. He was definitely attracted to her, but though he was feeling better about himself after three days at the spa, he had the nagging feeling that Beth had blossomed right out of his reach....

"You'd think there were sharks in the pool the way you're beating the water to death!"

He had reached one end of the pool and turned to face Jill, who had swum up beside him. He'd taken one of her classes earlier in the day, and had chatted with her for some time afterward. He liked her. She was down-to-earth and funny—but she wasn't Beth.

He grinned. "No sharks. Just working off those anxieties."

"Those anxieties—they don't happen to concern my dearest friend and former roommate Beth Finlayson, do they?"

Sam looked at her. "I didn't realize you were that close."

"Couldn't be closer." Jill, who had been treading water alongside Sam, leaned up against the edge of the pool. "We were college roommates, then we got an apartment together, and now we're business partners and best friends. There aren't many secrets between us." She said this with a pointed look at Sam that was obviously intended to let him know she knew all about what was going on between the two of them.

Now Sam, too, stopped his determined motions and grabbed hold of the ledge. "Okay, Jill," he said straightforwardly. "There's obviously something on your mind. Why don't you come right out and say it?"

She hesitated for a moment. "I'm sorry, Sam. I didn't mean to come on like gangbusters. It's just that I know Beth so well, and she's told me a little about what's going on...."

"And..." Sam prompted.

Jill took a deep breath. "Well, I don't want to sound presumptuous or anything. But I feel I just have to say something—"

"So say it!"

"Okay, okay. It's totally unprofessional for me to say this to a client, but here goes. Sam, I've only seen Beth act the way she has in the past couple of days when she met her two—count 'em, *two*—previous boyfriends. I know there was something between you two way back when, though she hasn't shared a lot of the details, and you nipped it in the bud." She peeked at a grim-looking Sam. Her tone softened. "I just wanted to tell you that Beth is the dearest person in the world to me, after my family, and I couldn't bear to see her hurt. So be gentle, okay? Oh, God, I can't believe I said this to you. I've got such a big mouth. Sam, say something!"

But Sam didn't say anything for a long time. Finally, looking straight ahead, he said, "Do you think I feel good about the way I treated her in the past, Jill? I have news for you. I don't. Beth was one of the finest girls I knew and she deserved better. I would like to get to know the woman Beth a whole lot better, but I still can't offer any guarantees about the future."

He turned to look at Jill. "Did it ever occur to you that *she* might enjoy toying with *me* this time around? I asked her to dinner last night and she made me feel like dirt. She called to apologize and accept my invitation a while later, but I don't know how to deal with the hot and cold signals she's sending out. Besides, there are a million other potential problems—geographical distance, life-style differences—" He broke off helplessly.

"All of which can be worked out if two people love each other," Jill said softly.

"Isn't it a bit early in the game to be talking about love?"

Jill smiled. "It's never too early to be talking about love."

Sam returned the smile. "Words to live by."

"You do that." She climbed out of the pool, looked at him and said, "I think you're a good man, Sam. Don't disappoint me. Whatever you feel you have to do, do it honorably." With those words, she turned on her heel and walked to the ladies' change room.

Sam stayed in the pool and treaded water, not at all sure what else to do....

HE TRIED TO KEEP Jill's words in mind the rest of the week. He and Beth were wary around each other; he suspected that she felt as awkward about having responded to his kiss as he felt about having initiated it and saying the words he had. He forced himself not to push things—he'd go slowly, as he'd promised himself. But he hated the wariness; it seemed they were always feeling each other out, always looking for meanings beyond the words, emotions behind the actions. Sometimes he just wanted to grab her and crush her against him, tell her they were made for each other.

But he didn't. He made himself live day by day. He was quite enjoying his workouts now—and the food. Already he noticed that his pants were considerably looser and his muscles firmer. And considering his and Beth's ambivalence, they managed to spend quite a lot of time together—every minute of that time enjoyable and precious. They ate dinner together almost every night, and when Beth had a spare hour or two, she would often join him for a swim or a long walk. The air around them was always charged with sexual tension, though, and so activities that normally would have been relaxing, most definitely were not.

True to Sam's suspicions, Beth *was* feeling awkward about having shared that sensational kiss with him and thinking the thoughts she had—especially since Sam appeared to have withdrawn slightly. She wondered if he felt bad about taking advantage of her in a weak moment, misleading her.

She was glad when Thursday rolled around. It was her day off, and she went to town alone to do some errands—hoping time to herself would help her sort out her feelings. But though she usually enjoyed her days alone in town—living at the spa sometimes got on her nerves, as there were always so many people around—today she only felt lonely. She caught a five o'clock movie—a comedy that wasn't the least bit funny—and found herself longing for the variety of choice in Toronto. After the show, she grabbed a hot dog at the Dairy Queen—even dietitians sinned sometimes—went home, and climbed into bed at 8:30, eager to sleep and banish thoughts of a certain handsome mustard mogul from her mind....

On Friday, she didn't see Sam, either. Tied up with appointments all day, she only had time to grab a quick sandwich for dinner before heading over to Mike's place for meeting number two.

"Okay, guys," he announced when everyone was present, "let's get this show on the road. I realize some of you think you have more important concerns than the survival of this venture." He looked pointedly at Joel.

"Ouch!" Joel said, scrunching his face. "My, but you do know how to wound a poor doctor."

"There's an oxymoron if I've ever heard one," Jill said, grinning. "I don't believe I've ever heard those two words together before—poor and doctor. Nope." She shook her head. "Just doesn't go."

"What is this? Pick-on-Joel night?" he asked in an aggrieved tone. "Sheesh. And to think I gave up a hot date for this."

Beth, who was standing with Selma at the fireplace, came over to the couch and sat next to Joel. "How's the hot and heavy romance going, anyway?"

"Not so hot and heavy. Nora wants to take it slow. Her divorce just came through and she's a little gun-shy. We're taking it one step at a time." He shook his head. "I must say I'm getting impatient, though."

Beth saw the love shining on Joel's face and felt her eyes mist. Quickly she brushed any sign of moisture away. She was so sensitive these days! "That's really nice, Joel," she whispered, not trusting her voice to say any more.

Joel looked at her curiously. "And what's going on with you? Jill told me—"

"Social hour over," Mike said loudly. "We're here to save the spa, remember?"

When everyone had gathered around him, finally, he said, "Okay, I'll go around the circle and each of you will offer your suggestions for cutting costs and/ or increasing business. We'll start with you, Selma."

"Well, there isn't too much I can do to cut costs since my area doesn't require a lot of overhead. I suppose I could type a lot of my own reports instead of having Cheryl do them—she does them after 5:00, usually, and gets paid overtime. As for increasing business, I suppose I could advertise and try to get some media attention. Ads in the local papers should be cheap enough. I thought there was enough business here for me, so I never considered advertising, but it might be worth a shot. I could probably get quite a few town people in."

Mike nodded. "Good. I think you're right. And if you could type some of your own stuff, that would be great." He clasped his hands together. "Let me throw something else at you, Selma—Joel and Beth, too." The others looked at him expectantly. "How would you feel about using a sign-up system for scheduling clients and answering machines for taking calls—instead of Cheryl."

A chorus of arguments met his suggestion and he held up his hands. "Just listen to me for a moment," he said in a quietly persuasive tone. The clamor died down. "Cheryl's young and not a top-notch receptionist, but we're paying her pretty big bucks. A lot of professionals use answering machines. Selma, I've heard of psychologists and psychiatrists in private practice using them...and Beth, dietitians, too. A sign-up system means the patients would schedule your appointments for you, and with an answering machine, you'd be able to screen your calls—like Cheryl does now."

The group was silent. Finally Beth said hesitantly, "I guess I'd be willing to do it if you thought it would help that much."

"It would be a huge help, Beth. Cutting out that salary would lessen our burden by half. With a lot of little cutbacks on top of that, we'll be fine. And Cheryl hasn't been here long enough for anyone to get too dependent on her. Believe me, it's far better to get rid of someone when she's only been here a couple of months."

"But she likes it here so much," Selma said sadly.

"She's a nice, responsible girl and she'll get another good job," Mike said firmly, knowing the tide was turning in his favor.

"And if it doesn't work—after, say, three months, can we get a receptionist back?" Joel asked, his eyes narrowed.

"It's a deal," Mike said.

Beth expelled a breath. "I guess it's settled then."

"Fine." In a businesslike manner, Mike said, "Since she's been with us such a short time, we're only required by law to give her a couple of days notice. I'll tell her in the morning, and she can stay for the weekend—"

Beth broke in. "But Mike, that reporter is coming on Monday. Shouldn't we keep her on for a week? For appearances?"

Mike shook his head. "Beth, this is a crisis situation. We should have implemented these measures last week. Anyway, the sign-up board is such an efficient tool, I don't think there will be any mix-ups or crises. Trust me."

"Famous last words," Joel mumbled.

"Okay, now on to you, Jill." Mike turned a brilliant smile and supposedly mesmerizing eyes on the fitness director. "Any cost-cutting ideas?"

"Yeah, yeah. Distribute only one towel at the change room door instead of two, no free O.J. after classes, and we stick to the standard bikes and rowers, not upgrade like we were planning to."

Mike nodded. "Wonderful." He turned to Beth. "Beth?"

"Well, like Selma, I don't use equipment, and with Cheryl going, there's not much else I can do. I can tell Jane to cut down on the real expensive ingredients in the kitchen."

"Fine. I'm going to tell the room staff to cut down on some of the extras, too, like fruit for new arrivals, the number of towels in each room, and so on. And later on we might want to talk about cutting a couple of the other service people—maybe one of the cosmeticians or massage therapists. But we'll leave them be for now." He turned to Joel. "And finally, our joker-in-residence. Joel, any ideas?"

Joel shrugged. "I can only try to move my patients along quicker."

Mike looked at Selma and Beth. "Something you two should do, too." He smiled for a moment, then became serious again. "I have one more thing to suggest to everybody. It's not going to be popular, but it's standard business practice in times like these—"

"Salary cuts," Joel said, his voice indicating his disgust. "Jeez, Mike, is that really necessary?"

Mike shrugged. "Joel, if we're not all willing to cooperate, we're in a lot more trouble than we think."

"He's right," Jill said, sighing. "So much for the rest of my furniture."

"And mine," Beth echoed glumly.

"How much are we talking about here, Mike?" asked Selma.

"Twenty percent, I'd say."

"Ouch!" Joel exclaimed.

"It could be worse."

Beth nodded. "It sure could be. We could all be out of our jobs. And we will be if we don't all pull together. Come on, guys, twenty percent isn't tragic. Our living costs are pretty low. All entrepreneurs have to sacrifice a little before they make it."

Mike nodded approvingly. "Good girl. Okay, gang. Let's set what we've discussed in motion this weekend, and we'll reevaluate the situation once every couple of weeks or so. Is that okay with everybody?"

The others murmured their consent and got up to leave. Beth, trailing behind Selma and Joel, was just about to head out the door when she saw Mike corner Jill, who looked decidedly annoyed. Sensing that Jill needed some help, Beth called out to her friend, "Jill, are you coming?"

At the same time that Jill said, "Yeah, I'm coming," Mike said, "No, she's staying here for a bit."

Gently, Beth said, "Well, which is it?"

Jill glared at Mike. "Okay, Michael Petrie. I've had just about enough of you. You've been putting the moves on me for weeks now, and I've tried to be nice, tried to be polite, to no avail. I like you a lot as a friend and co-worker, but that's all we can be. Now just *cool* it, okay?" With that, she stormed out, never even looking back to see if Beth was following.

Beth guessed Jill wasn't particularly interested in pouring her heart out at the moment, so she decided to take the opportunity to have a little heart-to-heart with Mike. It wasn't in her nature to butt in to other people's love lives, but she sensed that things were coming to a head with her partners; both Jill and Mike were obviously quite distressed, and Beth did have a vested interest in seeing that all ran smoothly between her business partners. If their personal relationships deteriorated, the business was sure to follow.

She turned to Mike. "I think we need to talk," she said softly.

Mike ran both hands through his hair and sank onto a couch. "No lectures, please," he muttered. A moment later, he sighed and said, "I'm sorry, Beth. I know you're just concerned. Look, I like Jill—I like her a lot—and I'll tell you the honest truth, I'm not giving up yet. In business school the first thing you learn is to wear the customer down—persistence gets the sale every time."

Now Beth was really concerned. She sat down beside him, composing her speech in her head. She'd have to tread very lightly, she knew.

"Mike," she began, "Jill's obviously upset right now. Why don't you give her some space for a few weeks, date some other people in the meantime—"

"I don't *want* anybody else," Mike said sharply. He groaned. "There I go again. Beth, I'm going crazy." He jumped up and started to pace. "It's like, you know when you're a kid and it's so important to take the candy for recess that all the other kids love? Anything less—even the candy that tastes the same but has a different label—just isn't good enough. And then when you're a little older, it's the clothes. If the jeans aren't Levi's or Calvins, you're a nobody. You so desperately want these things! And when you're even older, and working, you have to have all the right status items in your apartment or your house, right down to the Alessi kettle...."

Beth was definitely worried at this point, but she didn't know quite what to say. There was an almost hysterical edge to Mike's voice, and she could only stare helplessly as he turned to her and said in a pleading tone, "Don't you get it, Beth? There's all that stuff that we're told every day we have to buy, and we think we need it, but we really don't, and it gets to the point where you think you'll go nuts if you don't have it."

Finally he stopped and took a ragged breath. Beth ventured cautiously, "So you don't necessarily want Jill, but you've talked yourself into thinking you'll go nuts if you can't have her?"

Mike seemed to snap back into reality and he gave her a confused look. Shaking his head tiredly, he said, "No, I wasn't talking about Jill. I was talking about—" he waved his hand vaguely "—everything." He sighed and said slowly, "Jill is the one person who might be able to help me—oh, I don't know—find the center of things, I guess."

Beth was thoroughly confused. Still, she said gently, "Mike, you can't just bend people to your will. If

Jill doesn't want to get involved with you, there's nothing you can do."

Mike only said tonelessly, "Go home, Beth. I know you're just trying to help, but...go home."

Slowly Beth got up and walked to the door. She turned around to say one more thing, but Mike was gone.

A chill ran down her spine. She had the sudden dreadful feeling that Mike's problem with Jill was only the tip of the iceberg. Somehow, she knew that something else in Mike's life had gone terribly, terribly wrong.

BETH STOPPED at Selma's cabin on the way home and apprised the psychologist of her strange conversation with Mike. Selma told Beth she'd try to talk to Mike, but warned her that unless he wanted to talk to her, she wouldn't be able to help. Somewhat reassured, Beth went back to her cabin and fell into bed, emotionally drained from the bizarre scene at Mike's. Her nightmares were filled with Alessi kettles and expensive pieces of art—and Mike's leering face urging her to "Buy, buy, buy!"

When her alarm rang in the morning, she groaned. And when her phone rang immediately afterward, she barked into the receiver, "Hello!"

"Hello, yourself!"

It was Sam. She took a moment to collect her thoughts. Before she could speak, he said, somewhat contritely, "I'm sorry. Did I wake you?"

"Oh, no!"

"That means yes, right? I'm sorry. It's just that I've missed you these past couple of days. I wanted to be sure to catch you before you left your house. Any chance I can make an appointment with you sometime today? And I don't mean to discuss the progress of my diet."

She couldn't help but smile. Maybe she was torturing herself too much about Sam. She'd missed him, too. Moreover, he was nice, seemingly sincere, handsome and wealthy. Didn't everybody deserve to have their adolescence obliterated? And with everything going on at the spa, she surely deserved some happiness. Then and there, she vowed to relax and enjoy her time with Sam.

"It would be my pleasure. How about lunch—at my place?" The words came out of her mouth unbidden. She had gone grocery shopping on her day off, and she did have the ingredients for quick and easy omelets and salads, but she wondered if it hadn't been a bit forward of her to ask him over.

But he didn't make a big deal out of it, for which she was grateful. All he asked was, "Will my dietitian approve?"

Beth smiled into the phone. "She'll be watching you like a hawk."

"Then I'll accept."

"Great. Around one?"

"Perfect. See you then."

Beth buried herself under the covers again and wondered how it was that her world seemed to be turning upside-down these days....

SAM SURPRISED HER with a bouquet of wildflowers he'd bought at the spa gift shop, and she thought she'd melt when he blushed as he gave them to her. "Thanks, Sam. That was so sweet, but unnecessary. Come in, come in."

"Nice place," he remarked as he stepped inside.

"Thanks. It's home—but not quite where I want it to be yet."

"Decorating a place takes time."

"It sure does. Tell you what, why don't you have a seat in the living room while I whip up a couple of omelets in the kitchen? Can I get you a drink?"

"Oh, no. We're partners in this. I'm a whiz with a frying pan."

He followed her into the kitchen, and Beth leaned against the counter and said, "Is that so?"

He looked affronted. "Do you doubt me? I am in the food business."

She crossed her arms over her chest. "Okay, big shot. Tell you what. Why don't we have a little contest?"

His eyes gleamed. "A cook-off?"

She grinned. "Yeah."

"Hmm. On second thought, you do have the home advantage..."

"I'll assemble all utensils and ingredients on the counter."

"You're on. We eat each other's omelets at the end and be scrupulously honest."

Laughing, she stuck out her hand. "It's a deal."

Beth soon discovered Sam was telling her the truth; he was a whiz in the kitchen—far more organized and conscientious than she was, and utterly engrossed in his task. Beth had never been more surprised in her life. Sam Sarnoff, the jock incarnate, taking tremendous pride in his perfect omelet! If only the football team could see him now! Interestingly enough, this aspect of him made him even more attractive in her eyes. Now *this* was a real man—one who looked great in jeans, especially since he'd lost a few pounds and firmed up substantially, and yet wasn't at all uncomfortable with doing what was traditionally "women's work."

Soon, they were seated at the kitchen table.

"The moment of truth," Beth announced as she prepared to cut into Sam's omelet. After chewing a bite slowly and swallowing, she said, "Uh-oh, I think I'm going to have to eat a little crow, too. Sam, this is *terrific*. Where did you learn to make such a divine omelet?"

He grinned. "Cordon Bleu."

"Aha! You're disqualified for withholding information. I can't believe you've been to the Cordon Bleu! When? Why?"

"Just before I went into business. I figured it couldn't hurt to learn about food from the pros—especially since I was going to be working in the industry. I did pretty well, though I must admit, I don't do this kind of thing very often anymore. As you know, I'm shamelessly addicted to fast food—a condition left over from my childhood that my Cordon Bleu friends would find thoroughly appalling, I'm sure." He took a bite of her omelet. "Hey, this isn't bad," he pronounced. "A little primitive, but it definitely has potential...."

She stuck out her tongue. "Very funny."

As they ate, they talked of myriad things—mutual acquaintances, hobbies and interests—but the time came soon enough when they had to part. Beth was sad that their "date" was over. She'd had a wonderful time. They'd been easy and relaxed with each other, and she actually found herself feeling optimistic about a relationship. They were taking things slowly, and it felt comfortable. Well, not comfortable, exactly. Before he left, Sam kissed her, and even though it was not a particularly passionate or sexy kiss—it was more tender than anything else—the effect it had on her was tremendous. She felt as if she'd been hit by lightning....

Soon, things began to look up on the business front, too. Over the weekend, the partners instituted the measures they'd discussed on Friday night, and all went fairly smoothly. Customers seemed willing to accept the decreased services with good humor, and on

Monday, Beth woke up smiling and humming, feeling better than she had in days. Even the problem with Mike seemed to be straightening itself out. Jill had indicated that he had been civil but distant over the weekend, which was just fine with her.

But when Beth came into the foyer of the main building on Monday morning, she got that chill down her spine again. Grouped at the front desk were Joel and Selma, smiling brightly, as well as a tall, gawky-looking stranger, and Jill—looking at the stranger with interest. Mike was standing a short distance behind Jill, his hands shoved into his pockets. He was glaring at the object of his desire.

Something was definitely wrong with this picture.

CHAPTER FIVE

"OH, HERE'S BETH!" Selma called out brightly. The group turned in synchronized movement. Beth had the distinct impression that they were insanely happy to see her.

Selma sauntered over to Beth and took her arm upon reaching her. As she guided Beth over to the others, she whispered, "Karen's sick with the flu, and Jane is having a delayed reaction to your suggestion about cutting costs in the kitchen. She's throwing a fit as we speak. Smile."

Beth immediately pasted on her standard phony smile.

As they met the group, Selma said, "Tom, I'd like you to meet Beth Finlayson, our in-house dietitian, and another partner in the spa. Beth, this is Tom Seldrake, from *City Life* magazine."

"I'm very pleased to meet you, ma'am."

"Likewise, Tom." While expressing this in a delighted tone, Beth was thinking she'd never seen an unlikelier looking reporter. Tom definitely didn't fit the mold of the urbane sophisticate who wrote for trendy city magazines. In fact, he looked as if he'd just come off the farm.

As Beth came to this conclusion, she noticed that Tom's bags were still on the floor. "Tell you what, Tom. Why don't we get you settled in your room, and then we can all have breakfast together."

Joel cleared his throat and said, "Uh, Beth, Karen has taken ill, and, uh, none of us can seem to find the reservations list. Do you happen to know where it is?"

Thankfully she did. Karen had recently confided to Beth that she'd begun to lock the list in a drawer—because of that "mischievous Mike."

"Yes, I do," she said, realizing that they couldn't have gotten off to a worse start. She walked behind the reservations desk, took a small key out of a drawer, and opened another one with it. She smiled weakly. "Karen's very security conscious."

Tom nodded. "Have you considered using a computer?"

So he wasn't just a naive farm boy, Beth mused as she retrieved the precious list.

"That's something we've been thinking about," Joel said briskly, looking frantically down the list over Beth's shoulder.

"Room 302," she finally announced.

"Wonderful," Joel said. "I'll help you with your bags."

"No porters?" Tom asked in a surprised tone.

"No porters," Joel answered through gritted teeth.

"Joel, I know you've got patients to see. Why don't I help Tom with his bags?"

Beth was surprised to hear Jill speak. She'd forgotten the fitness director was standing there. But one look at Jill and that horrible feeling came back.

"Don't be ridiculous, Jill. They'll only be a minute," Mike said smoothly. He'd been standing well behind them, but now he walked up to join the group. Beth wondered if everyone else could tell that the air was fairly crackling with tension.

"I insist," Jill said. And before Mike could make another comeback, she hefted Tom's bags with ease and walked jauntily toward the stairs. "Coming, Tom?" she asked in a singsong voice.

"Sure am," he said, and added, "Those are pretty big biceps for a little lady."

"Well, I guess our fitness program really works. I have to set a good example, you know...."

Jill's voice trailed off, and the others stood staring after them. After a moment, Selma said, "Well, that was certainly interesting."

"How long is he staying?" Beth asked in a barely audible whisper.

"Only till Sunday," Joel replied grimly. "He's doing one of those 'My six days at a spa' pieces."

"Well, six days isn't so bad. Remember, there was a time when we were actually looking forward to his arrival."

"That was before Karen got sick, Jane threw a fit and Jill caught a glimpse of Tom-boy," Mike said darkly.

"Well, we'll just have to make the best of it," Selma pronounced, smiling. But the others only glared at her.

When Jill and Tom came back downstairs, the group headed off to the dining room.

"Isn't he cute?" Jill whispered to Beth, who just stared at her friend. "He seems so honest and decent—like Jimmy Stewart in *Mr. Smith goes to Washington.*"

Beth couldn't seem to find any words, and for a split second she wondered if she was dreaming. Tom Seldrake seemed incredibly ordinary to her. Obviously attractiveness was very much in the eye of the beholder.

When they were seated, Selma and Joel—the only ones of the bunch who seemed to be playing with a full deck, in Beth's opinion—began to draw Tom out. Soon, he was telling them all about the farm he'd grown up on, near a small town just outside of Barrie, Ontario—*Aha,* thought Beth—and how his father had run the town's newspaper.

"I decided when I was still a pup that I wanted to be a reporter just like my daddy," he said proudly, then grinned and shook his head. "I went to journalism school out in Ottawa, at Carleton University, and that was some shock to an old farm boy like me, let me tell you. Those big-city boys sure kept me on my toes."

"Oh, I'm sure you had some things to teach them, too," Jill said smoothly.

At the compliment, Tom's face turned pink—in contrast to Mike's, which went so white, his dark eyes seemed like small black pits.

"Well, I probably did teach some of those guys a thing or two about small-town honesty and decency." At this, Jill shot Beth a triumphant look. Tom shook his head. "What some of those sharks wouldn't do for a story. Boggles the mind, I tell ya."

At that point, Mike rose and threw his napkin on the table.

"Mike, where are you going?" Joel asked with eyes that said, "What the hell are you doing?"

"You'll have to excuse me," he said grimly. "Suddenly I feel sick to my stomach." With that, he turned on his heel and walked away. The others, who had been struck dumb by Mike's actions, looked down at their plates.

Except for Jill, who said cheerily, "Well, we can't let him rain on our parade, can we? I'm starving. What's for breakfast, anyway?"

ON TUESDAY EVENING, Beth took her time getting ready for the "California Beach Party" that had been planned for the guests and staff by Polly. It promised to be great fun, though Mike had insisted on substantially cutting Polly's original budget. He did relent on a few points when his partners had vehemently insisted that it was important to impress Tom. In the end, the plans for the evening pleased everybody. There would be chicken dogs roasted on open fires—

Beth had insisted on chicken as opposed to beef—
"lite" beer, Beach Boys music, Hula Hoop competitions and a lip-synch contest. And if it got too chilly by the lake, they could always move to the dining room.

Beth had chosen to wear faded Levi's and a Camp Beverly Hills sweatshirt that she'd bought on a trip to Los Angeles five years earlier. She'd put her hair up in a Barbie doll ponytail and finished the look off with a pair of Keds sneakers—in white, of course. She wanted to look as though she was getting into the spirit of the thing, but at the same time she didn't want to overdo it. She intended to look her very best for Sam, and her stomach was already fluttering in anticipation of seeing him again—possibly kissing him again...and more...

When Jill showed up at her door, Beth shrieked with laughter. In black stretch capri pants, a neon-pink off-the-shoulder top, Ray-Ban sunglasses and a Sony Walkman, she was the epitome of the modern California beach bunny.

"Oh, stop laughing," Jill muttered. "How does anybody expect me to see anything at night with sunglasses on? Whose idea was this, anyway?"

"Yours, partly. Like, let's split, okay?" Beth's imitation of a valley girl was truly awful, and Jill couldn't help but laugh. On their way over to the lake, they rehearsed their hastily put together rendition of "Respect Yourself" for the lip-synch contest.

"Thank the good Lord we don't really have to sing," Beth said, laughing.

"Amen, sister," Jill responded.

Soon they arrived at the lake and approached the large circle of staff members already there, including Mike, Selma, Joel, Jane and Polly. Polly was giving her standard preevening program talk. Mike and Joel looked relatively bored; Selma, indifferent, and Jane, resentful. Undoubtedly the temperamental cook had been haranguing Mike about the cutbacks. And in all likelihood, Mike had tried his best to ignore her.

"Okay, guys," Polly was saying cheerfully, "let's really have fun tonight, okay? And remember, be sure to mingle with the guests!"

"It never ceases to amaze me that somebody around here is even more perky than you," Beth said to Jill, grinning.

Jill quirked an eyebrow. "Polly's not a someone, she's a something. No human being can be that happy all the time. She's going full blast at dawn. Believe me, I know whereof I speak. She's always the first one at my early class, so bubbly she makes you dizzy just looking at her."

"Oh, stop it," Beth admonished her friend playfully. "Polly's a good kid."

"Yeah, she is," Jill admitted. "I'm probably just jealous. People think I'm always happy, but I'm not. She really is!"

Beth shrugged. "Who knows? I thought the same thing about you in school—that you had no problems. Then I saw you cry for a week over a man, throw up all over our carpet after eating three cartons of ice cream in one night and dye your hair purple."

"It was supposed to be red," Jill mumbled.

"Whatever."

Just then, Beth saw Karen approaching. Apparently her flu had been of the twenty-four-hour variety, but she was still feeling under the weather and was clutching her sweater around her shoulders and sniffling loudly.

"Karen!" Beth exclaimed. "Why are you here? You should be at home in bed."

Karen smiled a weak martyr's smile. "Oh, no, I couldn't miss this. Polly's been planning it for so long. And besides, as a part of the Couchiching team, it's my duty to set an example."

Jill poked Beth in the back surreptitiously, and Beth had to struggle to hold back the smile she felt creeping around the corners of her mouth. The woman definitely had an exaggerated sense of her own importance.

"Besides," Karen continued, "we need all the staff members we have available tonight. I checked my records and there are more people at the spa today than at any other time in our history."

"You're kidding," Jill said. "Does Mike know that?"

Karen's lips tightened. She and Mike had never gotten along. "I suppose he does."

"Strange that he hasn't mentioned it," Jill murmured.

Beth shrugged. "He probably doesn't want us to think we're out of trouble. Can't get too confident and all that jazz."

"I wonder..." Jill's words trailed off, and she was just about to say something else when Beach Boys music came on full blast.

Guests were beginning to approach, and Beth spotted Sam immediately. Her eyes were drawn to his like magnets. He looked sensational in faded jeans, a white sweatshirt, deck shoes and sunglasses. His high school body was reemerging and it was definitely hot. Beth smiled when he approached. "Very cool," she said. "Very hip."

"Likewise, babe." He looked at her approvingly. "Totally awesome."

Beth groaned. "I refuse to call you 'dude,' so don't even ask, okay?"

"It's a deal," he said, grinning, and at his smile, Beth felt her insides flip-flop. Suddenly she felt giddy and crazy, the way she should have felt at her high school dances but never did because she was too self-conscious.

Sam pointed toward Mike and Joel, who were busy cooking hot dogs over an open fire and piling them on trays carried by Polly and Selma to large tables spread out on the beach. "Now there's something I could get into," he said. "Care to join me?"

"Don't get all excited. They're chicken dogs—I insisted."

"A dog is a dog is a dog," he said blithely. "Come on."

When they were happily digging into their dogs, Beth commented between bites, "You know I wasn't completely sure you'd show up tonight."

"Oh? How come?"

"I dunno." She took another bite of her dog, chewed and swallowed. "I guess I figured you might lock yourself in your bungalow and catch up on work or something."

"You know, it's funny about that. I did bring work with me—a ton of it—and I keep meaning to do it, only I find myself continually making excuses. To tell you the truth, I'm enjoying it here a lot more than I thought I would. I just can't seem to get into a working mode."

"Then we're doing our job," Beth said, smiling. "You know, I can see a difference in you already. When you first got here, I could see the tension in your face."

She was about to go on, but Mike was approaching, and Beth knew what he wanted before he even said a word.

"Don't tell me," she said, grimacing. "Duty calls, right?"

"You got it, Finlayson. Snap to it. The rest of us have been working our butts off." He turned to Sam.

"You must be some charmer to have kept Beth away for so long."

Beth was grateful it was evening so Sam couldn't see her blush. "Sam, this is Mike Petrie, the spa's business manager. Mike, this is Sam Sarnoff, an old friend of mine."

"So you're Sam Sarnoff! It's great meeting you, Sam. You're in the food business, right?"

"Right. The Great Canadian Condiment Company."

"Super name! So the mustard business is good, eh?"

Beth decided it was time to make a graceful exit. "I'll leave you two financial geniuses alone. If you need me, I'll be slaving over the open fire...."

"Spare us, Finlayson." When she'd gone, Mike turned back to Sam. "So, I hear that's some successful company you've got there."

"Pardon?" Sam, preoccupied with watching Beth walk away, turned back to Mike. "Oh...yeah, well, I've been lucky. The business has done very well."

"I'm sure your business acumen has had more to do with it than luck," Mike said smoothly.

"Thanks for the compliment, but I don't know that anybody else couldn't have done it. I was pretty green when I started. Basically it's been a trial and error thing." He decided to change the topic. "You seem to have quite a success here yourself."

Mike shrugged. "It's a constant struggle. You wouldn't believe the upkeep costs on a place like this—grounds maintenance alone costs thousands a month."

Sam's eyebrows lifted. "That sounds awfully high."

"I kid you not. I'm talking about everything now—pool maintenance, landscaping, general caretaking, snow removal in the winter. It's never ending."

"Do you use that new maintenance service—the one geared to industry in this area...I forget the name...."

"Total Maintenance. Yup, we use them. I used to work for them before I started here—I ran their operation. I'm getting the discount rate, believe it or not."

"That's funny," Sam said slowly. "I know someone else who uses Total. It's a residential spread, a ranch, not usually what they do, but it's so huge a place, it made sense for him to use them. His needs are quite different than yours, but the acreage would be about the same and they charge him much, much less. I don't remember the exact figure, but it's nothing close to thousands a month."

"Well, like you said, his needs are different. Hey, Sam, it's been great talking to you, but I'm supposed to mingle with the other guests. Catch you later, dude!" With a wink, he was off, leaving a puzzled Sam standing there alone, trying to figure out why he didn't quite trust Mike....

Beth returned to his side shortly after Mike left. "Phew!" she said. "Looks like the rush is over. I think the entertainment portion of our evening is about to begin. Let's try to get good seats."

He glanced over to where a makeshift stage had been set up on the beach. Blankets were spread out in front of it. "I'm impressed," he commented.

"So am I," Beth said as they walked toward a blanket. "Polly really outdid herself tonight."

"Polly?"

"Polly Palmer. She plans all these programs. She lives in town and she's really great—so enthusiastic and energetic."

"Seems like you've got a real motley crew working here."

Beth smiled as they lowered themselves onto one of the blankets. "You're right—we're all so different it doesn't seem like we should work together, but we do—very well."

"That's great. Really." So great, he felt a bit of a pang. Beth and the others had so much fun with their work. His job had long since ceased being fun for him. But what was he to do about it?

His thoughts were cut off when Polly announced "The First Annual Couchiching-Disguised as California Beach Party Lip-Synch Contest!"

To his surprise, Beth's name was announced along with Jill's and she bounded up and onto the stage, where she and Jill strutted and laughed their way through a campy bump-and-grind version of "Respect Yourself." They were rewarded with rousing applause at the end, Sam's being the loudest. How much she'd changed since high school! The shy bookworm he'd known, while charming in her own way, would never have risked making a spectacle of herself in front of such a large group. Nor would she have acted so unselfconsciously, so...sexily!

"You've come a long way, baby," he told her, grinning, when she came back to the blanket.

"I won't ask if that's good or bad," she said breathily, still flushed with excitement. To Sam she had never looked more beautiful.

"Oh, it's good. It's definitely good," he murmured. He was about to reach over and kiss her when Andy Erdrich's name was called, and Sam found his head turning out of sheer curiosity.

Everybody hooted as he hammed his way through a scratchy recording of "Talk to the Animals." At least he had a sense of humor, Sam thought, in such a good mood he could afford to be magnanimous even to the fellow who irked him no end.

There were a couple more acts, then the Hula Hoop contest, at which Beth and Sam failed miserably, and after that, things died down fairly quickly. Sam remained behind with the staff members to help clean up, above Beth's protests. He insisted on walking her home, and at her door, he said softly, "Thank you for a wonderful evening."

"Thank you."

He leaned over and placed a soft kiss on her lips. She was about to speak, but he put a finger over her mouth. "I'll see you soon, okay?"

"Okay," she whispered.

"I don't want to ruin this by rushing it. We've got all the time in the world...."

Beth nodded weakly, and as he waved goodbye and walked down the path to the road, she touched her lips and wondered exactly what kind of roller-coaster ride she was in for.

ON WEDNESDAY, Beth didn't see Sam at all; she was too busy keeping Tom occupied. She and her partners were determined to fill his every moment. He seemed to be enjoying the place, but it was hard to tell, really. Jill kept reassuring the others, saying that she knew he loved the spa—and she should know.

Indeed, the fitness director was spending an inordinate amount of time with the farm-boy-turned-ace-reporter. Unfortunately the happier Jill seemed to get, the more withdrawn Mike got. And to add to the confusion, the odd complaint from a guest would come their way—a new development in the spa's relatively short history. It seemed some customers did not appreciate the cutbacks, after all. Beth was thankful *City Life* had sent the farm boy. Originally she'd been excited about any reporter coming, but now, upon reflection, she realized that a city reporter used to posh, upscale fitness clubs would probably have laughed their modest spa right out of existence.

She was also eternally grateful when Thursday—her day off—rolled around. After mustering her courage, she had asked Sam to join her for a day of fun and frolic in Orillia. He'd accepted with pleasure, though he'd expressed surprise at the fact that she'd "allow" him to leave the premises.

"Don't be silly, Sam," she'd said, laughing. "This isn't a jail. You're free to come and go as you please."

"You mean there are no guard dogs at the entrance?"

"No guard dogs at the entrance."

"Then it's a date."

"Great. By the way, we'll be swimming at least thirty lengths in the lake and eating only salad all day." At his silence she added, "Joke, Sam."

"Oh!" He'd laughed weakly, obviously relieved.

Beth found herself humming as she got ready and planned their day. It was 8:30 a.m. First, they'd eat at her favorite greasy spoon—a cozy little place with A-1 breakfasts. She'd try not to think about cholesterol today. Then they'd walk around town for a bit and flop out in the sun at Couchiching Beach. She'd play dinner by ear. If the day went well, perhaps they'd do that, too.

She looked at herself in the mirror critically. *Not bad, Beth,* she said to herself. She'd thrown a big red T-shirt and khaki walking shorts over her black maillot and had added dangly silver earrings for a casual but chic effect. She'd achieved the look she'd wanted: thoroughly stylish but not so much that it looked studied. Heaven forbid he should know that she'd spent almost an hour deciding on the color of her shirt.

When she heard a knock on her door, her stomach fluttered in excitement. *Be calm,* she ordered herself. But when she opened the door, she couldn't keep herself from staring. He looked sensational! He was wearing a classic white polo shirt and navy walking shorts. He had acquired a golden glow over the past couple of weeks, and his body was on its way to becoming nicely toned again. Beth thought he looked like a model in a summer issue of *GQ*.

"Hi," she said, trying desperately to keep her breath under control.

"Hi, yourself," he said, smiling almost shyly. "You look great. All ready for a day of fun and sun?"

"You bet. Let me just grab my purse and we can be off." She dashed to her bedroom, took one last critical look at herself in the mirror, and thought, *I can't do much better than this.* Then she dashed back downstairs.

They'd agreed to take Sam's car, and Beth was not all that surprised to see it was a white Saab.

"Nice car," she commented.

"Thanks," he replied, opening the passenger door for her. "It was one of my first indulgences when the business became a success."

"Really? That's my plan, too. But I'm still waiting."

Sam shut her door, then came around to the driver's side and got in. As he started the car, he grinned and said, "I know—that's why I offered to take us in style. Was that the same car you were driving in high school in your driveway?"

"Very funny. But too close for comfort. I bought that baby in college. I've had it for so long, I can't bear to give it up. Though I must say, I'm getting closer to that point every day—in direct proportion to the amount of trouble it gives me."

As they drove off, Sam said, "I know how you feel. You get attached to a car. I think I'm closer to my car than I am to most people."

Beth looked at him curiously. "That's not the Sam Sarnoff I know."

He remained silent for a moment. "You're right. I'm not the Sam Sarnoff you know—or knew."

She wasn't quite sure how to react to that. She sensed he wasn't ready to talk about their past relationship or its awkward demise, despite his words. She decided to hit the ball back to him, anyway.

"In what ways have you changed—aside from growing more handsome and fulfilling all that glorious potential?"

"My, my. You're quite the flatterer. You're almost as good as I was in high school."

"Only I meant it." The words slipped out before she could stop them. "Sam, I'm—"

"Don't, Beth." He stared straight ahead. "You're absolutely right. I cringe when I think of some of the stunts I pulled back then, the numbers I did on people. I was given a little attention and it went straight to my head." He chuckled wryly. "What a fool I was, thinking I could get everything I wanted with a great smile and a tan. By the way, where are we going?"

Lost in thought, Beth realized they were quickly approaching downtown Orillia, and she instructed him toward the restaurant she had in mind, on Mississaga Street. "It's a bit of a greasy spoon," she told him, "but the food's great—and cheap."

Soon they were ensconced in an old-style leatherette booth, poring over the diner's straightforward menu. Sam grinned and said, "I love places like this. Spare me the eggs Benedict and the mushroom quiche—give me scrambled eggs, hash browns and black coffee and I'm a happy man."

"The dietitian in me feels compelled to tell you that eating a breakfast like this is okay once in a while, but remember that in restaurants, the eggs and the potatoes tend to be fried in very fatty oils. And besides, everyone should limit their egg intake to three servings a week—and you should watch the caffeine, too."

"Hey, I've been a very good boy. Don't I deserve a treat?"

"Of course you do. Remember, everything in moderation."

"Yes, ma'am."

When they had placed their orders, Sam said, "So you want to know how I've changed since high school."

"Oh, Sam, I didn't mean—"

He held up a hand. "Beth, it's okay—really. I told you, I know I was incredibly thoughtless back then.

I'm just glad I woke up in time, started to take things seriously. It seems I've gone overboard with that, too, but that's another story.''

"So what caused this turnaround?" Beth asked as their waitress placed two glasses of orange juice on their table.

"The death of my father."

"It must have been horrible for you," Beth said softly.

"It was. My father was a quiet man, a proud man— an honest man. He worked hard and didn't make much money. But you know what? He didn't care. I was unhappier about it than he was.''

"Your father was certainly extraordinary, Sam. And you have many of his wonderful qualities."

He looked her straight in the eye. "You can still say that about me?''

"Of course. At one time you were a good friend to me. That last year in high school you were definitely a jerk, but I guess everybody should be forgiven their high school days sooner or later, right?''

Well said, Beth, she congratulated herself. *You acknowledged that he made a mistake without making a specific accusation. He can take it as a joke if he likes.*

But he took her words quite seriously. "I was never a very good friend to you, Beth. I could have done much better. It seems I've paid too much attention to the wrong people and not enough to the people I should have."

"Your parents?" she asked softly.

He nodded. "I think I told you I was in my first year of university, at Windsor, when Pa died. I was just coasting along, like I did in high school, and boom—tragedy struck. He went pretty quickly. My mother was never the same. It was as if she couldn't live without him. She died when I had just started my business."

"They never saw you become a success," Beth said sympathetically.

Sam shrugged. "It wouldn't have been a big deal to them. And I probably wouldn't have become the driven businessman that I am if my dad hadn't died. He was constantly warning me against becoming too materialistic. A big reason I threw myself into work was so I wouldn't have to deal with the pain of losing them. Work was my escape, my salvation. And a way of paying tribute to my mother through her recipes. Yummy," he added appreciatively after enthusiastically gulping down some hash browns. The waitress had brought the rest of their meal while he'd been talking.

"Oh-oh," Beth said teasingly. "I can tell it's going to be tough to get you back on spa food."

Grinning, Sam replied, "Maybe the secret is to give everybody a meal like this once in a while."

When they were finished breakfast, they strolled along Mississaga Street and Beth pointed out some of the town's landmarks, such as the Orillia opera house, and the more popular shops and restaurants. Then they walked at a leisurely pace back to the car, from which Beth retrieved the beach bag she'd brought along, and they headed toward the lake.

When they got to the beach, they spread a large blanket on the ground, and then Sam began to strip down to the swimming trunks he was wearing underneath his walking shorts.

At the sight of his broad, tanned torso and his muscular legs, Beth caught her breath—and began to panic. Would she be able to stay rational while lying beside him on a blanket for the remainder of the day? She certainly hoped so!

When she realised that he was looking at her questioningly, as if to ask why she wasn't getting undressed, she removed her clothes. She didn't notice that Sam was looking at her almost exactly the same way she'd looked at him just a few moments earlier, as though he wasn't sure his equilibrium could take a whole day of lying beside her.

In fact, he was thinking he'd never seen such a beautiful body before—curvy in all the right places, but well toned, and exceedingly graceful. And it was shown off to perfection in a sexy black one-piece suit. Her skin had a luscious golden glow to it, and it looked as soft as velvet. How he longed to reach out and touch her, stroke her, caress her....

Stop it, he told himself firmly. *You're in for a whole day of looking and not touching.*

They smiled awkwardly at each other for a couple of seconds, then lay down on the blanket—Sam moving to the farthest end of his side, and Beth moving to the far end of hers.

But Beth began to relax as the warm sun began to envelop her. "Mmm, that feels nice," she murmured.

"Sure does," Sam replied, wishing her words could have been in response to his touch instead of to the sun's. But soon he, too, began to fall under its spell.

Since it was a weekday, the beach was relatively empty, and the only noises were those of the sea gulls on the shore and the occasional child laughing or crying. A slight breeze wafted over them, and they lay perfectly still.

After a few moments, Beth said, "This is why I love Orillia."

"I completely understand," Sam said. "It's so peaceful here. You can almost feel the tension leaving your body. I never get that feeling in Toronto."

"Well, don't get too relaxed," Beth said, dumping a handful of sand on a surprised Sam's stomach.

"Hey," he boomed, sitting up and scrambling behind her to the shore, where she was heading with a graceful jog.

When they reached the water's edge, Sam landed a neat handful of sand on her back and she shrieked playfully. She retaliated with a few splashes of water, then ran into the lake and dunked before he could get her back. Sam followed suit. They came up for air at the same time, and Sam promptly splashed her face. She pushed him, and he grabbed on to her shoulders. But as soon as he touched her, the playful mood evaporated. All he could think of was how smooth and silky her glistening wet skin felt and how incredibly sexy she looked, the water molding her suit to every curve so there was nothing left to the imagination.

Beth, too, was suddenly breathless. Dripping wet, Sam looked incredibly powerful and attractive. She imagined his strong arms enfolding her, his hands tenderly but confidently stroking her, causing her to lose control....

Their eyes met, and each read the desire in the other's look. As if in a trance, Sam moved closer to her, and Beth, equally mesmerized, lifted her head to meet his lips. At first, his mouth touched hers tentatively, questioningly. But it only took a moment for a soft sound to escape her mouth, and her own lips to move against his in a way that invited him to give in to his desire and kiss her like a starving man. His darting tongue teased her lips until she had to open her mouth fully and respond to his every move.

This kiss was entirely different from the first tender one they'd shared that night at the spa. Then, they'd been shy with each other, unsure of how to proceed. Now they drank each other in, gloried in the passion they were experiencing.

When they were on the brink of sinking into the water and wrapping their legs around each other, they broke apart breathlessly. But Sam did not let go of her. "I've wanted to do that since high school," he murmured against her hair, nuzzling it with his lips.

"Me, too," Beth said softly.

Sam tilted her head up so that he could see her face. "You don't regret it, do you?" he asked quietly.

Beth smiled tremulously. "Regret giving in to my teenage fantasy?"

Sam said seriously, "I don't intend to hurt you again, you know."

Beth smiled again, bravely. "Yeah, sure. That's what all you heartbreakers say." She looked away, unable to stop an inexplicable tear from running down her face. She cursed herself for being so emotional. If he wasn't already thinking of running, he would surely begin to do so now.

But he just held on to her tightly, and murmured, "It's going to be all right, Beth."

And somehow, she knew that their relationship had reached a new plane and there would be no turning back. . . .

WHILE BETH AND SAM were discovering each other in a glorious new way, Mike was sitting huddled in the corner of his living room. Damn! Nothing was working out the way he'd planned—nothing! Things had been going so smoothly for a while, too.

But then, he'd never had it easy—not like his partners. He spat the word out in his mind. He'd known he was different from them as soon as he'd met them, way back in college. They'd all—with the possible exception of Beth—come from disgustingly happy, middle-class homes. He, on the other hand, had been the son of a bitterly unhappy, violent man, and a young and mixed-up woman. He'd never even met his mother, but he'd heard stories over the years. His father's relatives had never bothered to censor their thoughts in front of young Michael.

Unlike his fancy friends, he'd grown up in a slum, with nobody caring if he was "content" or "fulfilled." His father hadn't thought happiness was particularly important. Maybe it was a matter of wanting to bring those around him down to his level. If he wasn't happy, nobody else would be, either....

It had escaped dear dad's eye that his son, Mike, possessed a keen intelligence. And since he also possessed a fiercely determined spirit, it became a goal of his at a very young age to escape his place of birth and create a new life, a new identity for himself. And he'd done so, by working his butt off in high school, winning an entrance scholarship to university.

It was there he'd met his future partners. Even though he'd scorned them on a certain level, he'd also envied them. Joel Green was everything Mike knew he'd never be: easygoing, happy, fun, relaxed. He would have bet a million dollars that Joel had never felt completely alone, completely unloved. And there was no way his partner had ever known how it felt to be at the mercy of someone who was completely unbalanced, completely unpredictable....

And then there was Jill—the all-American blonde, the girl next door. She, too, was everything he was not, but now he wanted her—*needed* her. With her on his side, he could still pull it off. But it wasn't working, dammit! Jill had fallen like a ton of bricks for that wimped-out reporter—anybody could see it.

And on top of that, he was beginning to get nervous about his "perfect" plan for paying back his creditors. Unfortunately the initial small amounts he'd "borrowed" from the spa coffers had become larger and larger as the collectors had leaned on him more and more. They weren't exactly the most upstanding citizens, and Mike could have kicked himself for having gotten involved with them in the first place. Somehow, he sensed that they'd never stop demanding payments....

At least his partners had given him a free hand with the books, naive souls that they were. He'd been doing plenty of creative accounting of late, in the form of fabricating fees for Total Maintenance, mainly. When he'd gotten the idea of skimming funds to pay back his debts, he'd had a few drinks with his old friends from Total and had managed to sneak the office key away from one drunken deadbeat. He'd taken a huge pile of invoices, and each month, he paid Total's legitimate fee, then destroyed the original invoice and replaced it with a phony one. He'd also come up with an elaborate plan for keeping dummy ledger books, hence his insistence on cutbacks—so he could pocket the extra dough. Bringing the reporter here after instituting the cutbacks was part of his plan, too. Hopefully Tom's article would cause a real drop-off in bookings. Hereby justifying even more cutbacks.

Only recently had he really started to panic. Having Tom around really made him nervous—not to mention mad as hell for attracting Jill's attention. And he'd started questioning himself. Had he gotten too sloppy, too obvious? Why in hell had he talked to that Sam guy about Total Maintenance? He'd had a few beers too many that night and couldn't remember things too clearly. *Damn!* He was a sharpie, that Sam. Maybe he'd catch on!

And he'd almost spilled the beans to Beth a few days ago! Thank God he'd caught himself before he'd done any real damage. At the time he'd wondered why it had been Beth he'd come close to confiding in. After having had a few days to contemplate the matter, he'd come to the conclusion that of all of them, Beth was the one he had the most in common with. She'd always been on the edge of things, too—not quite as cheerful, relaxed or easygoing as her friends. Unlike the others, she rarely mentioned her family. Something was awry there, he was sure of it.

But she wasn't as smart as he was. In fact, she was pretty stupid, getting more like them all the time. Now she was making a fool of herself over that bigwig. Making her an ally would be foolish. Anyway, she didn't even like him all that much.

As for Selma, she was hopeless with her phony middle-class sympathy. She didn't know anything. Talk about naive! And she actually thought he might talk to her about his problems! Fat chance.

No, they weren't like him at all. But he'd never felt more different from them than he did now. Funny, he knew they all thought they knew him. They had fit him into the slimy-but-successful mold. What they didn't realize was that they could never really know him. Nobody could ever really know anybody else. Just as they had no idea where he had come from, what he had been—long ago he'd fabricated a tale of parents who died in a fiery car crash—they couldn't know what went on in the dark, hidden chambers of his heart and mind.

Sure, they'd had some laughs together, but what did that mean? Yeah, they'd been the closest he'd ever come to friends, but he'd have to distance himself even more now. He'd never been like them, but he'd crossed over some invisible boundary of late.

He'd become a criminal.

CHAPTER SIX

RATHER INCREDIBLY, Beth and Sam managed to get through the rest of the afternoon and the early part of the evening without ripping off each other's bathing suits. Lying on the beach, they talked about their work and their friends, as if there was an unspoken agreement between them to learn even more about each other now that their relationship had undeniably changed.

Beth even told him a little bit about the problems at the spa, hoping he'd be able to offer some suggestions. But Sam seemed surprised when she said the spa wasn't doing well, and said it sounded as if they were taking the right steps if, in fact, the place was in trouble. He'd added that only someone familiar with the ledger could really know what was going on. Of course, he had vague suspicions about Mike, but he didn't dare tell Beth about them at this critical point in their relationship. Mike was her friend, and she would surely take offense.

As it came closer to the time for them to pack up, Beth tried to quell her rising feelings of nervousness. She knew that when Sam took her home, she wouldn't be able to send him away. She wanted to be close to him in every way a woman could be close to a man. They already knew each other's minds intimately; now she wanted to know his body intimately. She couldn't help but imagine how he would feel against her, inside her. . . .

But at the same time, she was apprehensive. She tried valiantly to recapture the light, teasing atmosphere she'd managed to create earlier in the day, when she'd thrown sand at him, but no matter how hard she tried, she couldn't act casually around him any longer. And not just because she thought of him as a potential lover now. The fact was, such behavior just wasn't her usual style. She'd always thought that had been part of the reason Sam hadn't stuck with her back in high school—aside from his not being courageous enough to defy his friends. No doubt the cheerleader types with their quick, teasing laughter had been a lot more fun to be around.

Beth sighed. In the past few years, she had managed to develop a fairly healthy sense of self-esteem, but in one afternoon with Sam, all her insecurities had risen to the surface. Surely he'd see she really hadn't changed, despite her new shell. He'd soon grow bored of her. After all, it was only her new appearance attracting him now. . . .

But a small voice told her that he did feel deeply for her—that he saw her as far more than just a pretty face, and that perhaps over the years, he'd come to see the mistakes he'd made, the biggest one being letting her go.

And indeed, that was exactly how he felt. The depth of Sam's emotions almost scared him. When he'd kissed her, it was as if he'd come home. He'd never experienced such a strong connection with a woman. There hadn't just been a physical desire; it had been as though each had wanted to get at the very essence of the other, to intimately know the other in a way they had never known each other before. And afterward, they'd talked their hearts out. But now, Beth was terribly, eerily quiet.

He sensed that the intensity of the whole experience had frightened her—either that, or memories of the past had come to the fore, memories he was determined to eradicate. They'd both changed, and he was bound and determined to prove it to her—and to make her see that they had something very special between them, something too special to let die. But he didn't want to scare her....

And so, as they lay beside each other in the twilight, each thought private thoughts, afraid to do or say anything that might threaten their fragile new relationship.

But the air was turning chilly, and Beth was uncomfortable, so she finally said, "Maybe we should start to pack up."

"Oh, sure," Sam said quickly. "Whatever you like."

Somewhat nervously, they threw their clothes back on and rolled up the blanket. When their hands met,

Beth pulled away quickly, dumped the blanket into her beach bag and stood awkwardly.

"All ready?" Sam asked.

"All ready," she echoed, hating that they were acting like strangers.

They remained silent as they headed toward the car, but when they got to it, and Sam was standing at the passenger door, ready to unlock it, he turned to Beth and cupped her face with his hands.

"We'll go slowly, okay?" he said in a low tone.

She smiled weakly, her insides melting. How could she resist him? "Okay," she answered in an equally soft voice.

He kissed her cheek gently, then opened her door. As she climbed in, Beth's spirits began to rise. Maybe things would work out, after all.

They were still relatively quiet on the way home, but the silence wasn't as tense, as nervous as it had been on the beach. It was a comfortable, thoughtful, natural silence.

When they were almost at the spa, Sam said, "I have an idea. Why don't we take showers and change, then go out for a swank dinner in town?"

"Sounds nice," Beth said, thinking that it really did sound nice, though not nearly as nice as dinner and torrid lovemaking would have sounded....

"Great," he said, and she wondered whether the tone of regret she thought she detected in his voice was a figment of her imagination. Had he been thinking the same thoughts she had?

When he pulled up to her house, he said, "I'll help you with your things," and she didn't object, even though his help was unnecessary.

He followed her in, and when she turned to thank him, she melted once again. He was looking at her as if he wanted desperately to come closer to her, but was afraid that if he did, she would wriggle away and be lost to him forever. He looked sincere, confused, and as though he needed her very much.

So she went to him and gently put her arms around him. He buried his head in her hair and held on to her as if for dear life. After a moment she pulled away, but still held on to his hands. There was a desperate desire and a questioning look in his eyes. She nodded almost imperceptibly and began to lead him to her bedroom. At the doorway, he stopped her and tilted her chin up. "Are you sure?" he asked softly.

"I've never been more sure of anything," she answered in a whisper. "I want you so much."

He pulled her to him, groaning. "Oh, Beth. You're so sweet, so beautiful. I want you, too—more than I've ever wanted anyone."

Silently she led him into the bedroom, and he watched in a trance as she slipped off her clothing, until she was standing naked before him like a goddess.

Slowly he walked toward her and allowed her to carefully undress him, and stroke the flesh on his arms and legs as she did so. Was she aware of how erotic, how teasingly devastating her motions were? he wondered. He doubted it. She was an incredible mixture of natural sensuality and sweet innocence. Dimly he wondered about other men she'd been with, but he tried to push the maddening thoughts from his mind. He was determined to make this experience one she wouldn't forget, one that would wipe out all previous memories.

When she sat on the bed and pulled him down with her, he thought he would come undone. Especially when she seemed to get shy all of a sudden. She lowered her eyes, but he tipped her chin up so she had to look directly at him. He saw a great deal of love there, but fear, too. He didn't know how truly afraid she was, afraid that she wouldn't be able to please him—after all, her experience had been limited—and afraid that it wouldn't be the magical experience he was hoping it would be.

He, too, was afraid—well, self-conscious, anyway. He certainly didn't look the same as he once had, and she was a knockout. Was she repulsed, disappointed? Was that the reason for the lowered eyes? No, somehow he sensed instinctively that she wanted him as much as he wanted her. But would he be able to please her? Only a couple of times in the past had he made love to women he really cared about. Now he was with the person he cared most about in the world, and he wanted desperately to make it good for her. He cupped her chin in his hands and kissed her gently. He waited for her to respond to his kiss. When she did, moaning softly and tilting her head back, allowing him to pry her mouth open and tease her tongue with his, he felt his control break.

Suddenly he could be gentle no longer. And she, too, seemed to want much, much more. They kissed passionately, intensely. They nipped, licked, stroked and sucked each other as if they couldn't get enough. Sam was amazed at how wild and uninhibited gentle Beth had become. When she whispered, "Let's make love, Sam," he thought he would die from sheer pleasure.

"Beth, I'm not—I don't have—"

"It's all right, Sam," she said softly. "I'm prepared." In one swift motion, she reached over to her night table and opened a drawer from which she withdrew a foil packet. Smiling a little shyly, she placed it on the table and resumed her explorations. Finally she knew he could wait no longer. Easing the condom onto him, she then guided him inside of her, and he marveled at how perfect they were for each other. They moved together wildly, in perfect synchronization.

Sam knew she was as out of control as he was. There was an expression of rapt wonderment on her face, as though she'd reached a peak no man had ever taken her to before, and her eyes were glazed with pleasure. When she shuddered in exquisite delight, he let go completely. They rocked together even harder, until they were both spent, and then they collapsed.

After a few minutes of lying entwined, breathing raggedly, Beth stroked Sam's cheek. "That was delicious," she murmured.

"It certainly was," he replied, pulling her closer to him. "Best dinner I've ever had."

She propped herself up on an elbow and nuzzled her breasts against him suggestively. "How about dessert?"

He looked at her in surprise. "You don't mean . . ."

She blinked. "Tired already?"

He grinned. "Woman, you amaze me."

She grinned back, and he said softly, "Now I'm really going to amaze you."

Her eyes glittered. "Go right ahead," she whispered seductively.

Holding her wrists down, he hoisted himself over her once again and bent so that he could lick her stomach sensuously. He delighted in her answering groan of pleasure. His tongue rose to the hollow of her creamy breasts and he sucked at her nipples until they were erect. When she arched her back wantonly, he was almost lost again, but, determined to give her as much pleasure as he could, he drew his tongue back down her stomach to her womanly crest, and teased her with it, until she was thrashing wildly. When he finally satisfied her completely by sliding back up the length of her body and entering her, she cried, "Oh, Sam," and once again, they rocked wildly until they were sated.

After a few moments, he turned languidly toward her and was surprised to see that her eyes were moist. He cupped her face in his hands, forcing her to look at him.

"What's wrong, darling?" he asked, concerned.

"Nothing's wrong," she said softly. "I'm just happy."

He pulled her against him and held her closely. His own eyes watered, and he marveled at the emotions she could make him feel. As in the afternoon, he sensed a connection of their souls, a mutual need to know each other intimately that went far beyond the mere physical or the mere intellectual. He knew she felt it, too—and it scared the hell out of her.

He stroked her hair and whispered comforting words to her, and they remained wrapped in each other's arms until they drifted off into a peaceful sleep.

Beth was the first to awaken, some hours later. She looked at the sleeping Sam, and thoughts whirled around in her head. Was there something undeniably special between them, or was this simply what great sex felt like? She'd always known her sexual experiences with Jim and Alex had been less than ideal, but instinctively, she sensed that there was a lot more to her feelings for Sam. Aside from the perfection of their physical union, there was that unspoken mutual need to establish a relationship that could be no closer. She snuggled against him. She owed it to herself to see where they could go together—even though she was scared to death.

Soon, his eyelids fluttered open.

"Sorry I woke you," she whispered.

"Don't be sorry," he said, reaching out to stroke her hair. "I can't think of anything nicer than waking up with you next to me."

She smiled. "Are you hungry?"

He looked at her.

"For food," she said, smacking his arm playfully.

"As a matter of fact, I am. What can we do to remedy the situation?"

"Make a midnight raid on my fridge. Come on." She scurried over to her closet and tossed on a bathrobe while he put his shorts back on.

Beth flicked on the lights as she went out of the room, and for the first time, Sam noticed how lovely her bedroom was. The bed they'd made love on was a brass one, with a lovely quilt atop it, and in the hall just outside the room were old photographs—of relatives, he guessed—and a lovely pine hall table.

"I've told you before, but this is a really nice place," he commented. "It's so comfortable, and still so elegant."

"Thanks," she said. "There's still a lot to do, but it will have to be done slowly. As you said, furnishing a house takes time."

"I know. I just finished decorating my condo."

They were quiet for a moment, and Beth wondered if he, too, was imagining what their life would be like if they lived together....

Once in the country kitchen, Beth opened her freezer.

"Ha! We're in luck—frozen pizza."

"Frozen pizza? You?"

Beth wagged her finger at him as she placed the pizza box on the counter. "Another misconception, Sam. A serving of vegetarian pizza is perfect for dinner with a tossed salad. All the major food groups are represented. It's only when you eat it between meals— or have megaportions—that you get into trouble."

"I beg your pardon," Sam said as she popped the pizza into the oven. "Believe me, you'll get no complaints."

"Soft drink? Beer? Wine?" Beth asked as she walked over to the fridge.

"Whatever you're having."

She brought a bottle of Chianti to the table. "I feel like celebrating," she said shyly.

"Me, too," Sam said softly, sitting down.

She retrieved two glasses and poured some wine for both of them.

When she sat down, Sam lifted his glass and said, "To a sweet, beautiful woman—and getting to know each other again."

"I'll drink to that," Beth said, her eyes glistening. "Cheers." After taking a sip, she set her glass down and said tentatively, "Sam...tonight was very... special to me...."

"To me, too, Beth," he replied, setting his own glass down and looking deeply into her eyes. "I've never felt the way I did this evening."

Beth caught her breath. Things were progressing almost too perfectly. "Really?" she asked.

He took hold of both her hands. "Really," he said simply. "There's something very special between us. At least I feel it, and I hope you do, too."

"I do," she whispered.

"But you're afraid of it?" he asked.

"Yes," she answered honestly.

"Beth," Sam said, choosing his words carefully, "we've both changed since high school. We're adults who share a tremendous mutual admiration and attraction. There are never any guarantees in life, but I think if we both want to pursue a relationship and we agree to work hard at understanding each other, there's no reason on earth why we can't do anything we want to."

Beth thought she had never heard such beautiful words. "I'm in if you are," she said softly.

He smiled. "I'm in." He reached over and tenderly kissed her cheek, and Beth felt happiness well up inside her.

After they had polished off the pizza, they went back to bed, and this time, their lovemaking was sweet and infinitely tender, as if both of them sensed, deep down, that in spite of their vows, their beautiful new relationship could not possibly last.

WHEN THE SUN CAME UP, Sam got out of bed, got dressed and kissed Beth's cheek tenderly.

Her eyes opened. "Don't go," she said dreamily.

He smiled. "My car's on your driveway. I don't want to be the cause of your getting a bad reputation this early in the game."

"This isn't high school, Sam."

"Thank the good Lord." He kissed her cheek again. "Just the same, I think I'd better go. But I want to steal you for lunch, okay?"

She smiled back, relieved. "Okay."

He winked and left. She fell back asleep for a couple of hours and dreamed some truly wonderful dreams. A loud pounding on her door woke her.

"I'm coming, I'm coming," she grumbled as she made her way to the front hall. She opened the door to find a surprised looking Jill on her doorstep.

"My, my, don't we look tired. Busy day off?" her friend asked mischievously.

Beth opened the door wider and signaled her in. "Why don't you just ask whatever it is you want to know. It would be far easier to answer a direct question than to try to figure out your cryptic remarks."

"Okay. Did you have a nice time?" she asked agreeably, following Beth to the kitchen.

"Yes," Beth said, taking a pitcher of orange juice out of the fridge. "Juice?"

"Sure. Thanks. Next question—how nice a time?"

Beth felt her face flush. "A very nice time."

"You're blushing!"

"Am not!"

"Are, too!" Her eyes widened as she put two and two together. "Oh, my God, I don't believe it. You slept with him!"

Beth rolled her eyes. "Jill, we're not in college anymore."

"This is *so* exciting! Are you in love?"

Beth brought two glasses of juice to the table and said cautiously, "He's very nice and very attractive, and there's definitely something...special...between us. We're going to see where it goes—"

Jill clapped her hands together gleefully. "Am I your maid of honor?"

"Jill!"

"Okay, okay. I'm just happy for you. Don't pick pink for the dresses, okay?"

Beth grinned and shook her head in exasperation. "What am I going to do with you?"

"You love me," Jill said blithely, "and you know it. Hey, maybe we could make it a double wedding— you and Sam, and me and Tom!"

Beth looked at her friend closely. "You really like him, huh?"

"And how. He's got such a sweetness about him— he's the total opposite of Mike."

"That he is," Beth agreed.

"Are you coming to the dining room for breakfast?" Jill asked.

Beth ran her fingers through her hair. "Nah. I think I'll just grab something here and take a nice long shower."

Jill jumped up. "Then I guess I'll see you later. Oh, is it okay if Tom comes to talk to you sometime today about your part of the program?"

"Yeah, sure. Tell him to take a look at the sign-up board to see when I've got some free time."

"Hey, how's that working, anyway?"

Beth shrugged. "Seems to be going all right. We've had a couple of complaints, but I think it's still too early to tell how well it's going to work."

"You could be right. Well, so long."

"Bye. Oh, and Jill, call before you drop by next time, okay?"

"Sure thing, sugar. Who am I to stand in the way of True Romance?"

Beth groaned.

"Okay, okay. I'm leaving...."

Just a few minutes later, as Beth was helping herself to a bowl of granola, the phone rang.

"Lord, can't a person have a few private moments around here?" she muttered as she went to answer it.

"Hello?"

"Hi, dear. How are you?"

"Oh, hi, Mom. Not too bad. How are things with you and Daddy?"

"Just fine, dear. Just fine. I called to tell you that we were planning to spend the day at the Wilsons' cottage on Saturday. It's right near the spa, and we thought it would be great if we could pick you up for dinner and have a nice meal in town."

"Sounds good," Beth said, even though she was thinking it was bound to be a hectic weekend, what with Sam and Tom still around.

"Super. Oh, and Beth, the Wilsons have this darling nephew around your age who'll be at the cottage, too—"

"Mom," Beth broke in gently, "I'm sort of...seeing...someone, so I'm not really interested."

"You are! Honey, that's wonderful. Tell me all about him."

"Well, actually, it's someone I've remet. You remember my friend from high school—Sam Sarnoff."

There was a slight pause, and then Beth's mother said, "Oh, yes. The one who lived in that run-down house."

Beth grimaced. Was this the beginning of the kind of thing she'd have to contend with from her mother, who definitely had snobbish tendencies?

"Yes, Mom. He lived in a run-down house. But he happens to be a kind, wonderful, intelligent, sincere person." She paused. "And he just happens to have made a truckload of money in the past few years."

"Is that right? What is it that he does?"

Beth grinned. Her remark had obviously caught her mother's attention.

"He has a company that makes and sells mustards and salad dressings. It's called The Great Canadian Condiment Company. You may have seen the label in grocery stores."

"Yes, of course I have. And not just in any grocery stores. He's in all the fine food shops."

Beth smiled to herself. She'd known exactly what buttons to push with her mother.

"Well, do bring him along on Saturday evening, Beth. I'm sure your father will want to meet him, too."

"I don't know, Mom. I'll see...."

"Well, I hope he can make it. We'll pop by your house around six on Saturday, okay?"

"Okay, Mom. By the way, have you spoken to Barb recently? I haven't heard from her." This was a sneaky way of trying to find out exactly what her mother knew yet—if anything.

"Oh, yes. She and Mark are going to the Blue and White Ball tonight. You know, the annual benefit for the hospital." Mark was a prominent physician at one of Toronto's largest hospitals. Apparently he and Barb were still trying to make a go of it—or trying to pretend they were happy. Lillian could still be in for the shock of her life....

"Oh, that's nice. Well, say hi to them for me and tell Barb I'll call soon."

"I will, dear. Bye now."

Beth frowned as she hung up. It was a very bad time for her parents to be visiting. And a simply terrible time for them to be meeting Sam—or remeeting Sam, as it were. Their relationship was so new and so delicate, she wasn't sure it could hold up to public scrutiny just yet. Maybe she shouldn't even tell Sam about the invitation....

Sighing, she sat down at the table and ate her granola, wondering why everything always had to happen at once.

The rest of her morning progressed fairly smoothly, but the best part of it was the end—when Sam popped into her office and planted a sensuous kiss on her lips.

"Mmm. Who needs lunch?" she said in a seductive tone.

Sam grinned. "I do. I'm starving. This morning I did thirty laps in the pool and one of Jill's aerobics classes."

"But don't you feel a better man for it?"

Sam rolled his eyes. "Spare me. Come on, I need your dining-room recommendation."

As they dug into seafood salads, Beth apprised him of what her morning had been like. She mentioned the call from her mother casually—and the fact that her parents wanted her to join them for dinner on Saturday. She avoided mentioning that her mother had requested his presence, too.

"That's nice," Sam said. "Maybe I'll pop by your house to say hello. It's been years since I've seen your folks."

"Well, uh, actually, they wondered if you might like to join us. I told my mom we were sort of . . . seeing each other, and that's when she asked. But don't feel obligated at all, because—"

"Beth," Sam interrupted her. "I'd love to join you and your parents for dinner."

"You would?"

"I would."

Beth sat back in her chair "Oh

"What's wrong?"

"Nothing."

"Uh-uh, Beth. You can't play that game with me. Something is definitely wrong."

She shook her head vigorously. "No, really. Nothing's wrong." She defended her answer until he dropped the subject, but something *was* wrong—and there was more to it than simply the fact that their relationship was still so new and fragile.

Visits with her parents always managed to upset her because they had not yet given up on the idea of Beth-as-a-baby-machine. They were sure to embarrass both her and Sam, as well as upset her by asking an inordinate number of questions about his career and very few about hers. They were incredibly old-fashioned that way, and their traditional values sometimes caused their actions and words to border on unfeeling.

Sam walked Beth back to her office and pulled her close to him. "Everything's going to be all right," he whispered before he kissed her, and for just a moment, that perfect moment when his lips met hers, she believed him.

MEANWHILE, IN HIS darkened office, Mike was contemplating his situation. It amazed him that he could still carry on the facade. If he had to run, maybe he'd go to Hollywood! He'd certainly proven himself to be a talented actor in the past couple of months. Hell, going to California probably wasn't even such a crazy idea. After all, nobody had a history there. He had the looks and the persistence to make it. Maybe there he'd find his blond dream girl, the one who would make it all better. . . .

His mind snapped back to the present. Things were moving at such a rapid pace. Outside he was perfectly calm, but inside he felt as though he was on a roller coaster, careening wildly. He would lose his grip any day now.

He poured himself another Scotch. The rich man's drink. That was a laugh. What a joke he was! A poor drunken sod, no better than his petty thief of a father, despite all his fine education. He had even surpassed his father in all his criminal glory! Such had been his destiny, he knew now. The sins of the father were visited on the son, and there was nothing he could do to prevent that. Somewhere there was a book in which some higher being recorded every human birth, and there was inscribed there a fate, a path, a destiny that could not be escaped.

All the others would find happiness: Joel with his mousy town girl; Beth with the fat-cat food executive; Selma, with her books and theories and patients; and Jill—his beloved, his golden girl—with that poor excuse for a reporter and an even poorer excuse for a man. Their happiness was written, and he knew it would come to be.

Only he would fall wildly in a downward spiral, never to rise again. Only he would know what it was like to never know happiness, never put down roots, never have children. Only he would know what it meant to live life in the shadows, always looking over his shoulder, watching his every word, guarding his tongue scrupulously, even in his sleep, so that his nights were filled with restless awakenings and unsatisfied dreams.

Only he would know what it felt like to be a failure.

He could admit it freely now—to himself, anyway. That was what led him to believe he'd crack under the strain soon. He'd always thought of himself as invincible, impenetrable, but he'd come to realize that he'd made grave errors, had arranged his life without thinking—in a manner befitting a failure.

Then again, if it was all predestined, he couldn't have done anything else....

Yes, he'd crack soon. And then what? Undoubtedly he'd have to run. But where? How?

He massaged his aching temples. There was too much to think about—far too much to think about.

And his strength was waning. He felt it draining out of him, like sap out of a tree.

He wanted to go home. But where was home?

He didn't have one.

Just then, he heard a hideous sound, like that of a wounded animal, and he covered his head in his hands to shut it out. It was a horrible wild shrieking, a tortured wail that spoke of pain and humiliation and great suffering. It was so terrible that he couldn't bear to hear it, and he pressed his palms against his ears and rocked back and forth, as if the motion would somehow make the awful noise go away.

He remained like that for a long, long time, and it was hours later that he realized the awful wail had come from himself—that he was the wounded animal.

CHAPTER SEVEN

IT WAS ACTUALLY WORSE than Beth had anticipated. Her mother had been hurtling questions at Sam for what seemed like hours, using an overly polite tone that Beth knew she donned only when she was trying to obtain information she could really sink her teeth into. It was becoming clear that she desperately wanted to know as much as she could about Sam's "people"—that is, what sort of background he had come from. Beth knew that along with her mother's practised facade of mannerly propriety came a woeful ignorance of other cultures. Sam's Russian heritage was a mystery to Lillian Finlayson. Beth was sure her mother's ignorance would reveal itself shortly, and she was worried that her mother might inadvertently say something that would offend Sam.

They were on dessert and coffee—finally, Beth thought—at The Ossawippi Express. Her mother's most recent question had been, "So, Sam, these are actually your mother's recipes you use in your business?"

Sam's answer was typically smooth. "Well, they were my mother's originally. I do have a team of experts who test and refine the recipes for mass consumption."

"How lovely," Mrs. Finlayson replied, slightly coolly. This was obviously not the answer she'd wanted. Then she inspired her daughter's wrath by saying, "I keep telling Beth that she should try out a new cook. That Jane seems to specialize in bird food, doesn't she, dear?"

In response, Beth gritted her teeth and managed to say, "On the contrary, Mom. Jane has an excellent reputation in the industry. Her methods may not suit you, but she's won praise from experts across the country for her innovative cuisine."

This was a slight exaggeration, but Beth was of the opinion that slight exaggerations were called for now and again in life, especially to show her mother that she, too, was the owner of a first-class business.

"I can surely attest to Jane's talent," Sam said, smiling at Beth and taking her hand. "I told Beth that I hope to wrangle Jane's low-cal salad dressing recipes out of her before I leave."

"Really" was all Beth's mother said.

"Really," Beth said firmly. She turned a bright smile on her father. "So, Daddy, how goes the banking business these days?"

Beth's father was a mild-mannered, oftentimes distracted bank manager who tended not to contribute to conversations unless asked.

"Oh, not too badly, baby. Can't complain."

"Well, good. It's nice to know not everybody is having problems at work."

Beth's mother pounced on that. "What's that, sweetheart? Are you unhappy? Is the spa in trouble?"

Too late, Beth realized her gaffe. "Oh, no, Mom. Just the usual thing—got to keep profits rising and expenses low. We've had to make a few cutbacks here and there, but nothing to be alarmed about. I'm fine—no need to worry."

Beth's mother clucked. "Still, dear, I wish you'd get a job that was, well, steadier—like Barb's. Being a part owner of a business is so stressful...."

Here we go, Beth thought. She'd had this conversation with her mother just about every time they spoke since the spa had first opened. It was a conversation into which Barb's name was invariably dragged. Beth's sister worked as a dental assistant, which Lillian thought was just one step away from president. If her own interest in life had been teeth, Beth thought, she'd have wanted to be a dentist, not the assistant. And knowing what Beth did about Barb's present troubles, her mother's pride seemed particularly misplaced today.

Steadily she answered, "I know you wish my job was more secure, Mom. I do, too, sometimes. But I really love what I'm doing, and the world needs entrepreneurs. Without us, there would be no jobs. Look at how many people Sam employs."

"Well, I know, dear. But Sam's a man. You'll be settling down with a family one day—"

"Maybe and maybe not," Beth interrupted her.

"Well, let's be optimistic, darling! You'll just have to give this up when you are a mother...."

"Mom, lots of women work and have children, too." Beth knew the wise thing would be to drop the subject, but she was getting sucked in the way she always did. She was about to expand on her reply when Sam spoke up.

"You know, Mrs. Finlayson," he said, "studies have shown that children develop very well with two working parents. They tend to be more individualistic, more independent and better equipped with life skills. Generally they get along with their peers better, thanks to increased participation in things like play groups. But most importantly, now little girls have role models to show them that they can do just about anything they set their minds to. They're more apt to set high goals for themselves."

Beth was wowed by Sam's response, but her mother seemed unconvinced.

"Well, I suppose so" was all she said. Conveniently she changed the subject. "Beth, how are Jill and the others doing? How thoughtless of me not to have asked."

"Everybody's fine, Mom," Beth replied, stifling a sigh. These conversations always exhausted her. Beth knew she'd never change her mother, and she didn't know why she even bothered trying. Was she so insecure that she needed everyone's approval all of the time? she wondered.

Yes, she thought glumly. And she knew she'd never change in that regard.

"Jill's a girl with a good head on her shoulders," Mrs. Finlayson commented.

Meaning I have a substandard one? Beth felt herself turn red, and she told herself she was overreacting to a simple compliment.

"She's another one who should be getting married and having babies. Tell me, Sam—" Mrs. Finlayson turned to him and smiled "—what do you think of these women who are so devoted to their careers?"

"I think they're wonderful," he said, grinning and squeezing Beth's hand.

Mrs. Finlayson did not reveal how she felt about his response. She only nudged her husband and he harrumphed.

"Yes, Lillian?" was all he said, oblivious to her obvious wish for him to participate in the conversation.

Beth stood up. "I think we'd better get going."

"But, dear, it's still early!"

"I'm tired, Mom, and I have to get up early tomorrow."

"Leave her be, Lillian," Albert piped up. "If the girl's tired, the girl's tired."

"Oh, all right. But I was hoping we'd all take a walk around town or something...."

During the drive back to the spa, Beth remained deathly silent. It began to irk her that Sam was being so accommodating and jovial with her parents. And her mother was actually being jovial with him! Strangely enough, that made Beth angry. She realized that Sam had, in fact, passed Lillian's test. She knew it was small of her, but she couldn't help feeling resentful. Her parents—her mother, anyway—had never accepted *her* for her real self. And she was their own flesh and blood!

When they turned in to the spa, Beth announced, "You can leave us both off at my place, Mom," which earned her a pointed glance from her mother via the rearview mirror.

Finally goodbyes were said, and Beth heaved a sigh of relief as her parents waved and pulled away.

"I gather you're about ready for a nightcap," Sam said, grinning.

"About two or three—no ice," Beth muttered.

Sam chuckled, linked her arm with his, and led her to the doorstep.

As she searched her purse for her keys, Sam said, "Your parents are pretty nice people. I had a good time."

Beth finally found her keys, and as she wrestled with the lock and flung the door open, she retorted, "Yeah, well, sure. They were fawning all over you. Try putting the shoe on the other foot. They don't give me the time of day."

NO RISK, NO OBLIGATION TO BUY... NOW OR EVER!

CASINO JUBILEE
"Match'n Scratch" Game

Here's how to play:

1. Peel off label from front cover. Place it in space provided at right. With a coin, carefully scratch off the silver box. This makes you eligible to receive one or more free books, and possibly other gifts, depending upon what is revealed beneath the scratch-off area.

2. You'll receive brand-new Harlequin Superromance® novels. When you return this card, we'll rush you the books and gifts you qualify for ABSOLUTELY FREE!

3. If we don't hear from you, every month we'll send you 4 additional novels to read and enjoy. You can return them and owe nothing but if you decide to keep them, you'll pay only $2.92* per book, a saving of 33¢ each off the cover price. There is *no* extra charge for postage and handling. There are *no* hidden extras.

4. When you join the Harlequin Reader Service®, you'll get our subscribers-only newsletter, as well as additional free gifts from time to time just for being a subscriber!

5. You must be completely satisfied. You may cancel at any time simply by sending us a note or a shipping statement marked "cancel" or returning any shipment to us at our cost.

YOURS FREE!

This lovely Victorian pewter-finish miniature is perfect for displaying a treasured photograph and it's yours absolutely free — when you accept our no-risk offer!

© 1991 HARLEQUIN ENTERPRISES LIMITED.

*Terms and prices subject to change without notice. Sales tax applicable in NY.

CASINO JUBILEE
"Match'n Scratch" Game

CHECK CLAIM CHART BELOW FOR YOUR FREE GIFTS!

YES! I have placed my label from the front cover in the space provided above and scratched off the silver box. Please send me all the gifts for which I qualify. I understand I am under no obligation to purchase any books, as explained on the opposite page.

(U-H-SR-09/91) 134 CIH ADE2

Name _____

Address _____ Apt. _____

City _____ State _____ Zip _____

CASINO JUBILEE CLAIM CHART	
🍒🍒🍒 / 🍒🍒🍒	WORTH 4 FREE BOOKS, FREE VICTORIAN PICTURE FRAME PLUS MYSTERY BONUS GIFT
🍒🔔🍒	WORTH 3 FREE BOOKS PLUS MYSTERY GIFT
🍒🔔🔔	WORTH 2 FREE BOOKS

CLAIM N° **1528**

Offer limited to one per household and not valid to current Harlequin Superromance® subscribers. All orders subject to approval.

▼ DETACH AND MAIL CARD TODAY! ▼

HARLEQUIN "NO RISK" GUARANTEE

- You're not required to buy a single book — ever!
- You must be completely satisfied or you may cancel at any time simply by sending us a note or a shipping statement marked "cancel" or by returning any shipment to us at our cost. Either way, you will receive no more books; you'll have no obligation to buy.
- The free book(s) and gift(s) you claimed on the "Casino Jubilee" offer remains yours to keep no matter what you decide.

If offer card is missing, please write to: **Harlequin Reader Service**   P.O. Box 1867, Buffalo, N.Y. 14269-1867

"You try putting the shoe on the other foot, Beth," Sam said quietly, following her into the foyer. "I don't have any parents."

Beth stilled. That was true. Still, she refused to feel guilty for being upset with her parents. They had treated her badly all night—her father's silence had been as damning as her mother's barbs.

"Look, Sam," she said softly. "I'm very tired. These battles with my parents wear me out. Maybe as an outsider, you weren't that attuned to everything that was going on tonight. Suffice to say, I've always had a tough time getting my folks to realize that I don't have to do everything their way." Her voice softened. "I'm sorry you lost your parents, Sam, but that doesn't excuse the behavior of mine tonight and other nights."

She paused for a moment, then decided to come out and say what was on her mind. "And to tell you the truth, I'm a little upset that you don't seem to understand my feelings." She felt herself going just over the edge of reason, but she was unable to stop herself. "I guess it's still difficult for you to empathize with me, just as it was in high school."

She saw a look of pain flit across Sam's face and then he said, "You know, Beth, your mother wasn't exactly all sweetness and light to me, either. In fact, for a while there, she put me through quite the little inquisition. But unlike you, I don't expect people to be perfect. She's only human, as I am, but you've never been able to forgive people for being imperfect, have you?''

''What exactly is that supposed to mean?''

''It means that maybe you haven't changed that much since high school.''

Beth felt as if she'd been stabbed. She thought he'd come to admire her sensitivity, her good judgment of character. It seemed she'd been wrong. She straightened and said, ''Well, it's a good thing, isn't it? Otherwise, my standards would be incredibly low, like yours were.''

''No, you would get a lot more pleasure out of life if you did change a little. Instead of finding fault with everybody, you'd enrich your life by allowing a variety of people into it.''

Beth was burning with anger now. ''How dare you tell me how to run my life when you know so little about it. Especially since you were such a spineless wimp in high school. Do you think I can forget how you treated me back then? I was your dream come true in private but you couldn't handle having an honest-to-goodness public romance with me. It's a damn good thing I haven't changed since high school. If I had, I would have become an oily, hypocritical creep like you.''

For a moment, Sam was silent. Then he pivoted and stalked out of the house, slamming the door behind him. Beth stood staring after him for long moments, and then she slowly walked into the kitchen, slumped down in a chair and cried her heart out.

ON SUNDAY MORNING, she was awakened by a pounding on the door. Bleary-eyed, she looked through the peephole. It was Jill. Groaning, she opened the door. "Jill—"

"He's gone and all men are scum," she muttered, bounding in and sinking onto a chair at the kitchen table.

"Who's gone?" Beth asked, confused, thinking for a moment that her friend was talking about Sam.

"Tom! He left early this morning without even saying goodbye! Can you beat that? I thought something really interesting was starting to happen. And to think I even told him about the problems we were having here. I *trusted* him. I *confided* in him."

Alarmed, Beth asked, "Jill, just how much did you tell him?" She felt a pang of guilt for jumping on Jill when she herself had been guilty of confiding in Sam, but there was one very important difference: Tom was a reporter.

Jill shook her head. "Don't worry. It was all off the record. I had enough sense to say that, at least. I told him it was confidential."

Beth was somewhat relieved—but not completely. It was clear to her now that no woman could trust any man. The two sexes were on completely different wavelengths. Tom *had* seemed to be unusually honest at first, but Beth had seen past that facade soon enough. That just-off-the-farm crap was as phony as a three-dollar bill. Nevertheless, she felt compelled to try to help Jill feel better.

"Jill, Tom was planning to leave today long before he met you. His six days are up. Maybe he'll call you when he gets back to Toronto."

She saw a glimmer of hope in Jill's eyes. Then it faded and Jill shook her head. "Uh-uh. I don't think so."

"Why not?" asked Beth. "It's possible."

"To tell you the truth, I think Mike scared him off. What a rat!"

Beth sighed. "What did he do, aside from the stunt he pulled when Tom first arrived?"

"That was nothing, my dear. He followed us everywhere, begged to join us—you name it, he did it. He *tormented* us."

"Oh, Jill." Beth was truly sympathetic. "I'm sorry. It must have been awful for you."

"It was. Really awful. I don't know why I'm even friends with that . . . person."

Suddenly Beth felt a terrible heaviness in her chest. Everything was going wrong!

"Well," Jill said, "I'm too depressed about everything to even think anymore. Maybe some exercise will do the trick. I won't bother you anymore this morning. But thanks for the shoulder."

"Anytime," Beth mumbled.

Jill looked at her friend more closely. "Hey, you don't look so hot yourself. Is everything okay?"

Beth sighed. "Not really. Dinner with my folks was a disaster, as usual, and Sam and I had a huge fight afterward."

"Oh, no," Jill said mournfully.

Beth nodded grimly. "I'm afraid so."

"What's the problem?"

She shrugged. "I'm not sure, exactly. All I know is that when the chips are down, Sam's never there for me. My mom was on my case all night, as usual, and Sam was pretty good about defending me in front of her, but when we were alone, it was a different story." She looked away. "He never understood my feelings in high school, and it seems he doesn't now." Taking a deep breath, she added, "And if he doesn't value me enough to try to understand, I don't think I want to be with him."

"Oh, Beth," Jill said, "he doesn't know what he's giving up."

"Neither does Tom," Beth said, putting her arm around Jill.

Jill grinned. "What a pair we are. We'd better tell everybody to keep a distance today."

Beth looked away. "I have the feeling it will take a lot longer than a day."

Jill stood and said, "Hey, where's that famous Finlayson fortitude? Keep your chin up, kid. He'll come crawling back soon. I can feel it. Your luck with men has been a lot better than mine since university."

"Well, it's about time," Beth quipped.

"Oh, keep it to yourself." Jill smiled good-naturedly, and added, "Well, I'm going to go fortify myself. It promises to be a very long day." She placed a hand on Beth's shoulder. "Take it easy, okay? Maybe Sam will surprise you."

Beth stood, too, and shook her head. "I'm through with waiting for Sam to surprise me. I did enough of that in high school."

Wrinkling her nose, Jill said, "I know what you mean. Sometimes I think I spent my entire four years in high school waiting for some guy to turn into Prince Charming. Seems I'm still not out of the habit."

Beth linked her arm through Jill's and walked her to the door. "Old habits die hard," she said.

"Personally I blame it all on Barbie and Ken," Jill said darkly. In a lighter tone, she asked, "Are you coming to the dining room?"

"Uh...I think I'll just grab something here. I don't really feel like facing all those people today."

Jill peered at her. "Is it all those people you're concerned about or one person in particular?"

Beth smiled wanly. "Whatever."

"Okay, okay. I won't push it. But you can't hide out the rest of his stay, you know."

"He's due to leave this evening. We've been avoiding talking about it. Before the fight, I just assumed we'd keep seeing each other, I guess, despite the geography problems. Now, I don't know..."

"Aw, honey... I'll talk to you later, okay? Don't work too hard today."

"Will do. You take care, too, okay?" The two embraced.

As Jill walked away, she called, "Who needs *Knots Landing?*"

Beth grinned as she shut the door. And then she promptly burst into tears. It occurred to her that she hadn't cried so much since high school.

BETH WAS JUST LOCKING her door, about to set out for her office, when she saw a silver-gray sports car pull onto her driveway. It was Barb, but what was she doing at the spa?

She walked over to her sister's car to greet her. When Barb emerged, Beth saw she was visibly distraught. "Hi, sis, what's going on? This is a real surprise."

Barb took a cigarette out of a package in her purse, and with shaking hands, lifted it to her mouth and lit it. "Sorry for the smoke, kid, but it's one of the few pleasures left me. I can't eat a thing and there's been no sex for quite some time. I know you have appointments on Sundays, but I really needed to talk to someone...."

"Oh, Barb..." Beth put her arm around her sister's shoulders and led her along the walkway to her door. "Come on in. We'll make some tea and have a nice long talk. I'll tell somebody to post a sign on my office door saying I won't be in this morning."

After preparing tea and making a quick phone call to Selma, who agreed to take care of the sign, Beth settled down at the kitchen table next to Barb.

"So, what's up?" she asked.

Barb took a deep breath. "He says he's in love with her."

"Oh, Barb, I don't know what to say..."

She shook her head. "Don't say anything. It's so ridiculous, there's nothing you can say." She laughed mirthlessly. "His nurse. It's insane. I never thought stuff like that happened in real life. Of course, someone who answers to Mark's every word is perfect for him. Then again, in a few years, she's bound to turn into as big a nag as he says I am."

"What are you going to do?"

"I'm leaving," she said, her voice trembling. After she cleared her throat and paused to regain her composure, she said, "I need a place to stay until I find an apartment. I thought of asking you if I could stay here, but I couldn't handle the commute. So I guess the logical thing is to stay with Mom and Dad until I get a place."

Beth's eyebrows went up. "You're kidding!"

"Can you think of any other options?"

After a few moments, Beth sighed and said, "No."

"I rest my case. Listen, I don't like it any more than you do. I have the feeling my every move is going to be scrupulously analyzed and recorded. But I don't have a choice. Anyway, it's only temporary."

"True. Still, I could never do it. I wish you the best of luck."

Barb looked at her sister carefully. "Well, you could probably never do it because Mom would make your life miserable."

Beth looked at her in surprise. She'd never before heard Barb acknowledge that they'd been treated differently. They'd always managed to skirt that issue, somehow. "Yeah, that's probably true," she replied.

Barb sipped her tea and said slowly, "All my life I've tried to please Mom and Dad. Sure, I loved Mark when I married him, but the love died pretty early on. For a while I thought kids might be the answer. I was misguided there, of course—kids shouldn't be brought into a loveless marriage under any circumstances—but that didn't work out, either. I never devoted myself to a career because all I ever wanted was to be a wife and mother, and in the back of my mind, I knew Mom and Dad approved of that. And now I have nothing."

Beth started to protest, but Barb interrupted. "No, let me finish. I just wanted to let you know how much I admire you. I've never said that before—" she swallowed and looked down "—I guess because I felt pretty superior in our younger years. But I do. You've done so much—and all on your own, too. I—I wish I was more like you...." She broke down and sobbed, covering her face with her hands.

Beth rushed over to her and hugged her. "Don't be silly," she told her sister fiercely, overcome by a strong wave of love. "You have so much going for you—

you've got a loving, generous spirit and a real gift for putting people at ease. Sometimes I still wish I could be more like you!'' She saw Barb smile through her tears and wipe her eyes, so Beth loosened her hold on her sister and rubbed her shoulders.

"Something between us is the perfect woman," Barb quipped

Beth grinned and sat back down. "Right."

"So tell me about this new man of yours. Mom says you've met someone."

Beth could tell Barb was feeling a little embarrassed over her outburst and was trying to put on a brave face. So she went along with the change of topic, telling her sister a little about Sam—whom Barb couldn't be expected to remember since she had already been married when Beth had first met him. Beth took care not to make her deep feelings too obvious. She told Barb she wasn't at all sure that it would work out, which was true, and she thought Barb would be grateful for the knowledge that she wasn't the only one having man troubles, though hers were considerably more serious.

When she was done, Barb shook her head. "How we've all changed since we were kids."

"You said a mouthful there," Beth responded.

Barb rose and came over to hug her sister. "Things will work out for you. They always do."

"And things will work out for you, too—whatever happens."

"I sure hope so. Anyway, I'm going to be off now. I . . . I just wanted to tell you in person what my plans were. Thanks so much for listening, Beth. It meant a lot to me, knowing you were going to be supportive."

Beth walked her to the door. "If you need *any-thing,* all you have to do is call."

"I know." Barb hugged her again. "Take care, little sister."

"You, too, big sister." As she watched Barb walk to her car, she thought about Barb and Mark's wedding and how happy they had been—and how young. She thought of herself and Sam, too. And she wondered if somebody up there didn't get a perverse enjoyment out of turning people's expectations upside down.

NATURALLY, BETH SPENT the next few hours in a daze. When she allowed herself the small pleasure of an afternoon nap, she dreamed of Barb and Mark and of high school. She was thoroughly exhausted when she woke up. Why did one's subconscious always have to dwell on what was going on in one's life, she wondered.

"The mind works in mysterious ways," she muttered.

After splashing her face with water, she set out for the main building to look over her sign-up board. When she arrived at the front door, she decided to face facts. Slowly but surely she walked over to Karen.

"Hi, Karen," she said to the grim-looking receptionist. "I'd like to find out the status of a guest—Sam Sarnoff. Has he checked out yet?"

When Karen looked at her suspiciously, Beth realized it would be wise to give the woman a plausible reason for wanting the information. "I forgot to give him a couple of brochures he'd find especially useful," she lied.

Karen glared at her, harrumphed, then checked her reservation list. A moment later, she said, "He's checked out, all right. Left a couple of hours ago."

Beth's heart sank. "Did he leave any messages?"

"Not a one."

"Oh. Well, it's his loss," she said, knowing she'd have to force herself to believe that....

CHAPTER EIGHT

SAM WAS WISHING he was anywhere but where he was. After the couple of weeks he'd spent taking care of himself—eating properly, getting plenty of rest, exercising and not being obsessive about his work—it felt very wrong to be at a "power breakfast" with a business acquaintance, stuffing himself with cholesterol-laden eggs Benedict.

Moreover, it felt wrong to be sitting across from an extremely attractive woman who wasn't Beth. Joan Hartley was a very competent and very beautiful buyer for an exclusive new department store on Bloor Street. She had proven a delightful breakfast companion and a veritable business whiz. Together, they'd negotiated a deal in which Sam would be the sole purveyor of mustards and salad dressings at her store. Now, over coffees, they were double-checking the fine points of the contract.

During a lull in the conversation, Joan asked, "Sam, is something wrong? You're a million miles away."

No, only about a hundred, he thought. He looked critically at Joan. A cool blonde, men would have fought duels over her in another time. She was the epitome of the smart, confident beauty. And he was sure he hadn't imagined the signals she'd been sending out all through breakfast. She'd been subtle, but not subtle enough that he'd missed the too-direct looks, the slightly flirtatious smile, the very sexy blouse underneath the very businesslike jacket...

Normally he would have given answering signals in a flash. But this morning he felt ambivalent. Things might have died before they'd started with Beth, but he knew he had to come to terms with what had happened between them before he entertained thoughts of getting involved with another woman.

"No, nothing's wrong," he told Joan as he toyed with his coffee cup.

"But nothing's right, either," she said in a sympathetic tone.

"Well, some things are great." He attempted to smile. "Business, for instance." He raised his cup. "To a delightful new business associate."

They clinked coffee cups, then sipped. After a moment, Joan said softly, "Is that how you think of me, Sam? As a business associate?"

Oh-oh, he thought. *Here it comes.* "Joan," he said quietly, touching her hand with his, "You're a beautiful, smart, funny, desirable woman, and under any other circumstances, I'd jump at the chance to take you out on a real date, but—"

"But you're involved with someone else," she finished. "I'm sorry, I didn't know. I figured that since you weren't wearing a wedding ring..." She looked down. "So, who's the lucky lady?"

A terribly sweet and terribly insecure wallflower who's blossomed into a confident, beautiful woman. "Someone I knew a long time ago, who I met up with recently," he said vaguely.

"You mean she let you get away the first time?" Joan shook her head. "Silly woman."

"Actually," Sam said ruefully, "it was the other way around."

"Sounds as if you don't want to talk about it. I also get the feeling, somehow, that you're not absolutely sure you want her back in your life," Joan said. She smiled. "Either that or it's true love and you're scared to death."

He didn't answer her, and she nodded, as if his silence had answered for him.

"Maybe we'd better go," she said gently.

Rather reluctantly, he pulled out his charge card. Though it hadn't felt quite right being out with Joan, he didn't particularly want to go to the office, either. His lack of enthusiasm about his job was only getting worse. Nor did he want to go home. Last night his professionally decorated condominium in the heart of downtown Toronto had seemed cold, empty. Moreover, his sleep had been racked with troubling dreams. *Damn Beth Finlayson, anyway,* he thought as he nodded distractedly when Joan announced she was going to the ladies' room.

It was possible that he *had* made a mistake on Saturday night. He'd thought about that a long time, and he'd realized that he had, in fact, been shortsighted. Beth's parents' treatment of her *was* rather distressing, and he could see that she needed support, not lectures. Yes, he did miss his parents, and yes, he was very sensitive to the matter of children—even adult children—taking their parents for granted, but that didn't mean he believed parents had the right to act unfeelingly toward their children.

But the fact of the matter was, his problems with Beth went far beyond the incident that had occurred on Saturday evening. She was so insecure, so unsure of anyone's love for her or belief in her, that she could tolerate nothing less than total agreement with her views. Granted, his behavior in high school had been despicable, but he knew, somehow, that she'd never be able to get beyond that—that he'd constantly have to prove himself, bend over backward to make her believe in him.

And he didn't deserve that. He *was* trustworthy. He *was* decent. He was constantly telling her he admired her intelligence, her skills, her beauty. It seemed that for every three steps taken forward, there was a giant one to take back. Each wrong move was worth three right ones. And unfortunately, Beth interpreted every mistake he made as proof that he hadn't changed, that he'd never change.

Maybe the trick was to find someone who hadn't known him until quite recently—someone like...Joan.

He looked at her carefully as she made her way back to the table. She was stunning, all right. But when he looked at her he felt nothing like the way he did when he looked at Beth. Beth only had to smile and he'd feel as if he'd died and gone to heaven. No, there was no question in his mind that he was in love with Beth.

But what on earth was he supposed to do about it?

HE WAS DEFINITELY WEAK, Beth thought angrily, swatting violently at a particularly pesky fly. With a hard *thwack,* she got it and smiled triumphantly. "That'll teach you to fool around with me," she muttered to the insect's remnants, thinking she'd like very much to say those words to a certain mustard manufacturer....

She slumped in her office chair. Try as she might, she couldn't keep an edge to her anger. The more she thought about it, the more she suspected that maybe she'd overreacted on Saturday night. No, Sam hadn't been completely understanding, but then, he hadn't been completely unsupportive, either. She certainly hadn't given him a chance to say too much when they'd been alone. She'd pounced on him as soon as he'd said he liked her parents.

Way to go, Beth, she thought glumly. She nibbled at her nails—something else she hadn't done since high school. For the life of her, she just couldn't decide what to do. If she'd been certain their relationship was a good thing, she would have called immediately and urged him to meet with her and talk. But she wasn't at all sure their relationship *was* a good thing. After all, they'd known each other for years once upon a time, and nothing had come of that. Why should things be any different now?

Her thoughts were interrupted as Selma opened her door and peeked through the crack.

"Care for some lunch?" she asked.

Beth had been ready to avoid people for yet another day, but it occurred to her that Selma might be a good person to talk to. "Yeah," she said slowly, "hang on a sec while I get myself together." Beth retrieved her purse from a desk drawer and took out her compact to freshen her lipstick and powder. Selma came in and perched on the arm of a chair.

"I hope your morning was better than mine," she said to Beth.

Beth smiled. "It was probably about the same. I treated a compulsive junk-food eater and a bulimic, both of whom, I'm told, are going to you for counseling."

Selma nodded. "Ah, yes. What do you think?"

"It's hard to tell," Beth said. "The fact that they've come to the spa seems to indicate that they really want to become healthy, but you and I can do very little here. They'll have to work closely with their own psychologists and dietitians once they get home." She slipped her compact back into her purse and rose. "All set."

Selma got up, too, and they headed out the door.

Once they were downstairs, Beth asked, "Selma, you met Sam Sarnoff. Can I ask you—well, what you thought of him?"

Selma looked at Beth and raised her eyebrows. "He seemed to me a very nice man—a bit of a workaholic, but I think he really wants to change that. In our sessions—"

"You *treated* him?" Beth asked incredulously.

Selma seemed surprised. "Oh, dear, I thought for sure he'd told you. I don't like breaking client confidences...."

"Don't worry," Beth said hastily. "I won't say a word. Anyway, I did know he was trying to change his habits. After just a couple of days here he said he felt better enough to want to completely change his lifestyle. Naturally he'd talk to you about that." Meanwhile, she was wondering what else he'd discussed with Selma....

Selma was still looking at her closely. "Beth, obviously you're feeling lousy about something. Why don't you tell me what it is?"

They had arrived at the dining room, and they managed to find a secluded table. Once they were seated, Beth took a deep breath and began.

"Oh, God, Selma. I don't even know where to start. Sam and I went out with my parents on Saturday night, had a huge fight afterward and he checked out immediately—I haven't spoken to him since."

"Oh, dear," Selma said, truly concerned. "I didn't know."

"Well, I haven't exactly advertised. Jill knows, but that's about all. I'm quite confused about the whole episode, to tell you the truth."

"Do you want to tell me what happened?" Selma asked gently.

Beth sighed. "I'm not exactly sure. As I said, we went out with my folks, and you know that's always stressful for me."

Just then a waitress came over to take their orders. When she left, Beth toyed with her water glass and continued on with her story. When she finished, she crinkled her nose and smiled.

"Well, am I nuts?" she asked.

Selma smiled indulgently. "Far from it, Beth. Everyone feels ambivalent when they experience very powerful emotions. It's a scary thing to become intimate with someone and hope for a future with that person. And the fact that you had a relationship with Sam in the past that didn't work out the way you might have hoped only complicates matters."

She reached over to grab hold of Beth's hand. "Beth, you're very astute when it comes to your parents, and you're right—you deserve more respect than they accord you. And maybe Sam doesn't see the whole picture. He's obviously got some of his own problems to deal with, because of his own life experience. But my impression was that he was a good man, a man of honor. I think he at least deserves a chance to explain himself. If his explanation doesn't satisfy you, well, then you'll have to think about your situation and come to some conclusion."

She withdrew her hand, took a bite of her julienne salad, which had just arrived, and continued. "I get the feeling from what you've told me that you're perfectly aware you were reacting not only to what was going on that evening, but to what went on between the two of you in the past. As well, you were probably transferring some of your anger with your mother to Sam. You'd do well to think about those things and try to head off that sort of behavior in the future."

That silenced Beth. Sam had said almost the same thing. Just then the waitress brought her the oriental chicken salad she'd ordered—one of Jane's experiments. After taking a few bites, she said, "Mmm, not bad. Selma, you should try this the next time Jane makes it." She had a few more bites, then said, "So, you think I should talk to him?"

"I think you should talk to him."

Beth looked away. "It's going to be hard."

Selma said softly, "Of course it's going to be hard. Unfortunately most good things in life don't come easily."

As Beth was about to respond to that, Mike rushed up to their table. He looked agitated.

"Have either of you seen Jill?" he asked hurriedly.

"Uh-uh," Beth said. "Anything important?" she asked, hoping to draw Mike out. She still wanted him to talk to Selma. Out of all of them, Selma was probably the only one who'd be able to make him see how silly his fanatical pursuit of Jill was....

But instead of answering, he just ran a hand through his hair and said, "Well, if you see her, tell her I was looking for her, okay?" And then he scurried off.

Selma watched him go, her eyes narrowed. "Something is not right with that man these days."

Beth nodded. "Tell me about it. Jill says he was intolerable when Tom was here."

Selma shook her head sadly. "What do you suppose is the matter?"

"I have no idea, but I get the feeling it's much more than unrequited love."

"I second that emotion. I think this stuff with Jill is a reaction to something else."

Beth smiled. "And you get paid to say stuff like that?" She shook her head. "Unbelievable."

Selma had just tossed a serviette at Beth when Jill rushed up to their table. "Thank heavens I found you two. Mike is driving me *crazy*. Since Tom's left, he's been insufferable. Tell me he's been here already and I can relax."

"He's been here already and you can relax," Beth said obediently.

"Phew." Jill plopped down on a chair. "I'm beat. This constant pursuit is more exhausting than a high-energy aerobics class."

Beth grinned, but Selma frowned. "Jill, I can't help but think he's very deeply troubled about something.

I've thought that for a long time, but he hasn't asked me for help. Do you have any idea what it might be or how we can help him?''

Jill shrugged. ''I've thought for a long time that there's been something wrong. He's been so extravagant that for a while I thought some investment he made panned out and he hit the jackpot. Now I think it's just the opposite—something's gone really wrong...and not just with the spa. After all, he hasn't said too much more about that and I know this sounds weird, but I know him so well and there's this... desperation in him now....''

''You know, I sensed something like that, too,'' Beth said thoughtfully. ''A while ago we had the most bizarre conversation. Remember I told you about it, Selma?''

''I do. And I'm going to tell you now what I told you then. There isn't a lot we can do to help Mike if he doesn't want to help himself.''

Jill rolled her eyes. ''Can't a person have a simple conversation around here? Gee whiz, you'd think we were all health professionals or something. I vote we change the subject, since I am heartily sick of talking about Mike Petrie.''

''Done,'' Beth said, at which point she and Selma ordered desserts, and Jill, her main course. Beth asked Jill about Tom, but she brushed off the question, saying merely that she hadn't heard from him. As far as Beth could tell, her friend was trying desperately to forget that she'd ever met the man.

In a way, Beth was glad Jill wasn't in the mood for a heart-to-heart conversation. She was sick of discussing her own man troubles. It was with relish that she participated in the ensuing lighthearted banter about the latest assortment of crazies at the spa and how male chauvinists had to be behind panty hose.

It was a couple of hours later when Beth realized that that half hour or so was the only time during the day in which she hadn't been consumed with thoughts of Sam....

So FAR, Sam had landed thirteen baskets. The hoop had originally gone up in his office for decoration—as a symbol of the "playful" part of his nature. It was the little touches like these, combined with a quality product, that brought clients back to him again and again. He was a master at such salesmanship games. Only now he was spending more time playing with the damn thing than working!

Before he'd gone to the spa, his heart hadn't been in his job, but now it wasn't anywhere. He was thoroughly confused about both his work life and his love life. Breakfast with Joan, though a professional success, had been a personal embarrassment, and had only confused him more. He couldn't seem to concentrate on anything.

Margaret O'Hara, his secretary, poked her head into his office, interrupting his thoughts. "Nice shot," she commented as he sunk another ball.

"Thanks. What's up?"

"Do you have a few minutes?"

He looked at her. Something in her tone told him he wasn't going to like whatever she had to say. *Please don't let her quit,* he prayed. He had enough problems right now without having to deal with losing the best secretary the world had ever seen. She'd been with him since the beginning and was his right hand. But she was getting along in years, and he'd known for a while that it was just a matter of time before she retired.

Margaret settled herself in a chair across from his desk and smoothed her skirt. It was a few moments before she spoke, and Sam knew instinctively that he'd been right.

"Sam," she began quietly, "this is one of the most difficult things I've ever had to do. I won't beat around the bush. I think you've known for a while that I've been thinking of taking it a little easier now that Frank's retired and my girls are on their own. I've truly enjoyed working here, but my time has come, I'm afraid."

Sam sighed. "I don't suppose a hefty raise could entice you to stay...?"

She shook her head and smiled. "I'm afraid not, Sam. It's just... time."

"Ahh, Margaret, what am I going to do without you?" The question was heartfelt. Margaret was far more to him than just an employee; more, even, than a close friend. She was forever trying to get him to eat better and go out more. She and her husband, Frank, would often invite him over Sunday evening to dinner. She felt like family.

"Oh, Sam, there are plenty of bright young women out there just waiting to take my place. And I intend to have you over to dinner at least once a month. Hopefully soon you'll have a wife and some little ones to bring along!"

He couldn't help grinning. "You'll never give up, will you? I bet you're going to call the office everyday, not to see how the business is going, but to see if I've had any dates!"

She smiled back at him. "You bet that's what I'll do." More seriously, she added, "I'll stay for as long as you want me to, Sam. Take your time. Find the right person. I want someone to be here who will enjoy it as much as I did. I've really come to care about this business of yours."

He reached across the desk and took her hand. "I know you do, and you've made life a hell of a lot easier these past few years. I meant it when I said I don't know what I'm going to do without you. I suspect you're a dying breed, Margaret O'Hara. I don't know how many other secretaries would take the time and trouble to do all the little extra things you always did."

She squeezed his hand. "Well, it was more than professional concern. I care about you a lot, Sam. You're like a son to me." She took a tissue out of the box on his desk and dabbed at her eyes. "Oh, look at me, getting all sentimental." She stood up and said,

"We'd better cut this short before I start bawling. And Eddie should be here any minute."

Edward Nichols was the owner of a chain of specialty food shops in Toronto. His flagship store was just down the street from Sam's headquarters and he often popped in to chat about business or just to see how Sam was. The two were friends as well as business associates, and Sam was glad he'd be seeing him today. A hard worker, Eddie was also an irrepressible, fun-loving guy who always brought a smile to Sam's face.

He stood up. "Right. Before he gets here I want to check on things in back." He walked around his desk and put an arm around Margaret as he walked her to the door. "And don't you worry about me, Margaret. I'll be fine. You just enjoy your retirement with Frank. Of course, you might get phone calls now and then for the first few weeks...."

"I certainly hope I will," Margaret replied, smiling. "If I don't, I'll feel horribly expendable."

When Margaret returned to her desk, Sam continued on back to the warehouse part of the operation, where the products were actually refined and bottled. He had lucked out a couple of years ago in finding his current place of operations. Previously, he'd been located in a broken-down old building in the east end of the city, but when the business had started to really take off, he'd decided a more prestigious address would be beneficial, as the products he produced were relatively high-end. His real-estate agent had managed to find an old warehouse on currently trendy King Street, in the heart of downtown Toronto; it had been in dire need of renovations, but was going dirt cheap. Within a few months, the place was operational, and Sam was infinitely glad he'd had the foresight to move.

But now even the vitality of the area wasn't enough to keep him from getting down. What had once been a pleasure was getting to be a royal pain. The majority of his days were spent trying to push his already well-established products. He often thought about how nice it would be to spend his days doing something he loved without having to force anything on anybody. Memories of the spa came to mind suddenly. During his stay there he'd been struck by how much everybody seemed to love their work. A job like Mike's would really be terrific, he reflected. The challenge of running a place like that was tremendous, and at the same time, one would be in an atmosphere that was fun and spontaneous. . . .

The image of Mike stuck in his mind. He couldn't help but think it odd that Mike had told everyone the spa was in trouble when on the surface the place looked like a runaway success. Then there was the issue of the Total Maintenance costs. He made a mental note to ask Eddie about that.

"Yo, Sam!" Vito, Sam's foreman, called to him.

"Vito, my man, what's shakin'?"

"Nothing's shakin', man. Everything's smooth as silk."

Exactly, Sam thought. *This business could run itself. It doesn't need me anymore....* He thought about his staff. Vito was great, and so were the rest of the men and women who worked in the back, but he didn't have too much contact with them except when they were developing a new product. Otherwise, he left them pretty much alone—for efficiency's sake. Margaret was the one he had the most contact with, and now she was leaving. Perhaps it was time for him to make a choice....

After a cursory check to assure himself that all was well, Sam returned to his office, and shortly afterward, Eddie popped in.

"Hey, good lookin', what's cookin'?" Eddie asked.

"An awful lot, my friend. Hey, nice outfit. Spending the evening in Rosedale?" Sam's tone was sardonic. Their business successes had come at about the same time, and Eddie's shop was the one currently favored by the city's wealthy hostesses and food mavens. Eddie thrived on his new celebrity status as the city's foremost in-the-know foodie and was often seen at parties and charitable benefits attended by the well-heeled. He often regaled Sam with ribald tales about the rich and famous in Toronto.

He pivoted for Sam's benefit. "Like it? Sweater by Hugo Boss, pants by Armani. What a life, what a life." He plopped into a chair. "Hey, buddy, you really do look great. Your holiday definitely agreed with you." He narrowed his eyes. "But I sense somehow that you didn't agree with it. Why so glum? Can't be woman troubles. The last time you went on a date was ... oh, 1973, wasn't it?"

"Very funny. For your information, I do have woman troubles. And various other troubles, to boot."

"Sorry to hear it. Anything I can help you with?"

"Thanks, anyway, but I think I've got a few things to sort out in my head. You could do one thing for me, actually. Keep your ears open for news of any secretaries looking for work."

"Margaret's leaving?" Eddie exclaimed.

Sam nodded glumly.

"Bummer, man."

"You bet."

"You know what? You need to learn to relax, buddy. You'll find someone else. Yeah, Margaret's terrific, but you'll find another secretary who's just as terrific. You, my friend, need to buy a place in the country. I tell you, my farm is my salvation."

Sam smiled at Eddie's use of the term "farm." His spread in nearby King City was more like a resort, complete with horses, a man-made lake and guest cabins. It was the place Sam had mentioned to Mike in their conversation about the spa's upkeep.

"I dunno. If I did buy a getaway home, it would be a cottage, not a mini-hotel. The upkeep on that place must kill you. The spa I just came back from uses Total Maintenance, like you. Their spread doesn't look much bigger than yours, and their business manager told me the upkeep was thousands a month."

Eddie's eyebrows went up. "You must have heard wrong. There's no way."

"That's what I was told."

Eddie shrugged. "Well, their needs are different, I guess. Anyway, I'd love to stay and chat, but duty calls. I just wanted to tell you to double up on the Russian Mustard in your next shipment. The stuff's going like hotcakes!"

"Great! That's my personal favorite—it was my original recipe, you know."

"Just goes to show you. Don't fool with a good thing." He jumped up. "Well, *ciao,* my friend."

"Bye, buddy."

When Eddie had gone, Sam sat at his desk toying with his pencil for some time. A horrible theory had emerged in his head—a theory that had to do with the seemingly slippery Mike and his obvious exaggeration of Total Maintenance's fees. The right thing to do was confront Beth with the theory. But she already thought he was unsupportive. What would she say if he questioned the honesty of her co-worker? Anyway, he'd decided to apologize for being unsupportive. He couldn't tell her about his theory just yet. He'd wait for the right time. He only hoped it would come soon....

HIS CALL CAME late at night, when she was just about to shut off her bedside lamp.

"Hello," she answered quickly, concerned that something was wrong somewhere.

"Hello," he replied softly.

"Sam!" was all she could manage to say.

"Beth, before—"

"Sam, I—"

They both laughed at the same time. "Okay. You first," Beth said.

"I just wanted to say that I'm sorry if I didn't seem completely supportive of you on Saturday night. When you said what you did about your parents fawning over me and not giving you the time of day, I just went with a knee-jerk reaction—I didn't think." He paused for a moment. "I've been doing a lot of thinking since then, though, and there are a lot of things I think we need to talk about, get out in the open. That is—" he stopped awkwardly "—if you want to talk about them..."

"Oh, Sam," Beth said happily. "You don't know what that means to me. I accept your apology, but I'm sorry, too. I hardly even gave you a chance—I just shot my mouth off." She chose her next words carefully. "I've been doing a lot of thinking, too, and I've come to the conclusion that at least part of my reaction had to do with what happened between us in the past. And I was much more angry with my mother than with you—you were right about that." She didn't know quite what else to say. Thankfully, Sam took the ball from there.

"Well, I can't help you with your feelings toward your mother," he said, "but I can help you with the past. Maybe we should talk about it—then leave it there. Are you interested?''

"I sure am.'' Beth breathed a small sigh of relief. "I was so afraid to speak to you.''

"Don't ever be afraid to speak to me, Beth,'' Sam said in a low tone. "If you are, then there's no chance for us.''

"Is there still a chance for us?'' Beth asked softly.

"I think so. How about you?''

"I think so, too.'' Beth smiled into the receiver. Joy was beginning to bubble up inside her. "I...I've missed you so much. When and where should we meet?''

"You have Thursday off again?''

"Uh-huh.''

"Come to Toronto.''

She thought about it for a minute. "Don't you have to work?''

"This will be a golden opportunity to show you that I've changed my evil ways. I've missed you, too, and I need an entire day with you. Anyway, I have good people working for me. At least I do for now. My secretary—my right hand, actually—just gave me notice.''

"Oh, Sam, I'm sorry.''

"So am I. Margaret's virtually irreplaceable. But she is getting on in years, and she's going to stay on as long as I need her, so I can afford to wait until I find someone who's perfect. But I guess I should take advantage while she's still here. I don't know if I want to leave a brand-new person all alone."

"Okay—if you're sure. Just give me your address and I'll pray ol' Betsy makes it in."

He chuckled and gave her the information.

"Not a bad place," she said as she wrote down one of the most exclusive addresses in the city.

"It'll do. Let's say eleven o'clock or so. We'll have brunch."

Beth groaned. "Brunch! Oh, that is *so* Toronto."

He laughed. "Remembering why you left the place?"

"You bet!" She lowered her voice. "You're not going to try to seduce me into staying there, are you?"

"*Moi?*" he asked innocently. "Heaven forbid. But just in case, what's your favorite wine...."

"Plying me with spirits won't work, I'm afraid."

"No, I think honest-to-goodness lovemaking always works better."

"It sure does." Her voice became more emotional. "Bye, Sam. See you Thursday."

"Goodbye, sweetheart," he replied. "I'll be counting the minutes...."

CHAPTER NINE

ON WEDNESDAY NIGHT, Beth had another very vivid dream. This time the mise-en-scène was that of an erotic film. In the dream, she and Sam were doing things to and for each other that she'd never even thought about before. She woke up in a sweat, amazed at all the desires apparently bottled up inside her.

In the morning, she took her time choosing what to wear, and ultimately decided on a sexy white leather miniskirt and a close-fitting black sweater. Admiring herself in the mirror before leaving her house, she said aloud, "You've come a long way, baby." Then she grabbed her purse and left.

She stopped off at Jill's for a few minutes and was distressed at her friend's obvious sadness.

"You still haven't heard from him, huh?" Beth said sympathetically when they were seated at Jill's kitchen table.

"Nope. The bum. I hope he goes to reporter hell and has to type until his fingers fall off."

Beth laughed. "At least you haven't lost your sense of humor."

Jill grimaced. "I wish I had. It seems that Mom was right. Funny girls don't get men."

"Oh, Jill, that's hogwash and you know it. You just haven't found the right guy yet."

"I'm not sure the right guy exists." Jill looked at her friend suspiciously. "Say, what are you so happy about, anyway?" At Beth's guilty look, she exclaimed triumphantly, "You and Sam made up!"

Quickly Beth said, "Well, sort of. I'm going into Toronto today to talk to him. Hopefully we'll straighten some things out."

In a soft voice, Jill said, "Beth, please don't feel bad about feeling good. I hope our friendship is stronger than that. I'm glad for you—really, I am."

In a grateful tone, Beth said, "I know, Jill. I just wish things had worked out for you, too."

Jill bounced up. "Hey, I've got plenty to be thankful for. I'm not about to sit around moping because my Prince Charming hasn't come around. Women don't do that anymore—do they?"

Beth got up, too, and grinned. "Most definitely not. Well, I've got to run." She patted her friend on the back. "You take care, okay?"

"Uh-huh. And say hi to your hunk for me."

"Sure thing," Beth echoed as she walked down the hallway. When she reached the front door she turned to ask Jill when Tom's article was going to be coming out.

"I'm not sure, exactly. But I don't see why it wouldn't be in the next issue."

"Well, it's bound to be positive. I believe we kept him busy enough." Beth glanced at her watch. "Now

I really have to go. Bye, hon. See you later." With that, she walked slowly to her car, and once inside, put on an easy-listening radio station for the long ride.

She couldn't help but think about her friend during the ninety-odd minutes it took to get to Toronto. Jill really did deserve someone special, and it was too bad that someone couldn't have been Tom, whom she'd obviously started to care about.

Funny, Beth mused. He hadn't seemed oily or insincere. Still, she recalled guiltily, she had pegged him with such labels immediately after learning he'd left Jill. But then, at the time, she, too, had been suffering a severe case of general anger toward the entire male sex. In truth, she *had* detected a certain sweetness and innocence in Tom. Then again, he'd also surprised her with some of his sharp observations. The man was an enigma, she concluded.

That thought led to ruminations on Sam. He was another person who probably wasn't what he seemed. He must have changed since high school—even though on Saturday night she'd reacted to him as though he hadn't. But *she* had changed since then—and not just on the surface, but inside. She definitely possessed more confidence, more inner strength. Granted, she still had a lot of work to do, but the groundwork had been laid....

It was exactly eleven o'clock when she arrived at Sam's condominium. An elegant, rather intimidating building in the prestigious Bloor-Bay area of the city, it was a residence of choice for Toronto movers and shakers. Once she'd parked and entered the building, Beth took a few moments to observe the opulent Art-deco-style lobby, complete with Erte prints and granite floors. After clearing her throat and throwing her shoulders back resolutely, she walked over to the concierge's desk.

"Mr. Sam Sarnoff is expecting me. I'm Beth Finlayson," she said, at which point the concierge nodded, smiled stiffly, dialed, and announced her presence.

"Very good, sir," she heard him say a few moments later. After he turned to her and said, "You may go up, madam," she walked cautiously—for fear of bringing one of the marble columns crashing to the ground—to the elevator, which turned out to feature mirrored walls, plush carpets and piped-in music.

Finally she arrived at Sam's apartment. When he opened the door, her heart did a strange, but not entirely unexpected, little dance. He was wearing faded jeans and a denim shirt; his tan was still in evidence and his muscles remained well toned. He still had some weight to lose—about ten to fifteen pounds, she guessed, which meant he hadn't been vigilant about his diet since leaving the spa—but even she had to admit that the extra weight lent him an appealing solidity, an aura of power.

She was so busy admiring him that she didn't realize until a few moments later that he wasn't dressed for a restaurant.

When he smiled and silently opened the door wider to admit her, she saw why. The dining-room table was set beautifully, with fine china and crystal, fresh flowers, and an abundance of enticing-looking foods.

She looked at him in amazement and said in a soft voice, "Oh, Sam, I can't believe you went to such trouble. Everything looks fabulous."

She was delighted when he actually blushed slightly. Was he nervous? The thought was flattering.

"Thanks," he said. "It wasn't much trouble, really. This area is so convenient. Everything was at my fingertips."

I'll bet, Beth thought, her eyes wandering. His apartment was a decorator's dream. The furniture and accessories were of the highest quality, she could see. Nevertheless, the place lacked something—a lived-in feeling, a warmth. Her own little house, she thought, with its homey, country-style furniture—what little of it she had collected thus far—held much more appeal for her. Still, Sam's place was like a museum, and she was dying to see the rest of it.

"Can I get the grand tour?" she asked him, her eyes shining.

He looked embarrassed, but he only said, "Sure," and as they walked around, first through the spacious foyer and then the large living and dining room, he filled her in on the origins of the pieces she expressed an interest in. He also entertained her with hilarious stories about his temperamental decorator.

But it was the bedroom that really knocked her socks off. Practically as big as her whole house, it was sleek and sensuously appealing, with gray carpeting and a huge black lacquered canopy bed, the likes of which she'd never seen before. It was all she could do to drag herself away; being with Sam in such a luxurious, sexy room was almost too much for her. She saw that he, too, had to muster the willpower to leave....

Back in the dining room, Sam ordered her to sit while he served her.

"But Sam, I want to help—"

"Uh-uh. You and your partners waited on me hand and foot while I was at the spa. Now it's my turn."

She smiled. "Okay, but if you need me for anything, just call."

He clicked his heels, saluted, then marched into the kitchen.

When he returned with platters of delectable-smelling breads, cheeses and smoked fish, she licked her lips and said, "How did you know this is *exactly* what I wanted?"

He laughed. "I didn't get any of this stuff when I was at the spa, and I missed it like crazy. I had the feeling you would appreciate it, too."

"Just so long as we don't get too used to it," Beth warned him.

He shot her an innocent look. "Speak for yourself. I'm a good little Boy Scout now." *Sort of,* he amended silently.

They dug in and munched ravenously on the food. Beth was in heaven. *Forgive me, Joel, Jane and everybody else,* she thought. *Once in a while, a body needs a good bagel....*

When they were sipping coffee, Sam said, "Beth, I really want to talk about what happened on Saturday."

She put her mug down and sighed. "I guess we had to get around to it sooner or later."

Sam smiled. "It doesn't have to be a depressing conversation, you know. The more honest and open we are, the better. I'm looking at this discussion as a positive thing."

"I guess you're right." Beth smiled wanly. "How did you get so smart? I was the brain in high school, remember?"

"I had a good example to follow," he said warmly. "Anyway—" he reached over to envelop her hand in his "—I want you to know before we start talking that I'm completely crazy about you, Beth Finlayson. I will do anything I can to help keep this relationship on track. I lost you once before, and I'm not about to do it again."

Beth felt a lump form in her throat. She swallowed thickly. "I—I'm crazy about you, too, Sam," she whispered. "I only hope you don't disappear like you did before...."

"That's what you're afraid of, isn't it?" he asked seriously. "That you won't be able to count on me— that I won't be there for you in the crunch."

Beth's silence answered him.

He got up and began pacing. "I wish I could snap my fingers and blow the past away, Beth. I really do. I know I wasn't the strongest person in high school—athletically, yes, emotionally, no." He walked back toward her and sat in the chair beside her. Taking her hand again, he said, "I've changed, Beth. I don't know what it will take to convince you—I wish you would just believe me. My family situation, my work—these are things that helped shape me after high school." He paused for a moment. "People keep growing—in the nonphysical sense—throughout their lives. But because you didn't know me in the period following high school, you don't believe I could have changed that much." He looked into her eyes. "I have—believe it."

"I'll try," she said, affected by his speech.

He shook his head vigorously. "You have to do more than try, Beth. You have to do it." He gathered the courage to say what he had to. "You have to because it's not fair to me to do otherwise. How do you think I'm going to feel knowing you don't believe in me, that you'll always be expecting the worst from me?" More softly, he said, "You're going to have to let go of the past, Beth. Or the future will be very, very difficult."

Beth looked away. "That's easier said than done."

He rose, went to her and pressed her head against his stomach. Softly caressing her silky hair, he whispered, "I know. Believe me, darling, I know. I wish I could forget the past, too, sometimes...."

Beth just clung to him tightly.

Still stroking her hair, he said, "But I try to remember the good things, not the bad. That's the way it should be."

They remained locked in the embrace for a few moments, hearing nothing but the steady ticking of the hall clock.

Eventually Beth said, "I do tend to do that, don't I—look at the bad and not the good. I do that with my parents, too."

Thoughtfully, Sam said, "Probably to a certain extent. But it's obvious they provoke your anger, even if they don't mean to. You shouldn't feel guilty about that. If parents want their kids to respect them, they have to show some respect themselves." After a moment he added, "You're surprised I said that, aren't you?"

When she started to speak, he put up his hand. "Beth, I told you before, what you were privy to on Saturday was a knee-jerk reaction. I saw what was going on, believe me." He shook his head. "Maybe I just wanted to defuse the situation afterward so that we'd have a good evening, anyway." He laughed. "That plan backfired pretty nicely, don't you think?"

She beckoned for him to sit back down, saying seductively, "But look how much fun we're having making up."

He sat down again, smiling at her response. But he continued on in the same solemn tone. "Seriously, honey, I jumped all over you because of my sensitivity about parents. I'm jealous, basically. That old saying is so true—you don't know what you've got until it's gone."

They were quiet for a while, and Sam finally said, "You thought my saying I liked your parents was an example of my not being supportive of you, didn't you?"

Beth nodded, and Sam sighed. "I'm sorry, Beth. Truly I am. I guess I'll have to be extracareful for a while." He leaned toward her. "If you'll promise to cut me some slack for a bit. Like I said on the phone, we won't be perfect together right away. All couples need time to learn about each other."

"I know," she said, and she, too, released a sigh. "I just wish it was easier."

"If it was easier, it would be deadly dull," he pronounced, standing and pulling her up with him. "Now, my lady, it's time to get out and see the town— my town, my way."

A FEW HOURS LATER, Beth found herself exclaiming, "Sam, this is wonderful! I never even knew this existed!"

It was midafternoon, and they were exploring Little Italy, just northwest of Sam's area, near St. Clair Avenue and Dufferin Street. On just about every block, there were a couple of noisy cafés, where the younger members of the largely Italian, working-class community hung out. As well, there were numerous bakeries and unique gift shops, filled with curios of all kinds.

Sam put a hand on her shoulder, and when she turned toward him, he pried her mouth open with his fingers and shoved in a piece of ultrarich, cream-filled pastry.

"Ohh," she groaned when she had swallowed. "This is *so* sinful."

As they continued to stroll the bustling streets, Beth felt more alive than she had in a long time. Young men and women were walking arm in arm, kissing, or just plain flirting, and there was a spirit of romance in the air, which the hot summer sun turned into a smoldering sensuality. Beth's senses were finely tuned, and her body hummed with the delicious knowledge that Sam wanted her—and loved her, though he hadn't yet said the words.

But then, she hadn't, either. She wondered why.

Because you're scared came the answer.

Which was exactly why she *should* tell him, she knew. After all, it had only been a couple of hours ago that Sam had told her she had to forget about the past, throw away her old insecurities....

Then and there she promised herself that she would tell him she loved him at some point during the day.

All of a sudden it was crystal clear that that was what he needed to hear, what he was waiting for.

They sauntered in and out of shops. At one point, Sam playfully shoved her up against an elaborate wedding dress, whereupon a plump saleswoman waddled up to them enthusiastically. Beth waved her hands in denial, blushing, but unable to stop laughing along with Sam.

At dinnertime, they found seats at a crowded corner café and had fun watching the dressed-to-the-nines teenagers perform age-old mating dances. They hungrily sipped steaming bowls of minestrone and dug into healthy portions of veal scaloppine. Over espressos and ices, they looked at each other warmly and whispered endearments to each other. But still, neither of them said, "I love you."

The right moment for Beth didn't come until a little bit later. They were still walking in the area and had slipped into a jewelry store just in time to see an earnest-looking young man slip an engagement ring onto a pretty young woman's finger, and whisper, "I love you, darling."

Feeling like intruders, they crept out, and Beth suddenly felt a distance between them as if they both realized they should be as intimate as the couple in the jewelry store, but somehow weren't.

Just then, Beth saw a gum-ball machine, and an idea came to her.

"Oh, look," she said. "I loved those machines when I was a kid." She ran over to it, plunked in a quarter and out came a gum ball inside a fat plastic ring.

She smiled in satisfaction, took Sam's little finger and slipped the ring on.

"I love you, darling," she whispered, and felt a little thrill when he looked at her wonderingly, as if she'd given him the greatest gift he'd ever received.

Before she knew it, he was crushing her against him and burying his mouth in her hair, saying, "I love you, too, Beth—so much. So, so much..."

And she suddenly felt as if absolutely nothing could go wrong.

Indeed, when they went back to Sam's place and made love, the experience was on a completely different level. They had felt an emotional connection previously, but now their lovemaking was a statement rather than a tentative question. They had bonded in a way that was undeniable, indelible, and the experience brought each of them a joy and pleasure they had never known.

Beth stayed at Sam's until dawn, and then she got ready to leave. He was still sleeping when she had to go, so she kissed him tenderly on the cheek and tiptoed out of the bedroom. She was in such a good mood, she only laughed inwardly when the concierge shot her a slightly disapproving look as she left the building. She drove back to Orillia as if in a trance.

And then the bubble burst. When she got to her bungalow, she was met by a white-faced Jill, sitting on her doorstep.

With trembling hands, Jill held up the newspaper she was holding, and whispered, "Tom's article is going to put us out of business, Beth."

CHAPTER TEN

BETH EXPERIENCED a strange sinking feeling in the pit of her stomach. For one crazy moment she told herself that Jill was joking, but she knew from the look on her friend's face that this was no joke.

Like an automaton, she took the newspaper from Jill and began skimming. She stopped after she had read the really painful parts. Then, tossing the publication aside, she sunk slowly onto the step.

"What are we going to do?" Jill asked mournfully.

"What can we do? There's no point in worrying about it—what's done is done." Beth couldn't keep an edge of annoyance out of her voice. In his article, Tom had named a "confidential source" on the Couchiching spa staff, and Beth had no doubt that Jill had been that source. Apparently Tom had had no scruples about printing information that had been told to him "off the record."

His article was essentially concerned with how he spent his six days at the spa, but in a sidebar comparing various Canadian spas, he had commented rather extensively on Couchiching Spa's "lack of extras," which he attributed to the rumored financial difficulties. Beth couldn't help but wonder if Tom would have even noticed the "lack of extras" had he not been apprised of the situation.

Just then, Beth spotted Selma and Joel walking purposefully toward her house. She stood and rooted through her purse for her keys. "I think we're having a meeting," she muttered to Jill. "You'd better come in and have some caffeine fortification."

"Oh, Beth," Jill wailed, "you're all going to hate me now, but I swear I never would have told Tom anything if I'd thought for one minute that he was going to print it! What a slime bucket! He even *sent* it to me! The nerve!"

"Well, it's a bit late for regrets," Beth said sharply as she bustled around in her kitchen for coffee makings. She knew as she said it that it was cruel, but she was unable to stop herself.

"Don't, Beth, please," Jill said imploringly. "Don't you think I've asked myself a thousand times why I trusted him, why I told him everything? I *know* I was a stupid, naive fool. Don't make it worse."

"I'm sorry, hon," Beth said contritely, coming over to her friend, who had plunked herself on a kitchen chair. She placed a hand on her shoulder. "I'm certainly not blaming you. Heaven knows we've all confided in men we shouldn't have. Look at how I trusted Sam in high school."

Jill smiled wanly. "Yeah, but that turned out all right. I assume it went swimmingly yesterday."

Beth sat down beside her and said, "Yeah, it did. But you know, Jill, it might still work out with Tom. Maybe if you talked to him—"

Jill shook her head vigorously. "No way, Beth. The guy's a total rat. He took my confidences and *printed* them, for heaven's sake!"

Beth, too, shook her head. "I just can't believe he did that. I thought he was a little odd, but this kind of thing is downright unscrupulous. It doesn't jibe. And *City Life* is such a reputable newspaper. They can't possibly condone tactics like those." She shrugged. "I guess a bad apple has to slip in now and then. But I still can't believe it." She paused. "Then again, my record on character judgment is far from perfect."

Jill was about to speak when there was a hard rapping at the door.

"It's open," Beth called, and Joel and Selma strode in.

"I guess you've seen the latest edition of *City Life,*" Joel said, tramping through the hall and slumping down in a kitchen chair.

"Uh-huh," Beth said in a dull tone. "I guess he sent us all copies. How sweet of him. That's what we get for asking. Any suggestions as to how to deal with this little crisis?"

"Little crisis?" Joel asked, pacing. There was nothing lighthearted about him today. "I don't think this can be termed a 'little crisis.' It's a crisis that could sink us. Without our Toronto guests, we've got nothing."

Selma said, "I'm afraid Joel's right. I think it's imperative that we come up with a counterstrategy."

Beth had noticed that both Joel and Selma had avoided blaming Jill, who was remaining silent, and she was grateful for their sensitivity. On top of their external problems, the last thing the partners needed was a lot of infighting and petty clashes.

Unfortunately the civilized atmosphere declined as soon as Mike stormed in after pounding furiously on the door. When he saw Jill in the kitchen he said sarcastically, "Way to go, Jill. See what happens when you trust strangers?"

Quietly, Selma said, "Mike, please calm down. Yelling at Jill won't solve anything."

"It will make me feel better," Mike mumbled, leaning against a counter and crossing his arms.

"Well, if you hadn't made us institute cutbacks before Tom came, none of this would have happened," Jill cried, and then Joel and Selma joined in the argument. After a couple of minutes Beth whistled.

"Whoa, people! Come on. If this meeting is going to be productive, we have to discuss things in an orderly fashion." She turned to Jill. "Now, Jill, is there anything you'd like to say to us?"

"Yes," she said resolutely. "I'm terribly sorry if I contributed to Tom's negative opinion of the spa, but I do feel I'm being made a scapegoat here. We *had* put our cutbacks into effect before Tom came, so who's to say he wouldn't have come to the same conclusions if I hadn't told him anything? Secondly, I'd like to remind you all that I did tell Tom about our financial difficulties *in confidence*. An ethical reporter would have respected my request that our conversation remain off the record. I made a mistake in judgment, and again, I'm sorry for that, but I did take precautions...."

She trailed off, and the others remained silent for a few moments. In time, Selma said, "Mike, what do you have to say about our cutting back on services before Tom came? Was that wise?"

"Of course it was wise," Mike snapped. "You people don't know anything about business, so I'd thank you for not criticizing my methods."

"Mike," Beth said quietly, "I don't think that tone is necessary. We're trying to stay calm here, and it's not going to help us any if you lose your cool."

Mike ran a hand through his hair. "I'm sorry," he muttered. "It's just that this has all been very frustrating for me. You people chose to give me sole responsibility for managing the spa's finances, and now that something's gone wrong, you're jumping all over me. It isn't fair."

"Mike's right about that," Selma put in.

"Yes, but the question remains, was it a good idea to institute those cutbacks before Tom came?" Joel asked.

"I really don't think that's relevant right now," said Beth. "Obviously hindsight is twenty-twenty, and if we had the chance to do it all again, maybe we wouldn't have instituted the cutbacks until after Tom's visit. Mike is entitled to make a mistake once in a while." She surprised herself with that comment.

"Thank you, Beth," he said softly.

"You're welcome. Now, I think we should stop blaming each other and try to come up with some counterstrategies. Agreed?"

"Agreed," Joel said. "How about guided tours through Mike's bedroom, for a ten-dollar admission charge? No extras lacking there."

"Very funny," Mike mumbled.

Beth smiled. It was a good sign that Joel had started in on Mike. Maybe now they'd get somewhere.

"How about asking *City Life* to give us another try?" Selma suggested.

Mike snorted. "Are you kidding? First of all, that would be like admitting Tom was right when he implied our spa was substandard, and secondly, no newspaper would ever send a reporter to do a story over again just because the subjects didn't like it."

"I suppose you're right," Selma said glumly. Then she brightened and said, "Well, then, how about informing the editor-in-chief that a reporter acted unethically?"

"Wouldn't do any good," Mike said. "The damage to our business has already been done, and the information isn't wrong, so we can't get them to print a statement saying the allegations are untrue. That's about the only thing that would get us out of this mess."

"I've got an idea," Joel cried, jumping up from his chair. "Let's put on a show!"

Everyone turned hostile stares on him.

"You've obviously been watching too many Judy Garland movies," Mike said darkly.

"No," said Joel in an excited tone. "I was thinking of an open-house type of thing. We can put ads in *City Life* and some other high-profile publications and give people a free day at the spa! We can pull out all the stops, have Jane cook up a storm—"

"That would kill it right there," Mike responded sarcastically.

"Stop it," Beth admonished him. "I'm really tired of defending Jane. She does terrific work."

"Beth, even you have to admit that her culinary horizons are somewhat—limited," Jill said.

"And she's temperamental," Joel added.

"Okay, okay. But the customers love her stuff— flower food makes them feel like they're in a high-class place. Besides, she comes cheap. But Jane is not the issue here. This open house sounds expensive, and I don't know if we can afford it. Mike, what do you say?"

"It stinks," Mike said succinctly.

Joel sat down again and crossed his arms. "Kill-joys," he muttered.

"Coffee, anybody?" Beth asked, and when everybody grumbled yes, she poured five steaming mugs and distributed them.

"So," she said after a while, "I guess there isn't a whole heck of a lot we can do about this."

"You know," Jill said, sipping her coffee, "I never felt sorry for performers or artists before, but now I can imagine how it must feel to have to face reviews with every new work." She shuddered. "Courageous people."

"They certainly are," said Selma.

"I feel like I failed an exam," said Beth miserably.

"I feel the way I did when my tree house broke," Joel said in a mournful voice. "The year was—"

"Would you all just shut up," Mike said, exasperated. "It's not the end of the world."

"It might be the end of our world," Jill said quietly, and they all fell silent once again.

A sadness seemed to envelop them, and one by one, as they finished their coffee, they got up to leave. All agreed that it was pointless to try to come up with solutions in their present depressed states.

Jill was the last one left, and as she prepared to go, Beth asked her quietly, "Are you going to be okay?"

"Sure, sure," she said in a too-bright tone.

"Jill, I—"

She held up a hand. "Beth, please don't get maudlin on me or I'll cry. And I have a class to teach in about twenty minutes."

"Okay," Beth said simply. Deliberately lightening her tone, she added, "Well, one good thing might have come out of all this. Mike seemed pretty upset with you. Maybe he'll stop bugging you now."

"Yeah," Jill said slowly. "That was strange, wasn't it?"

"Strange?" Beth said, wrinkling her brows. "I don't think it was strange, exactly. Everybody was pretty riled up."

Jill shook her head. "No, Mike was almost too upset. I know him so well, Beth, and I really didn't think he'd make *that* big a deal out of it. His outrage rang falsely, somehow. It was almost as if he was putting on an act...."

"Why on earth would he do that?" Beth asked. "To show people he's not as obsessed with you as you say?"

"Either that," Jill said slowly, "or he's covering up." She looked at Beth as the idea took root, and then she exclaimed. "That's it! Beth, I know that's it!"

"What's it? What are you talking about?" Then she, too, paused, and said slowly, "Do you mean to say that you think Mike could have spilled the beans to Tom?"

"Yes!"

"But why would he have done that?" Beth asked, baffled.

"Who knows." Jill waved her hand vaguely. "It could have been a total accident. Maybe it just slipped out, and he realized too late that he'd said something he shouldn't have."

"That doesn't sound like Mike," Beth commented.

"Believe me, nothing about that man surprises me anymore. His behavior has been totally erratic." Jill put her hands on Beth's shoulders and looked into her eyes. "Beth, I know in my heart that Tom wouldn't have printed what I told him in confidence. You were right—it just doesn't jibe. Just because our relationship didn't work out doesn't mean he's a dishonorable reporter. Believe me, I heard many speeches about ethics in journalism from him. Why would he have gone on about that if he knew he was going to use information I provided him with in confidence? There's got to be another explanation, and I think we've got it."

"Well," Beth said pragmatically, "even if Mike did say something to Tom, there still isn't anything we can do. He obviously feels bad about it—as you say, he's overcompensating—and he won't do it again. What else can we ask for?"

"Revenge," Jill grumbled.

Beth smiled indulgently. "Honey, I'd just leave it be, if I were you. If what we're conjecturing is true, he'll feel too guilty about blaming you publicly to bother you privately, and after what he's put you through, I think that's worth a lot."

Jill sighed. "I suppose you're right." More enthusiastically, she said, "Hey, you haven't said anything about yesterday. Let's hear the sordid details."

Beth looked down shyly. "Things went very well," she said, unable to stop a smile from spreading across her face.

"Oh, Beth, that's wonderful news! When's the wedding? Remember—no pink dresses!"

Beth laughed. "Stop! We are very, very far from marriage. But I promise you, if the time ever comes, there'll be no pink dresses."

"I'll hold you to that, you know," Jill said in a threatening tone.

"I'm sure you will," Beth replied, smiling, and then Jill gave her a quick hug and left her alone to visualize a late-summer wedding, complete with a canopied altar near the waves lapping on the shore, a flowing white dress and an incredibly handsome dark-haired groom in a tuxedo...

AT THE VERY MOMENT that Beth was imagining a dark-haired man standing at the water's edge, there was such a man doing just that—only it wasn't Sam. It was Mike.

He knew the end was drawing near. He'd have to take some serious action soon—but what? His latest plan seemed to have worked well, but had he been a little overzealous in his attack on Jill over the leak? No, they couldn't know, he told himself, wiping the sweat from his brow. He was just being paranoid.

He knew, however, that he couldn't continue on this way. Something had to give. He was getting very tired of constantly thinking up the next strategy, constantly negotiating his next move. He was trapped. And he knew it was his inability to concentrate that had gotten him into the trap in the first place. But he had some fight left in him. He could still try to escape....

Just then, he heard a couple of guests approaching, laughing and joking, and he was off like a shot. Nothing made him run so much these days as the sound of happy people....

SAM HAD JUST ARRIVED at his office when he received Beth's call. Though he declared he was frighteningly busy, he sat down and settled in for a long chat. He'd seen *City Life* in the morning and knew that Beth needed his support today more than ever. He certainly couldn't reveal his suspicions about Mike now....

"Beth, I know it's hard to read something like that," he told her once she'd expressed her frustrations, "but believe me, no establishment gets rave reviews all the time. It's one article. You'll weather it." He hoped he sounded convincing. In truth, it was a blow devastating enough to effectively squash the modest three-year-old venture. They *might* be able to weather it, but things could just as easily go the other way. However, he sure wasn't going to be the one to tell Beth that.

"I know," she said, sighing. "But it's still awful for us—especially since everybody thought Tom liked the place so much."

"Yeah, well, reporters aren't known to be particularly up-front about their real feelings."

"But he seemed different, though I must say, I couldn't quite get a handle on him. And poor Jill. She thought they had a great romance starting, and he dropped her like a hot potato."

"That's too bad," Sam agreed. "But like I said, try not to worry too much. You guys have a wonderful operation going there—and I speak from firsthand experience. You'll get more and better publicity in the future. These rough parts are a necessary evil of establishing a business."

"Did you experience them, too?" she asked.

"Sure," he lied. In truth, his business had been phenomenally successful from the very beginning. "Anyway, hon, I've got to go. My phone's lighting up like a Christmas tree. I'll talk to you later. Be brave, okay?"

"Okay," Beth said. When she'd hung up after exchanging a tender goodbye with Sam, she set out to walk over to the main building, but before she could leave, the phone rang.

"Hello?"

"Beth? It's me. I've just seen the article. Darling, what's going on?"

Beth's heart sank at the sound of her mother's voice. This was all she needed!

"Oh, hi, Mom. Well, we thought some publicity would be nice, but I guess we were wrong, huh?" She tried to keep her tone light. The last thing she wanted was her mother knowing her business could fail miserably.

"Well, I must say I didn't think the reporter was very fair about the whole thing. He compared you to the most exclusive, luxurious spas, when you and your friends are attempting to provide a more homey atmosphere for your guests."

Beth was touched by her mother's observation. She was rallying to her daughter's side, after all. Would wonders never cease?

"That's exactly what we're trying to do, Mom. It's tough getting a business off the ground, though. Mike's a terrific financial manager, but even he can't get us out of the mid-level doldrums. If our fees were incredibly low, I'm sure we would have been judged quite differently. But because we are trying to offer some luxury services, we have to charge accordingly. We're pretty full up most of the time, but we've still had to raise our prices recently and institute some cutbacks."

"Well, I hope you'll give this reporter a good piece of your mind!"

Beth smiled, still somewhat amazed at her mother's reaction. "I don't think so, Mom. It's probably best just to let it die."

"Well, if there's anything we can do, darling, just let us know. Do you need any money to tide you over?"

That question grated on Beth. Sometimes it seemed her mother didn't ask those kinds of questions to be helpful, but because she thought her daughter was still too young and too inept to balance her budget!

"No, Mom. Believe me, I take these setbacks into account. We're still just starting out, and in a business time frame, three years is nothing. I've got to expect some lean times."

"Of course, dear." Beth could tell by her mother's now-distracted tone that she was tiring of the conversation.

"By the way," her mother added in a slightly tremulous tone, "you know Barb has moved in?"

Beth's heart went out to her mother immediately. The way she'd said those few words told Beth her mother's own heart was broken. But she was trying her best to be a trouper. "No, Mom, I didn't know. I haven't spoken to her in a while. She did say she was thinking about it, though." Beth felt a pang of guilt; she really should have called Barb after their talk to see how she was doing. "How is she?"

Lillian sighed. "As well as can be expected, I suppose. No woman should have to go through what Mark put her through."

Good for you, Mom, Beth said silently.

"I—I just wish Barb had, well, more going on in her life. She's just been moping, staring at the walls."

"Well, as you said, she's been through a lot."

"Yes, and she placed all of her hopes and dreams on a successful marriage. I'm no longer sure that's such a great thing to do...."

Beth could hardly contain her astonishment. It was the closest her mother had ever come to voicing approval of Beth's life-style. But she apparently had no intention of saying any more, because she abruptly changed the subject.

"Tell me," she asked, "how is your young man?"

"Sam is fine, Mom. We haven't had much time to see each other, but we talk quite a bit on the phone."

"Well, good. But, Beth, remember, you have to make time for your social life as well as your work life. All work and no play makes Beth a dull girl...."

Why did she always have to ruin their conversations, Beth wondered. "Right. I won't forget. I've got to run now. I'll talk to you soon, okay?"

"Okay, dear. Say hello to everyone for me."

"I will. Bye."

"Bye, darling."

Beth breathed a sigh of relief when she hung up— even though the call had been better than most. Her mother had seemed more worried than triumphant about the article; an I-told-you-so manner would have been more in character. But it seemed as if she realized she'd gone too far on that Saturday evening and was guarding against a repeat performance. And then there was her supportiveness of Barb, though she'd obviously been terribly disappointed about the breakup. She'd even gone so far as to hint that Barb needed more in her life. *Maybe she's learning,* Beth mused.

Over the next few days, Beth was too busy to speak to Sam as much as she would have liked. But then again, he was just as busy, and Beth was distressed at the new, clipped quality in his voice when she spoke to him on the phone. In one conversation, she told him how she felt.

"I'm sorry, Beth," he said, sounding frustrated and unhappy. "This is a really bad time for me. We're getting our fall orders tied up and things are just crazy. On top of that, I'm busy interviewing people for Margaret's job."

"Sam," she said gently, "I hope you're taking care of yourself. If you don't take time out for some rest and relaxation once in a while, you'll only end up hurting your business. You won't be in good enough shape to give it your all."

She heard him sigh. "I know. I know," he said. "And I have good people working for me, too. It's just that—well, old habits are hard to break, I guess." He didn't tell her that he'd gone back to skipping breakfasts and grabbing greasy fast foods for lunch. It was simply a matter of saving time....

"Well, if you ever need a break, you know where I am," she said teasingly.

"How about you come into Toronto again on Thursday?"

"Oh, Sam, I can't. To tell you the truth, it's been a bit crazy here, too. I don't think I'll be taking any time off this week. This is our busiest time, though there does seem to have been a slight decline in attendance—because of Tom's article, I guess."

"I'm sorry to hear that," Sam said sympathetically.

Beth sighed. "Yeah, it's pretty tense around here. Mike and Jill avoid each other like the plague, which is probably best, since he was making her life miserable when he followed her around like a puppy, but when they do have to talk to each other, they snap like pit bulls. It's really awful."

"It sounds to me as if things are coming to a head," said Sam. "You guys might just have to do some corporate restructuring."

"I know," Beth said sadly. "Don't remind me. Let this be a lesson to all potential entrepreneurs—don't go into business with friends."

"Here, here," Sam said. "Seriously, Beth, you can't continue to work in an environment like that. You—and everybody else, I'm sure—will start to hate the place."

"So what do I do?"

"Sit on it for another couple of weeks—maybe emotions are still running too high for everybody to be logical. But if you still feel that the situation is unworkable, you're going to have to think long and hard about what *you* want to do. You won't be able to force anybody else out. Either you make a change in your own life or sit everybody down to tell them you can't work like this."

"It sounds so easy when you talk about it that way," Beth said regretfully, knowing she'd have to make one of the choices Sam had proposed.

"Believe me, it's not easy at all. I've seen too many partnerships break down, and it's always messy. But you have to be happy in your work situation, Beth...."

They talked a while longer, but when Beth hung up, she didn't feel that much better. The situation with Jill and Mike was bad for staff morale and bad for business. Jill's mood, especially, spilled over into her classes, and Beth had actually heard complaints about Jill riding the clients too hard.

And Beth's state of mind was worsening every day, not just because of the situation with her partners and the drop-off in clientele, but because the one person who could have been a tonic and a support to her lived in a different city. And though she and Sam had expressed their love for each other, they hadn't had much opportunity to go beyond that. While it was still far too early in the relationship to be talking about marriage or moving in together, Beth felt decidedly unsettled. Would they ever be able to regain the level of closeness they'd achieved when they'd been together at the spa and in Toronto? She honestly didn't know, but she did know that she desperately needed that closeness now, when the other aspects of her life seemed to be crumbling before her eyes.

Her mother's typical words of wisdom in regard to her daughter's new relationship didn't help matters any—the latest line was "Why should someone buy milk when he can get it from the cow for free?" However, Beth was finding that she was more able to tolerate her mother's oblique comments about her love life. The remarks were, in fact, becoming less and less frequent.

As time went on, Beth became convinced that her mother's change of attitude toward her was at least partly due to the destruction of her illusions about her other daughter. And even Beth had to sympathize. Poor Lillian had deluded herself for so long, the disappointment had to be huge.

And the change in Barb was heartbreaking. Beth had phoned her shortly after her conversation with Sam and was more than a little distressed by Barb's behavior. The formerly vivacious young woman was listless and weepy and showed no interest in taking the steps necessary to get on with her life, such as finding an apartment or going out with friends. Beth assumed it was a delayed reaction to the breakup. She had seemed to be holding up admirably when she'd come out to the spa—in need of a shoulder, but in control.

It really was too bad, Beth thought, that Barb wasn't passionate about her career. Sure, Barb liked her job, but that wasn't enough. Beth knew that if things didn't work out with Sam, her work would be her salvation.

Strangely enough, even though she felt awful about Barb, she couldn't help feeling a tiny bit triumphant. With Barb in her present state, Beth knew Lillian couldn't help but make comparisons between her daughters and see that Beth hadn't been so silly after all, working her butt off to make a success of herself.

Beth found it surprisingly easy, all of a sudden, to forgive her mother—partially because Lillian had expressed her vulnerability, albeit in a roundabout way. But also because Sam's influence had made her see that she'd been at least a little to blame for the deterioration of her relationship with her mother. As he had pointed out, she tended not to forgive people for their errors too quickly. Just as it had taken her a long time to forgive Sam for having been a jerk in high school, Beth hadn't been able to forgive her parents for having made a few mistakes while raising her.

Then, too, these days Beth was generally more open to the possibility of change in people. Sam was a prime example of someone who had turned out to be the total opposite of what she'd expected. And in very different ways, Tom and Mike had surprised her, made her see that people weren't always what they seemed.

Deciding to shake her suddenly negative frame of mind, Beth went to bed. Once again, her sleep was filled with bizarre dreams, dreams that left her troubled and confused—and aching for the feel of Sam's arms around her....

SAM, TOO, WAS HAVING his fill of troubled nights and days. Since his sojourn at the spa, he'd been acutely aware that his life was lacking a couple of essential elements, namely enjoyment of his work—more and more he was beginning to resent his business—and important close relationships.

He found himself discussing his newfound insight with Bob over dinner one night. Bob had gotten in touch with him shortly after he'd returned from the spa, to find out how his vacation had gone. The good doctor had been delighted at Sam's enthusiasm—and the fact that he'd met someone—and he'd suggested the two of them meet. Both being busy professionals, the only day they could pin down was a Friday at the end of June, but it had arrived soon enough. During dinner, Sam vowed to make more time for his friends in the future. It felt good to be bouncing thoughts and impressions off Bob.

"So if everything's fine between you two now," Bob said between bites of sole—they were at a very trendy, new Bloor Street restaurant. "Why don't you move in together or something?"

Sam paused before taking another bite of his grilled shrimp. Then he said, "To tell you the truth, I'm not sure." He shrugged. "Yeah, we live in different cities right now, but we haven't even talked about the future, except in the most general of terms. It's almost as if we're both still afraid something might go wrong." Suddenly it came to him. "We've pledged our love, but not our trust," he said slowly. "I thought that when I heard her say she loved me, I'd feel she trusted me, too. But the truth is, I'm still waiting for her to tell me she doesn't believe I can make it through the long haul—and no doubt she's still waiting for me to screw up royally. Until those feelings are gone completely, there's no way we'll be able to make a go of it."

"I hate to tell you, pal, but those feelings will never be gone completely," Bob said practically.

"Hey, what makes you such an expert?" Sam asked playfully. "You never date the same woman twice."

"Ah, but I read a lot of psychiatry journals."

Sam chuckled. "If I read those, I'd probably be more confused than I already am."

"I gather you're confused about other things, too," Bob said casually as he took another bite of sole. "You're looking better than you did, but not as good as I expected from what you'd told me. I thought you'd started to eat right, exercise and get plenty of rest . . . ?"

Sam sighed. "I tried, Bob, I did, but it's so hard."

"Nobody said it was easy."

"I know, I know. But I tell you, my business is really getting me down. It takes so much of my time and energy, I can hardly stop to breathe. Did I tell you Margaret is leaving?"

"No!"

"Yeah. It's a real bummer. I can hardly muster the energy to do interviews. The ones I have seen so far have been singularly unimpressive. Anyway, I guess I'm feeling, well, sorry for myself, and food is my reward."

Bob looked at him critically. "Didn't you learn anything while you were at Couchiching?"

Sam looked down at his plate and in a mock-ashamed tone said, "Yes, I did, sir, and I'll never be bad again."

Bob grinned. "Whoops. Sorry—I didn't mean to sound so patronizing. But you said you'd done so well there..."

"I know." Sam looked away for a moment. "The other day I was telling Beth that she should be making some hard decisions in her life. It seems I'm not one to follow my own advice. I'm a master of avoidance techniques—like overeating and workaholism."

"That can be remedied. You are the only one in control of your life."

"Right as usual, doctor. I promise I'll make some decisions real soon."

With that, Bob changed the subject and during the rest of the meal, he chatted on cheerfully about his practice and his own love life. Sam was strangely silent. After Bob had said "You are the only one in control of your life," a plan had begun to form in his head; suddenly he had a clear vision of his future, and he knew exactly what it was that he wanted to do.

He set the plan in motion with a phone call to Beth when he got home.

"Hi, beautiful," he whispered when she answered.

"Oooh," she cooed. "No one's ever called me beautiful before."

"Well, now I know what to call you every time I speak to you."

Beth immediately felt her burdens fly off her shoulders.

"I've missed you," she said in a low voice.

"I've missed you, too, sweetheart," he said.

"Sam, I'm dying to see you. Can you take next Thursday off? It's the Fourth of July."

That was six days away, he calculated. That would be enough time, surely....

"Sounds great. Tell you what—I'll come to you this time. I'm in desperate need of a beach."

"Great," she said. "Just come straight to the bungalow when you arrive. What time should I be ready for you?"

"Honey," he drawled, "to be ready for me, all you have to do is stay in bed."

She chuckled. "My sentiments, exactly. We may never make it to the beach."

"Bed rest is even more therapeutic," he said suggestively.

Coyly, she replied, "Who'll be resting?"

"Beth, I'd better hang up before I have to take a cold shower. I've always hated those."

"Okay, darling." Her voice dropped to a whisper. "I love you."

"Love you, too," he whispered back.

When she hung up, he grinned. As he placed the receiver gently back in place, he wondered what she

would think if she knew that tomorrow he was going
to be shopping for the ring he would present to her
when he asked her to be his wife....

CHAPTER ELEVEN

WHEN SAM KNOCKED on the door, he hardly expected Beth to open it fully dressed and looking ready for an outing to the beach.

At his downcast look, Beth laughed, kissed him soundly on the lips and pulled him inside.

"Disappointed?" she asked, knowing the answer.

"I thought we agreed that you would stay in bed," Sam said, pouting.

Still smiling, Beth said, "I'm sorry, darling, really I am. And I promise you, later we'll come back here for a triple X-rated romp, but I've been dying to get out of here for so long, I just couldn't contain my enthusiasm."

Sam sighed. "Well, in that case, I guess I'll just have to contain mine."

Beth laughed again. "Don't look so upset. Some people would actually enjoy a day at the beach."

"Not when faced with the choice of frolicking in bed with you...."

"Believe me, many men have considered the opportunity a meager one."

"Fools, all," Sam pronounced.

"Well," Beth said, "shall we go?"

"Only if you promise to come to our favorite greasy spoon with me. I have to have my appetite satisfied one way or another."

"Will do," Beth announced happily.

And they were off, in Sam's car. On the way to the restaurant, they brought each other up-to-date on what had gone on in their lives over the past few days. On the way to Orillia Sam had decided to wait until just before going back to Toronto to present Beth with her engagement ring. He'd concluded the day before that he was going to give her the ring his mother had once worn. It was much nicer than anything he'd seen in even the finest jewelry stores, and the symbolism meant a lot to him.

Though it was difficult to keep his proposal in, he really was interested in hearing about the ever-increasing level of tension at the spa. At his request, Beth quickly described various incidents that had occurred since she'd spoken to him last, but she told him she didn't really want to talk about the spa—doing so only depressed her, and she wanted to have a good time today. He understood, and fought an urge to warn her about avoidance techniques, telling her instead about his restlessness vis-à-vis his business.

When they were seated in a booth and were digging into generous portions of pancakes and sausages, Beth said in a concerned voice, "Sam, you don't look so great. Are you back to your old habits?"

He smiled a little sadly. "You and Bob. Are you ever going to leave me alone?"

"That means you're not exercising, you're eating poorly, and you're not getting enough rest, right? I wouldn't have agreed to come here if I hadn't thought it would be a treat. I hope you don't eat this stuff all the time...."

He looked down sheepishly and played with a piece of sausage. Then he sighed and leaned his head against the wall behind him. "Like I told you, Beth, old habits die hard."

"So you *are* feeling tired and irritable?"

He shrugged. "I always do, to a certain extent."

"Did you feel that way when you were at the spa?"

"Well, no, but I was on vacation—"

Beth shook her head. "There's more to it than that, Sam. Eating properly and exercising have a positive effect on your mental health, too. Have you ever heard of 'endorphins'?"

"Yeah, but I'm not sure what they are."

"An endorphin is one of a group of chemical compounds that have pain-and-stress-relieving properties. Endorphins exist naturally in the brain and are released through exercise, so working out brings you an immediate feeling of well-being. It's not just a theory—it's been proven scientifically, in the same way that certain foods have been linked with heart disease and specific kinds of cancer." In a more personal tone, she added, "I'm not trying to lecture you, Sam. I'm just trying to help you enjoy your life more."

"I know," he said and paused for a moment. "But I don't think it's a mere matter of exercising more, or eating the right kinds of foods. The fact is, I'm not very happy with my life right now."

"In what ways?" Beth asked tentatively, hoping against hope that he would say something about his needing her to be with him all the time. . . .

"Well, first off, my job just isn't what it used to be," he said.

First off. That meant there was still hope. Aloud, she said, "Do you mean it doesn't satisfy you the way it once did?"

"Exactly," he answered, sounding down in the dumps.

"Well," she said slowly, "why do you think that is?"

He shrugged again. "Beats me. We've talked about this before. I do know I just don't get the same high, the same enjoyment out of it that I once did. I used to love getting up in the mornings and hustling and shmoozing with the buyers. But it's just not fun anymore—it's aggravating. And I told you about Margaret leaving. I still haven't found anyone to replace her. I've interviewed at least a dozen people, and I haven't been remotely impressed with any of them." He sighed. "I know it's childish, but it's not going to be the same without her. . . ."

"That's not at all childish, Sam. Margaret was a very important part of your business for you." Beth was quiet for a moment as she chewed thoughtfully on her food. Then she said, "Not too long ago you told me that I was going to have to make some choices. . . ?"

Sam grimaced. "I take it you're saying I have to do the same thing."

She nodded.

"I know," he said, running a hand through his hair. "It's just that it would kill me to give up the business. In a sense it's a memorial to my parents. How can I sell it?"

"Maybe you don't have to sell it. Maybe you could hire a good manager and remove yourself from the day-to-day hassles. Then you could spend the majority of the time doing what you want to do."

"That's a thought," Sam said slowly.

"It must have occurred to you previously," she commented.

"Yes," he replied cautiously. "Yes, it did. Only I'm not sure that I'll be able to give up control."

"Sam," Beth said gently, "you're no longer controlling the business—the business is controlling you. In order to live and work effectively, you have to delegate, have to let others take the load off."

"I know, I know." He took a mouthful of food and worked on it for a while. When he was ready to talk again, he said, "It's not something I'll be able to do right away—I'll have to take a good long time to think about it. Anyway, I'm not sure I'm entirely comfortable with the idea of a manager. No one works as hard for a company as the owner...."

"That's true. It's just a possibility. There are others." She softened her voice. "Keep in mind, Sam, that your parents, who were quite generous and understanding in spirit, wouldn't have wanted you to do anything you didn't want to. If you do sell the business, wherever they are, I'm sure they'll understand. But take your time making the decision. It's an important one, and there's absolutely no rush."

"I know. But I can't seem to help thinking about all the possibilities these days. Also, I don't know what else I would do. Business is all I know, and every business has its hassles."

"That's something you'll want to research. Talk to people, other professionals. Maybe something will click."

Suddenly he reached over the table to take her hands in his. "I do know that whatever I do with my future, I want you to be a big part of it," he said softly, coming very close to proposing, but stopping just short of saying the magic words. "I can't imagine my life without you, Beth."

Beth felt joy well up inside of her. "I can't imagine mine without you," she replied, squeezing his hands. "I was afraid of the future for a long time, but I really think we can make it now, Sam. I still have some reservations, but I'm sure every couple has a few concerns that are never completely resolved. At least I'm not afraid anymore."

"I'm glad." He squeezed her hands back, then took care of the check, which the waitress had dropped unceremoniously on their table.

In no time at all, they were parked at the beach. It was another gorgeous day, and Sam thought that life seemed perfect. Before they collapsed under the sun, they took a slow walk along the main pier and admired the many boats—some sleek and expensive-looking, and others more run-down but decidedly appealing. Sam took a whiff of air, redolent with the mingled scents of sun, sand, ice cream and fresh water, and imagined himself and Beth lounging on a luxurious boat anchored in the middle of the still lake. They'd feast at a leisurely pace on freshly caught fish and cold beer, then make love languidly in the cool cabin, rocking gently along with the slow, steady waves....

"It's perfect, isn't it," Beth said softly as they walked along at a relaxed pace, hand in hand.

"Just what I was thinking." He stopped and sat at the edge of the pier to dangle his feet in the water, and he motioned for her to do the same.

She did so, and they stayed silent for a few moments.

Sam broke the quiet by saying, "Every time I come here I'm so struck by how different the pace is. No one in Toronto stops to dangle their feet in the lake."

"That's probably because they're not allowed near it."

"True," Sam acknowledged, chuckling. "But I meant it figuratively as well as literally. Even on weekends I go crazy doing errands and things I haven't had time to do during the week. People here are more relaxed—happier, I think."

"Maybe," Beth said reflectively. "I know I'm happier here. But don't forget, you're looking at it from a tourist's point of view. If you lived here, you'd have to work, just as you do in Toronto, and you'd likely have a mortgage, as you do in Toronto, etcetera, etcetera." Even while she said all this in a common-sensical tone, her heart was fluttering madly. Was Sam actually toying with the idea of moving to Orillia? It couldn't be—but then, he'd already talked about changing careers....

She vowed not to get carried away with her thoughts.

"Even so..." he said thoughtfully, letting his words trail off.

She held a breath, then let it out when he said in a bright tone, "Ah, well, we can't all live the life of Riley, eh?" Jumping up, he grabbed her arm and led her over to a snack bar. "But today we can. Your choice, my dear—chocolate, vanilla or strawberry?"

"Decisions, decisions," Beth said gravely. "Frankly I've always been a purist. Vanilla for me," she said to the teenage girl behind the counter.

"Make it two," Sam supplied. "Without cones."

"Good for you," Beth said approvingly.

When they had their ice creams in hand, they walked back down the marina pier toward the beach, enjoying a comfortable silence on the way. By the time they reached the sandy shore, they had finished their snacks and were ready to flop out under the glorious, and by now very hot, sun.

Sam stole a glance at Beth's long, slender body as she stripped down to her bathing suit—a sensational black and purple bikini this time. He could hardly tear his eyes away. Her skin looked especially tanned and supple next to the thick, shiny fabric of the suit, and the fabulous shade of purple brought out the blue of her glorious eyes. . . .

He forced himself to look away, and as he did, Beth covertly checked him out. He'd gained a bit of weight since she'd seen him last, but there was no question that he still looked wonderful. His tan was still in evidence, and his muscles were well defined and very appealing. And of course, he had a wonderfully handsome face that never ceased to cause her heart to flutter each time they met.

But it was when his torso was bared that she could barely keep from swooning. He was an incredible specimen of a man; she wondered how she could have ever thought he'd lost his looks since high school. He had the kind of looks that were solid, that endured . . . or was it that she was so bowled over by the strength of his character and the beauty of his soul that the inside and the outside of the man were all jumbled in her mind?

When they were lying side by side on the blanket, Sam reached over and kissed her cheek lightly before lying back down and turning his face up appreciatively to the warm sun.

And she still felt the warmth of his tender kiss as she drifted off into a peaceful sleep, to dream about them making love on the beach, at twilight....

She woke up to feel Sam gently nudging her and to hear him say, "Beth, wake up. Beth...."

Groggily she lifted herself up onto her elbows. "How long have I slept?" she asked.

"Just about an hour or so. I wanted to make sure you didn't burn."

"I won't burn," she assured him. "I have a pretty good base." She stretched languidly. "Mmm, you interrupted the most delicious dream...."

"I was in it, I hope," Sam said in a seductive tone.

"You were the star," she said huskily.

"And you my costar?"

"You bet." She lay back down, and Sam, resting on one elbow, began to slowly and sensuously trace a pattern along her arms and legs.

"Tell me what the dream was about," he said, nearly driving her crazy with his touch.

"We were making love on the beach," she whispered.

"We can make the dream come true," he said. "But obviously not now," he added as a little boy dumped a bucket of sand on his legs, giggled, and ran off.

Beth, too, collapsed into a fit of giggles, and then scrambled to her feet. "I've got a better idea," she said. "Let's go back to my place, take nice hot showers and have dinner in."

"Sounds heavenly," Sam said and jumped up.

As they drove back to the spa, they sang songs from their teenage years when they weren't breaking up in helpless laughter.

"Oh, God," Beth said when they had parked and were unloading the car, "I can't believe we actually liked those songs. They were so corny!"

"Every generation thinks its music is the best—and fifteen years later, the worst."

"I suppose so," she mused as she unlocked the door. Dropping her load she turned to him and announced, "That was a terrific day. Just what the doctor ordered."

"You said it," Sam affirmed, lowering his bag and taking his shoes off. As he followed her down the hall into the kitchen, he said, "Are you hungry?"

"Sure am," she said enthusiastically.

"Me, too," he said, and grabbing her waist, he whirled her around. "But not for dinner..."

He led her to the bedroom, where he quickly caused the memory of the dream she'd had in the afternoon to recede. Skillfully and confidently, he excited her with very real sensuous experiments that took her to the point of no return. And then she amazed him by taking control, straddling him so that as they rocked together, her breasts moved sensuously with the rhythm of their union, and her hair swung to and fro. He moaned helplessly, thoroughly under her spell, amazed that she felt so free with him. It was a sure sign that she'd come to trust him. When she cried out, he came, too, aroused beyond his wildest dreams....

As they lay contentedly in each other's arms, Sam whispered, "Happy?"

"Mmm, hmm."

"Honey?"

"Mmm?"

"Now I really am hungry."

She opened one eye. "Same here. Let's go see what we can rustle up." Soon, they were digging into tossed salads and steaming platefuls of pasta with a tomato and basil sauce.

"Mmm, hmm." Sam shook his head in wonderment. "You are a sensational cook."

"Nothing to this meal at all, Sam. You saw."

"I know, I know. I should do what you do instead of grabbing fast food, right?"

"You said it, I didn't."

"Yeah, yeah, I know. But since I did introduce the subject, it's my prerogative to change it, which I'm going to do right now. Since we've had such a great day, maybe you can talk about what's going on at the spa now." He was more than a little curious, particularly about Mike.

She sighed and said, "You're right. I should talk about it. I'm awfully good at sweeping things under the carpet, it seems. And maybe you'll be able to help. I know you said you aren't familiar with the books, but maybe something I say will twig a suggestion. I hope you *can* help. Heaven knows we've made a lot of mistakes." So Beth told him absolutely everything that had happened from the last time she'd spoken to him until he'd arrived at her bungalow in the morning. She'd already spoken to him about the article, but not about Jill's theory regarding Mike.

When she asked him outright if he thought Mike might have told Tom about the problems at the spa, he remained silent for a few minutes and then said, "Beth, I know Mike is—was—a good friend of yours, but his behavior certainly has been very strange lately. I've known a few guys who have acted similarly in certain circumstances...."

His voice trailed off as he seemed to change his mind about saying whatever it was he was going to say.

"Sam, what is it? What are you thinking?"

He looked her directly in the eye. "Beth, have you considered the possibility that Mike might be stealing from you?"

CHAPTER TWELVE

BETH ONLY STARED at him. "Excuse me?"

Softly, Sam said, "I know it's a difficult concept, Beth, but quite frankly, everything you've told me points to the same thing. He's got total control over your finances, he claims the spa is going broke when it seems to everybody else—myself included—that it's doing just fine, he's been behaving strangely, and you think he leaked news of the spa's apparent difficulties." He leaned forward. "He may just have done that purposefully, you know—to bring about *real* difficulties. That way, no one would suspect his thievery was what caused the initial drop-off in bookings—"

"Whoa, whoa!" Beth shook her head vigorously. "Sam, I appreciate your trying to help, but you've got it all wrong. There's no way Mike would ever steal from the spa. We're all old friends, for heaven's sake!"

"People change," he said gently. "You know that better than anyone." He paused for a few moments. "I've had my suspicions about Mike for a while, Beth. Way back at the beach party he told me how much Total Maintenance was charging you. The sum he gave me was way off base. I know someone else who uses

Total. He could be faking expenses—either with phony invoices or double sets of books, or both.''

Beth fought to rein in her rising temper. Sam's matter-of-fact words had unleashed a strange and powerful resentment in her. How did he dare question her character judgment? Until recently, he hadn't even bothered to look beneath the skin when choosing his friends. Mike Petrie may not have been the greatest friend in the world to her, and indeed, sometimes their conversations were downright awkward, but Beth did think of him as a kindred spirit of sorts—and not just because they worked together. He, like Beth, hadn't ever quite fit in, and so there was an unspoken bond between them that transcended their differences. It was because of this that Beth had not thrown off Mike's friendship long ago. She, unlike Sam, was forever loyal to her friends.

Besides the fact that he was completely out of line, his treatment of her now was bordering on patronizing. How stupid did he think she was, anyway? She and the other partners weren't completely absolved from financial responsibility. They did examine the figures annually. But were they the right figures, a little voice asked. *Of course,* she thought, squelching the momentary doubt.

"Sam," she said, trying hard to keep her voice level. "I pride myself on being a good judge of character, and while I may not be as close to Mike as some of my other partners, he is still my friend, and I'll thank you not to accuse him of serious crimes lightly. Unlike some people, I am loyal to my friends.''

Sam looked shocked for a moment, and then, he shook his head and laughed mirthlessly. ''So, we're back to that, are we? I really thought we'd gone beyond that, Beth. Everyone who hasn't hurt you in the past is worthy of your loyalty, is that it? You can't get beyond the fact that I was an ass way back when, and you'll never forgive your parents for not being as understanding as Mr. and Mrs. Brady on *The Brady Bunch!* Well, I've got a news flash for you, sweetheart.'' He stood and leaned toward her, his eyes glittering. ''People can change! Unsavory people can turn into good people, and vice versa. But you're so stubborn—or so terrified of really living—that you won't take people out of the little compartments you've put them in. Face it, Beth, you're afraid of change. You can't handle it.''

She started to protest, but he leveled a cool glance at her and interrupted, saying, ''I'm glad I realized just now that I'm positively unable to live with your opinion of me. If we ever got married—heaven forbid—you'd always be expecting me to fail you in some way. With every mistake I made, you'd say, 'That's the real Sam coming out' instead of, 'Sam, who's a pretty terrific guy, made a mistake.' Hell, I don't even have to make mistakes for you to think badly of me. Just now I was trying to help you, dammit.'' He ran out of words and just stood there for a few moments longer, looking at her coldly. He was tremendously disappointed in her and tremendously hurt. How could she have possibly thought that he hadn't been acting in her best interests? Her reaction to the theory he'd put forth had astounded him.

Beth, too, was feeling as if she'd just been kicked in the gut. Surely loyalty to one's friends was an admirable trait—and one he obviously didn't appreciate. The other things he'd said—about her being afraid of change—merely told her that he wasn't sensitive enough to understand the hurts she'd sustained in the past, and he'd never be able to. He really hadn't changed, after all. Sam Sarnoff had always wanted things to come too easily. Apparently he wasn't interested in working hard enough to regain her trust. It could take months—years, even....

"I think you'd better leave," she whispered, feeling her eyes starting to mist, hearing her voice become shaky.

And before she knew it, he was gone, having collected his things in angry, sweeping movements. His behavior had only inflamed her own anger and despair. How could she have been so wrong about him? How had he presumed to criticize her friends and her judgment like that—and then get so hot under the collar at her disappointment in him?

It was quite clear that there was no future for them. Things hadn't changed; she and Sam were still fundamentally different. He wasn't at all surprised when people acted cruelly or irresponsibly—he'd had plenty of insensitive pals in the old days—whereas any kind of betrayal shattered Beth. She always expected the best of people, and that meant being tolerant and open to those who were different than her, and always giving people the benefit of the doubt. Yes, indeed, she and Sam were as different as two people could be.

But how it hurt. She'd wanted things to work out so very much. She'd allowed herself to become vulnerable, even when she'd been unsure of what the future held....

And so the tears came, slowly at first, then in torrents as she tortured herself by thinking of what they might have had, what might have been. She cried for about an hour, at the end of which she felt as if her body was completely dry. She glanced at her watch. It was ten o'clock. *Is that all?* she thought dully. She'd been sure it was well into the wee hours.

She dragged herself up from the kitchen table into her bedroom. Moving very slowly, as if life itself weighed her down, she pulled on sweatpants and a matching pullover. Then she went back to the kitchen and made a phone call.

"Selma?" she asked when the other woman had picked up the receiver. "Can you come over?" She heard her voice crack. "I need to talk to you."

THANK HEAVEN FOR SELMA, Beth thought. She always seemed to know just what to say and do—and just what not to say and do.

Shortly after coming in, Selma had put on a pot of chamomile tea, and when Beth burst into tears at her friend's ministrations, Selma grabbed a box of tissues off a counter, led Beth over to the table and tried to soothe her. Finally she said in a soft voice, "Do you want to tell me what happened?"

Between fresh sobs, Beth said, "God . . . Selma . . . I haven't cried . . . this much . . . since adolescence!"

Selma couldn't help but smile. "I'd say you've been doing well, then."

When Beth had calmed down a little, she tried to get the story out, dabbing ferociously at her eyes all the while. "I can't believe it. He actually suggested that Mike could be—well, taking money from the business accounts. The story he concocted! He even said that Mike might have spilled the beans to Tom about our financial difficulties on purpose!"

Selma knit her brows. "What was Sam's reasoning?"

"He said Mike may have wanted to bring about real difficulties, so that people wouldn't suspect that his stealing was what caused the drop-off in reservations. He—he also said he'd had suspicions about Mike for a while because of some maintenance-cost figure Mike had given him that sounded out of whack."

"Hmm" was all Selma said to that.

"I guess what made me so mad—apart from his accusing Mike of such terrible things—was his cavalier attitude. Every once in a while he does something that makes him seem like a creature from another planet. I know you're going to tell me—like you have before—that that's perfectly natural, but sometimes I just can't believe he's the same person I've fallen in love with.''

"And you get scared.''

"Yes,'' Beth admitted. "I get very afraid of the future—afraid we're too different to make it work, and that we won't see eye to eye on anything.'' She sighed. "I shouldn't even be talking about the future. It's over. He said he can't live with my fear. And I almost don't blame him for that—it must be hard for him to deal with my lack of trust. But he's put me in that position.''

"Beth,'' Selma said slowly, "it's perfectly natural for a couple to disagree on major issues. I'd say that two people who agreed on everything were exceedingly boring. You're bound to have a radically different perspective from your partner at times. You're coming from a different history, a different culture. The important thing is that you find a means of resolving disputes. Don't focus on winning or losing arguments. Try to work on problem-solving techniques.''

Beth realized that Selma's words made a lot of sense. But what good did they do her now?

She dabbed at her eyes and sighed. "That's all well and good,'' she said, "but like I told you, it's probably too late now. I guess I blew it. Me and my temper. Here I was attacking Sam for not being perfect when I'm far from perfect myself.''

"You know, Beth, you and Sam seem to be bringing more baggage from your high school days into your relationship than you even realize. Not only are you insecure about Sam because of the way he treated you back then, but even the structure of your present relationship is adolescent in nature."

"What do you mean?" Beth asked, not following.

"Well, every time you two argue, you 'break up.' It's just like high school. You're adults now. Either you commit and understand that you're going to fight now and then or you get together for good."

"But maybe it really is over this time...."

"Don't you owe it to yourself to find out?" Selma asked gently.

Beth knew she did. She also knew she was guilty of the adolescent behavior Selma had charged her with. Perhaps, she mused, she acted that way because she always feared being attacked, being hurt. She didn't want to commit: commitment meant risk. All of a sudden, things became quite clear. By lashing out at Sam, she'd tried to force the relationship to end, so she would no longer be vulnerable. She couldn't lose what she no longer had....

She decided then and there to try to work on all her faults. She would talk to Sam and—*Please God*—if he agreed to continue to try to make a go of it, she would promise to always work on solutions, on methods of compromising—if he did the same.

What if he doesn't want you back, a small voice whispered. She pushed the troubling thought away. She'd think about that tomorrow. Right now, she had to know if she'd been wrong about something else....

"Selma," she asked tentatively, "do you think there's a possibility that what Sam suggested could be true? Do you think Mike would really...embezzle funds?" She still couldn't say "steal."

Selma refilled her mug carefully and looked Beth straight in the eye when she said, "The thought had occurred to me long before you mentioned it."

"Really?" Beth said incredulously, and she was about to go on when there was a hesitant knock at the door. Hope leaped up wildly in her chest but died again when she saw that it was Joel.

"Oh, it's only you," she said disappointedly.

Joel saw Selma and gave an exaggerated shrug. "It's only you. The story of my life," he said. Turning back to Beth and following her into the kitchen, he said, "Sorry for coming by so late, but I saw the light on, and since I observed Mr. Wonderful pulling away earlier, I knew I wasn't going to interrupt anything." Once in the kitchen, he got a closer look at Beth's tear-stained face, and Selma's serious one, and when he spotted the box of tissues and the teapot on the table, he said in a concerned tone, "Hey, is something wrong? Anything I can do? If you want me to leave—"

"No, Joel, everything's fine," Beth interrupted him, determined to hold on to her composure. "Sam and I had a stupid fight and I was talking to Selma about it. But we've just started discussing Mike, so you've come at the right time. Pull up a chair."

"Tea?" Selma asked him.

He wrinkled his brow. "Got anything stronger, Beth?" he asked her over his shoulder. She was at the fridge looking for some snacks to put on the table, and at Joel's request, she brought out an unopened bottle of Chianti.

He nodded approvingly when she set it down along with three wineglasses and a corkscrew. "It seems appropriate," he commented. "Remember our gab sessions in university? They were really just excuses to talk about whoever didn't show up. We always drank the most godawful wine. I must say your taste has improved, Beth."

Selma grinned. "Perhaps some music is in order?"

"What say we retire into the living room?" Beth suggested. "I'm tired of these walls."

"Good idea," Joel responded, bouncing out of his chair and balancing the bottle, the corkscrew and the three glasses in his arms.

When Selma was seated on Beth's lone sofa, her feet curled under her, and Joel was sprawled on the floor, Beth put an old Chicago tape on the cassette player, and came to sit on the other end of the sofa. Joel uncorked the wine, then got up to hand out the glasses and pour. When he sat back down, he took a long, slow sip.

"Mmm, that's good," he said appreciatively.

"Brings back memories of college, doesn't it?" Beth said, a hint of wistfulness in her voice.

"Sure does," Joel affirmed. "Complete with Chicago. I nearly forgot about them. What album number are they up to—Chicago 58?"

"That's a brand of kosher salami, Joel," Selma said dryly.

"I knew that."

"Sure you did."

Suddenly Beth felt a warm wave of nostalgia wash over her. "We had some great times then, didn't we?" she said.

"We did," Selma answered firmly, and in a more gentle tone, added, "But they're in the past, Beth. We can have great times now, too."

"But everybody changes," she said sadly. "Sometimes I feel like I'm losing everything and everyone I hold dear...."

Selma nodded her head. "Everybody feels that way now and then, but change is an important part of life. And speaking of change..." She turned to Joel. "Joel, when you came in, Beth started to say that we were talking about Mike." Briefly she recounted their conversation. When she was done, she asked, "Well, what do you think?"

Joel took another slow sip of wine and then admitted, "I had some inklings in that direction myself, to tell you the truth."

Beth shook her head. "I must really be naive," she said.

"Not naive," Selma said, reaching out to touch her friend's hand. "Good-hearted. Optimistic."

Then, there was another knock at the door.

"What is this? Grand Central Station?" Beth muttered as she got up. When she opened the door, Jill burst in. "Hi, hon," she said as she flung off her lightweight jacket. "Saw your light was on and lover boy's car was gone, so I thought it was all right to come—" Upon reaching the living room, she narrowed her eyes and said, "Chicago? Chianti? Are we getting so old that we have to try to recapture our lost youth?"

Beth smiled as she followed her friend in. After pouring her some wine, she asked, "Couldn't you sleep?"

Jill sunk onto the couch, her glass firmly in hand. "I haven't tried. I've just come from Toronto. I saw Tom."

"Jill, that's great! What—"

Jill held up a hand. "No, it's not great. I didn't let him say one word about us. I did not go there to beg for explanations about why he hasn't called me, but I did want to resolve this business about the article. I needed to confirm my theory about Mike." She looked at Beth questioningly, but Beth only waved her hand dismissively.

"It's okay," she told Jill. "They all know. Moreover, we've got a new theory that fits in quite nicely with yours. Wait till you hear this one. It's a doozer."

"In that case," Jill said slowly, allowing the tension to build, "they'll want to know that I was one-hundred percent right. Tom wouldn't divulge any details, though, so I'm not sure how their conversation came about. All I know is that it *was* Mike who spilled the beans to Tom—and he didn't say anything about keeping it off the record. So he was just covering up when he pretended to be outraged.''

Nobody spoke—they just sighed collectively. Then Beth apprised Jill of their recent discussions.

''Well,'' Jill said slowly when Beth was done, ''I can't say it would come as a shock to me if it proved to be true. He's always been a bit of a jerk, but he seems to have gone way beyond that. In fact, I think in the back of my mind I knew it was something like this. There were zillions of hints. Beth, remember at the beach party Karen told us the spa had never been busier? That was right when Mike was telling us we were in trouble. We should have known then. No,'' she said more firmly, shaking her head, ''I wouldn't be at all surprised if he turned out to be a thief.''

''How can you say that?'' Beth cried, jumping up. ''Mike may be a jerk, but can he have changed so much that he'd steal from his friends? I refuse to believe it.''

''Beth, honey, this isn't college anymore,'' Jill reminded her. ''It's a big, bad world out there, and Mike has lots of other people in his life to influence him.'' She shrugged. ''He pals around with high-powered business types who use words like 'hostile takeover' and 'corporate merger.' Those yuppies with their original artwork and their designer watches must make Mike feel awfully inadequate.''

Selma sighed and said, "I think I knew, too. He's incredibly insecure to begin with, and I can see him really feeling the pressure to acquire, simply to fit in. He was bound to resort to illegal means."

Somewhat defensively, Beth said, "You make it sound as if all businessmen are bad. Sam's a businessman and he's not like that."

"Sam's special," Jill said simply, and Beth looked down.

"Yes, he is," she said softly.

At Jill's enquiring look, Beth said, "Later."

"This reminds me of the time..." As Joel eased into a long, humorous anecdote about an evening they'd all spent together in college, Beth drew her head back and shut her eyes. She knew instinctively that these people, these three very special people sitting in her living room, would be her friends forever—no matter how much they talked about the inevitability of change. Over the years they'd all influenced her enormously; they'd helped shape her, helped make her who she was. They'd spent many an evening like this— helping one another, supporting one another.

Sam was another one who'd helped her learn and grow—even back in high school. He, too, was a real friend. Deep down she knew that. She just had trouble getting past her pride. Back in high school he'd had mixed feelings about a romantic involvement, but so what? That was no big deal. It took some people decades to determine if they were right for each other. And he hadn't taken their relationship outside of school paper circles because she wouldn't have gotten along with his friends. That, too, was quite natural. It was time to let it all go; it was in the past, when they'd been teenagers, ill equipped to deal with the realities of life. Tomorrow she would talk to him. They *could* work it out. They *would* find a way. They had to....

She was jolted out of her reverie when the rest of them laughed at something. She smiled softly, and when the laughter died down, she asked, "So, what are we going to do about Mike?"

Joel shook his head. "Beats me."

"Put worms in his bed," Jill suggested.

"Jill!"

Selma finally butted in. "Folks, the only way we're going to get anywhere is by talking to him directly."

Beth looked at her apprehensively. "There's no other way?"

Selma's answer was firm. "There's no other way."

"Okay," Jill said brightly. "I nominate Joel."

"Now, wait a minute—"

"I'm afraid this will have to be a group effort," Selma interrupted him.

"There is strength in numbers," Beth added tentatively.

Jill sighed and got up to pace. "I suppose you're right. But how? What are we going to say? 'Mike, have you been fooling around with the books?' I don't exactly expect him to say, 'Well, gosh, you found out. You'd better take me away then.'"

"Maybe he won't admit it," Joel said practically, "but we might scare him into stopping—or looking for a new job, which may not be such a bad thing. Doing something is a whole lot better than doing nothing. It will force him to take action, though he may just take off."

"We're jumping the gun," Jill said. "Let's talk strategy."

And so they did—for another couple of hours. And as they talked, Beth had the eerie feeling that this one event was going to have a tremendous ripple effect on all their lives and that none of them would ever be quite the same—and certainly not as innocent—again.

CHAPTER THIRTEEN

SO THEY KNEW. He wasn't as smart as he'd thought, after all. They'd seen right through him. His time was up. He'd have to go now. But he was tired—so tired...

Maybe he'd just give himself up. It took far too much energy trying to cover one's tracks. He didn't want to look over his shoulder in fear anymore.

Then again, they'd surely press charges. He'd go to jail. Maybe he'd see his father there.....

His destiny was sealed. He wondered when it had all begun to go wrong for him. As a boy, he'd been determined to make it in the way that the privileged ones made it—hell, he'd even won a scholarship and come out on top in his business studies. But immediately upon coming into contact with the tweed-and-cashmere set, he'd felt unhealthy stirrings inside—stirrings of envy, jealousy.

Yes, he realized now, simple greed had been his downfall. He'd wanted too much too soon. He'd wanted to be like them, with their vacations in Florida and Aspen, their fancy cars, their fabulous clothes. Sure, he'd taken the straight road for a few years, but his nature had caught up with him. He'd wanted more than them—more than anybody had ever had!

Indeed, he'd bought so many things of late, he hardly knew what to do with it all. There were precious rugs, treasured pieces of art, one-of-a-kind furnishings. And now, he'd have to leave them behind while he lived out his destiny as a criminal on the run...a failure.

He rose from the flower bed outside Beth's window and looked around furtively before heading back toward his place. He had to prepare for departure. It was a good thing he'd investigated the noises he'd heard coming from Beth's house. If he hadn't eavesdropped tonight, he'd have been in deep trouble.

True to form, it had been Beth who'd been unable to believe he could have stooped so low. Poor Beth. She had a sweet nature, but she was doomed to be disappointed in life time and time again. Her boyfriend would prove to be her next big disappointment. Hadn't he already used her, taken advantage of her? And she had taken him back with barely a second thought.

He arrived at his front door and went in quietly. Upon turning on the lights, he walked over to the fireplace and stared at the painting that hung over the mantel. It was called *The Betrayal*, and it portrayed a group of children turning their backs on a lone little boy. One little girl—Jill, he thought—was laughing and flirting with another little boy....

Damn Jill, anyway. He'd wasted his hopes on someone who'd never had to struggle, never had to dream day in and day out because reality was just too hard to bear. She'd never understood him....

One little boy in the painting—Joel?—was standing between a couple of half-turned kids and the others, smiling stupidly. That was typical of Joel—always smiling, always laughing. Mind you, now he was involved with somewhat of a hard-luck case. No doubt he would soon get tired of the philanthropist routine. Yessir, he'd get real tired of the girl and stop laughing soon enough.

He stared at the painting a few minutes longer, and suddenly he was struck by a powerful urge to destroy it. Whatever had possessed him to purchase it in the first place? Those painted children meant nothing to him, nothing at all.

In a rage, he ran to the kitchen and retrieved a sharp paring knife from a drawer. Then he ran back into the living room and began to slash wildly at the canvas. With each cut, he became more and more determined to destroy the thing beyond all recognition.

Soon, he'd done it. Tattered shreds of color hung from the gilded frame, which was eerily tilted and swaying perilously. He looked at it for a long while, then he sunk to the floor, moaning, and began to sob wildly.

"ONE MORE TIME, Uncle Sam! One more time!"

Sam swung his niece Gillian around in the air so that she squealed with delight.

"Okay, children, time for brekkie." Evelyn flashed a grin at her brother. "Notice I used the plural."

"I chose to ignore it. I'm above responding to such cheap efforts to belittle me."

"I'm not belittling you," Evelyn said as she took Gillian's hand and started walking toward the house. They'd been relaxing in her backyard. She'd invited Sam to spend the day because she hadn't seen him in ages, besides which her husband, John, was on one of his frequent business trips and she craved adult company. It was Friday, a day on which Sam rarely considered doing anything but work, but he'd told her before he left for Orillia that he was going to make a long weekend out of it and not return to work on the last day of the week.

"On the contrary," Evelyn said, "it's nice to see you acting childlike for a change. You're far too serious and addicted to your work most of the time. I take it that Beth is responsible for this wonderful change...."

She opened the patio door and walked in. Gillian and Sam followed, the former immediately scurrying into the den to play with the state-of-the-art dolly Uncle Sam had brought her.

Sam sat down on a kitchen chair and stared at a fixed point on the wall. "I suppose she's had some effect on me."

Evelyn stopped retrieving items from the pantry and turned to look at him. "That isn't the most enthusiastic endorsement I've ever heard."

"We're having some problems. No, let me rephrase that. We're no longer together."

"Are you sure about that?" Evelyn asked carefully.

"Of course I'm sure. Why else would I have told you?"

"Well, it sounds to me as though you had a huge fight, threatened to leave, but didn't resolve anything one way or another."

"You guessed right."

"Amazing." Her voice was droll.

He quirked an eyebrow. "You aren't upset? I thought you wanted me to experience all the myriad joys of connubial bliss."

"I do, indeed. And I am upset—upset that neither of you can see the forest for the trees. Sam, you two have a tremendous love for each other—a love that's lasted for years. Now I can't speak for Beth, but I have noticed that *you* flip out every time you have a disagreement with her. Guess what, pal? Everybody fights. Welcome to reality, bro."

"You and John don't fight."

"Wanna make a bet?"

"What do you fight about? How many oranges to buy?"

Evelyn shook her head. "Sam, don't kid yourself. Solid relationships are difficult. They take hard work, understanding and lots of compromising. Believe me, this is far from a utopian existence. But if the good things outweigh the bad, you figure you're doing well."

"You make it sound thoroughly unappealing."

She laughed. "Do I? I don't mean to. Yeah, sometimes your 'better half' makes you so mad you think 'How on earth could I have married that person?' but at other times, you wonder how it is you got so lucky, how you met the perfect person for you in this world full of billions of people."

"That's all very touching, Ev, but I'm not at all sure that the good does outweigh the bad in our case."

"I would spend a lot more time thinking about that if I were you."

"Okay, okay. I promise I won't do anything rash." He wanted to change the topic; he was tired of thinking about Beth, tired of seeing her in his mind. And Evelyn's words *had* confused him. Maybe he had been too rash the previous evening. But she'd made him so damn mad! The bottom line was they couldn't escape their pasts, and they had very fundamental differences, which he'd begun to think were insurmountable.

Evelyn didn't say any more after that, and Sam got up to help her put bowls of fruit, yogurt and granola on the table. Unlike himself, Evelyn had always been devoted to eating healthily.

When Gillian came running in, Evelyn hugged her fiercely. "And then there's this little munchkin."

Inexplicably Sam found himself wondering what his and Beth's children would look like.

"I'm going to miss you when you go to school all day, pumpkin."

"I'm going to miss you, too, Mommy. But we can still play together when I come home."

"It's a deal. Come on, let's eat."

Soon, Sam was digging into a bowl of yogurt and fruit sprinkled with granola.

"This is terrific, Ev."

She quirked an eyebrow. "My brother telling me he likes yogurt? You've changed a whole lot more than you know, big bro. But thanks for the compliment. I made the granola myself."

"You're kidding!"

"Uh-uh." She shrugged. "Gillian's so independent now, I find I've got a lot more time on my hands. I don't have to watch her every single minute."

"You'll have even more time on your hands when Gillian starts Grade One."

"I know. That's why I've been thinking of going back to work."

"You have? That's great, Ev. Doing what?"

She sighed. "That is the sixty-four-thousand-dollar question. I'm not sure. I never did get my business degree...." Evelyn had followed in her brother's steps, enrolling in a business course in university, but she'd dropped out to work when she'd married John, and had given birth to Gillian shortly after that. "I'm not qualified for the kind of work I'd like to do."

"I've got an opening for a secretary."

"Yuck! Besides the fact that I'm all thumbs with a typewriter, I have a decidedly perfunctory telephone manner."

Sam grinned. "You do not. You're as sweet as pie to everyone. I've heard you. You even listen to those computerized sales pitches until the recording's over."

"I do not!"

"Do, too!"

"Do, too, Mommy!"

"See what you're doing?" Evelyn glared at Sam. "You're turning my own child against me. And you can forget the secretary idea. The very thought of you asking me to fetch your coffee makes me shiver."

"I don't have my secretary fetch my coffee."

"How very enlightened of you."

"So you don't have anything in mind?"

"'Fraid not. I'm smart, literate, assertive without being unattractively aggressive, and even a little bit witty, but the fact remains that no one in the business world will hire me for a responsible position without that degree."

"Why don't you go back to school?"

"I might have to, though I must say the thought of doing so turns my stomach."

Suddenly a vague idea popped into Sam's head, but he kept it to himself. There was no use getting her hopes up before he thought it through slowly and carefully. But it was very definitely a good idea...

A while later, he thanked her for breakfast, kissed her and Gillian and dashed home. He had a lot to figure out....

THEY KNOCKED for what seemed like an eternity to Beth, but there was no answer. It was midmorning and Mike should have been at home; on Fridays he usually wandered into his office around 11:00 a.m.

"Let me just take a peek through the front window," Joel said. "Maybe I'll be able to tell whether he's there or not." The entrance was actually at the side of the house, so they hadn't had the opportunity to see in. Joel went around to the front, and a few moments later, he returned, his mouth set in a grim line.

"What?" Beth asked apprehensively.

Joel's answer took the form of banging the door open—by running for it and bashing his left side into it, television detective style.

The others ambled in behind him, dazed by what they had just seen.

"Oh, my," Selma said weakly after a moment.

"I can think of a more appropriate reaction," Jill muttered.

The place was a mess. Obviously Mike had left in a hurry. A quick glance around told them that he'd taken only those things that were easily transportable—expensive knickknacks and various objets d'art. He'd left all his furniture and the large paintings.

"Looks like he left in a hurry," Beth said, not knowing what else to say. The others looked at her as if to say, "No kidding."

"I'm going to look for something that might explain this," Joel announced.

"Why don't we all do that—we can split up," suggested Jill.

"Good idea, Jill," Selma said. "I'll take the living and dining rooms."

"I'll take the bedroom," Jill said. "I've always had a morbid curiosity about what might be hidden in that den of iniquity."

"I'll take the basement," Joel said.

"That leaves the kitchen for me," concluded Beth.

"If someone finds something, shout," Joel suggested.

They all nodded, then went their separate ways.

"Oh, my God," cried Selma softly a moment later, and they all ran to the living room.

"Wow," Joel said, taking in a sharp breath at the sight of the brutally slashed painting over the mantel. "*The Betrayal* was a valuable painting. Why the hell would he have destroyed it like that?"

"It appears that Mike is even more troubled than we thought," Selma said grimly. "A senseless enraged act like this indicates very deep-seated, potentially dangerous hostilities. Let's work together to try to figure out what he's done and why. Maybe there are more clues around the house. Let's check."

Again they split up.

Beth saw it as soon as she entered the kitchen—a note on a sheet of white paper in the middle of the elegant ceramic-topped table. She opened her mouth to shout to the others, then clamped it shut. She wanted to read his words by herself first—to take a moment to be alone with Mike and his demons.

Slowly, with hesitant steps, she walked over to the table and lifted the note out from under an artfully sculpted acrylic napkin holder. She read it, dazed.

To Joel, Jill, Beth and Selma:

I guess it's all over now. Funny, somehow I thought it would never end. I thought I could keep going—like Spiderman. Remember when we used to collect Spiderman comics, Joel? Are college kids still into Spiderman? We always wanted to be like the webbed wonder. But he had Mary Jane, and I never could find her—Jill, you were the closest I could come.

To make a long story short, I heard you guys talking about me last night. Let me rephrase that: I heard you talking and then I eavesdropped. You were correct in your assumptions. It's way too late for regrets, but I am sorry I let you all down. Especially you, Beth. Of all of us, you're the one who was always the most hurt by betrayal. Your unflagging belief in the human spirit is admirable, my dear, but somewhat misguided.

As I said, I'm sorry I disappointed you, but that doesn't mean I'm into repentance. File charges, send the police after me if you must—I'll certainly understand—but I'll do everything I can to escape them. By the way, the spa never had any financial problems. That was all a smoke screen.

There doesn't seem to be that much more to say, guys. I've never been much for analyzing my actions and reactions, though I seem to have done an inordinate amount of that lately—and I'll leave you all to ruminate on why I did what I did. Telling you what I came up with would completely destroy my aura of mystery....

You were on the right track last night. Keep going, kids. I'm sure that after consuming a couple more bottles of Chianti, you'll come up with some more million-dollar theories. Oh, and don't think any of you could have "helped" me in any way. Except for one conversation with Beth in which I slipped some—but you were too touchingly naive to clue in, dear—I took great pains to cover my tracks.

I guess I'll sign off now. Maybe we'll meet again someday. It's been nice knowing you all. You're good people.

Mike

Beth sat perfectly still. How well he had known them, and how little they had known him. He'd called her "touchingly naive." She supposed she was. Yet she couldn't accept that her "unflagging belief in the human spirit" was misguided. That was a certain case of the fallen trying to drag everyone else down with him.

She felt sorry for him, in a way. He must have felt terribly alone to have risked so much and not confided in anyone. When had it all begun to change? she wondered.

It came to her then that perhaps they'd all started wanting too much at a certain point. Mike had taken things to an extreme, but maybe they had all been guilty of wanting more than they deserved.

As she stared out the window, Joel came into the kitchen, saw the note, picked it up and started reading. When he was done, he placed a hand on Beth's shoulder, and they remained that way for a long, long time.

"SO WHAT ARE WE going to do?" Jill asked practically after everyone had read the note and discussed its implications. Also, Joel had called Total Maintenance to confirm their monthly charge and it had been far less than the figure Mike had quoted to Sam.

"I guess we should press charges," Joel said, a trifle reluctantly.

"Do we have to?" asked Jill. "I mean, he said in the note the spa wasn't in trouble. That means we'll be able to turn it around, right?"

"We don't know how much damage Mike did," Beth answered. "So we really don't know if we'll be able to turn it around. Why are you so anxious to protect him, anyway? He made your life miserable."

Jill shrugged. "I don't know. I guess I feel sorry for him. And guilty, too. I know he said we couldn't have helped him, but dammit, I can't help but feel there's *something* we could have done to prevent this."

Selma walked over to the counter where Jill was standing, put her arm around her and said, "Jill, don't torture yourself like that. Mike didn't want our help, and we're not mind readers, so what were we supposed to do? As a fitness expert, you should know that you can't help anyone who doesn't want to help himself."

"I suppose you're right. But—"

"No buts about it." Selma turned to Joel. "Joel, I do agree with Jill that we probably shouldn't press charges. At least we should wait until we've assessed the damage."

Joel shrugged. "I guess we can delay pressing charges. Beth, are you in agreement?"

"I really have no idea what the right thing to do is," she said tiredly. "Whatever the majority decides is fine with me."

"Then it's settled," Selma said. "We'll have someone look at the books, and hopefully, we'll be in okay shape. Quite frankly, I think criminal prosecution would be too hard on everyone psychologically to justify. If we can recoup our losses, I'd like to see us all try to get on with our lives."

"I think Selma's right," Beth said. "I think prosecuting someone we once considered a trusted friend would be incredibly strange."

"Decision made," said Joel, getting up from his chair. "I'm going to go over to Mike's office and see what I can dig up."

Beth got up, too. "We can all go, I guess. But what do we do about all this stuff in here? You broke the door, Joel."

He just shrugged. "Somehow, I don't think Mike will care if anything gets stolen. And I don't know about you, but I don't feel particularly well equipped to deal with it just now. I do, however, have a great interest in finding out whether or not we're financially solvent. If you think it's necessary, shove something against the front door and leave through the back. I'll see you all later."

When he left, Selma said, "He's right, Beth. We shouldn't worry about this now. I've got appointments, anyway. We can meet again at the end of the day, if everyone thinks that's a good idea."

"Yeah, it is," Beth said absently. "Keep in touch."

"Okay. If you want to talk, pop into the office anytime."

"Right. See you later, Selma."

Shortly after Selma departed, Beth and Jill sat quietly at the table, just thinking. Then there was a soft knocking at the door. Beth and Jill exchanged a surprised look, and Jill went to the door.

At the kitchen table, Beth could peer down the hall to see who it was. And she was shocked to see that it was...Tom!

"Jill, we've got to talk," she heard him say in an assertive tone.

"I have nothing to say to you," she said stiffly.

"Then just listen," he begged. "I have to set things straight between us."

"You have set them straight," she told him. "You made it perfectly clear by your actions that you were not the least bit interested in me, only in whatever help I could give you with your story—even if it was Mike who handed it to you in the end."

Beth decided she'd heard enough and walked to the door.

"Uh, hi, Tom," she said, feeling more than a little awkward. "I know you two want to talk, so I'll leave you alone."

"No, don't go, Beth," Tom replied, holding his arm out to block the doorway. "I want you to hear this, too. I know you're Jill's closest friend, so I let you down, too. And if after hearing my story you think I deserve another chance, maybe you'll be able to convince Jill to give me one."

Beth didn't think that was likely, but since Tom wasn't about to let her go anywhere and she was emotionally drained from the events of the morning, she simply shrugged and led the way back to the kitchen.

"How did you know we were in here, anyway?" Jill asked suspiciously.

"I ran into Selma. She told me about Mike taking off. Puts my story in a whole new light, since he was my major source."

When they were seated around the table, and Jill and Beth were looking at him expectantly, Tom continued, "The fact is, I liked all you people—Jill, you know what we had was special, and so did I. I really enjoyed my time at the spa. But I had an obligation as a journalist to tell people about what I found out. I knew you'd all be disappointed in me for printing what I had to print, so I just cut off contact."

When he paused, Beth voiced her thoughts aloud. "That accounts for the strange vibes I was getting from you when you were at the spa."

Jill and Tom both looked at her. She shrugged and explained. "I couldn't put my finger on it. I guess I sensed that conflict in you. You can't be everybody's pal and stay objective, too."

He sighed. "Don't I know it. I guess it doesn't hurt to tell you this is my first job at a major publication. I aced my journalism school marks, then worked at a local paper for a couple of years—not Dad's, a bigger one—and then *City Life* hired me. I've only been with them a few months."

"No!" Jill said with great irony.

He made a face. "That obvious, huh? God, what I've been through. Jill, I couldn't bear to face you after the article came out, even though I did the right thing, professionally speaking. I knew you'd think I printed your confidences, but I couldn't betray Mike, either—he wanted to remain anonymous. He told me I could go ahead and print the information, that maybe it would force his partners—you guys—to work a little harder. And I had no reason to believe he wasn't a reliable source."

Beth fumed inwardly at that one.

"The nerve!" exclaimed Jill.

Tom turned away for a moment. "I didn't want to print that stuff, but I had to. If not wanting to hurt my friends makes me a bad journalist, then maybe I'm not meant to be a journalist. God knows the world needs people to print the truth, and not let friendships get in the way. I admire most of the reporters I know, but I'm not kidding anybody. I'm just not like the rest of them. You guys knew I was green right off the bat." He shook his head. "Heck, I shouldn't even have gotten involved with you in the first place, Jill. But I just couldn't help myself."

Jill opened her mouth to speak, but Tom cut her off. "Remember I told you that I wrote some short stories a few years back? Well, I'm working on one again—I think it's pretty good. I'm going to submit it to some magazines and see if anything comes of it."

"Oh, Tom," Jill said, her eyes misty all of a sudden. "That's wonderful."

"You forgive me, then?" he asked eagerly.

"Of course I forgive you. But it's you who should be forgiving me. I jumped to conclusions when I knew you had a good heart. You're so right about journalism, Tom. I admire reporters, too, but the fact is, it's a cold world out there. You've got to be real tough to get at the truth, and you're not tough at all—you're strong, but not tough. You've got to be a little bit mean to be tough.''

"Speaking of the truth," Beth interjected, "I think you're going to have to do some retracting, Tom. Much of what you said in your article was based on false information. Normally we do offer more services, more extras for the money—and as soon as we see some significant growth—which we were expecting to—we were going to do even more.''

"Fair enough," Tom said slowly. "But the fact is, you had decreased services by the time I'd arrived, so the comparative stuff wasn't wrong, per se. There's another hitch, too. If I print the piece now, I might have to reveal why my information about your difficulties was wrong. Do you want all that stuff disclosed?''

"I guess not," Beth said glumly.

"Tell you what. When you guys turn this place around—and I'm sure you will—I'll help you organize a massive media campaign, okay?''

"Of course it's okay," Jill said. "Oh, Tom, I knew you didn't have it in you to treat me badly. I'm so relieved.''

Tom smiled and grabbed Jill's hand. "I'm glad we've cleared all this up, finally. But speaking of someone who treated you badly, tell me more about what happened with Mike.''

Beth and Jill took turns filling him in, and when he'd heard the whole story, he just shook his head. "Hard to believe someone with all those advantages would just throw them away. And that he would betray his friends like that. And for what?''

The three conversed for a few more minutes, but then Beth realized that Jill and Tom probably needed some time alone. She made her excuses, then exited the bungalow of her former friend, and walked to her own house.

Once there, she flopped on the sofa and stared into space. She wanted to really think about the events of the past twelve or so hours, what it all meant and how she would be affected, but she didn't have the energy. And, she had something else on her mind.

She knew now that it was finally time to put the past behind her. Hadn't the whole episode with Mike proven that even so-called lifelong friends could betray people, that anyone could change? Sam, unlike Mike, had changed for the good. And Beth realized, in retrospect, that he'd tried to convince her of that in a relatively gentle manner. Yes, he could have presented his ideas with a little more sensitivity, but on the other hand, it must have killed an experienced businessman like him to have kept quiet about his suspicions for so long.

She knew now that she could trust Sam implicitly, believe in him with her whole heart and soul, place her utmost faith in him. What more could she ask for in a mate?

Somehow, she'd have to make it through the day's appointments. Then she'd drive like a madwoman to Toronto to tell him she'd made a dreadful mistake—

that she was sorry, and she'd never again accuse him of not acting in her best interests.

She only hoped that it wasn't too late, that she hadn't already lost him....

CHAPTER FOURTEEN

BETH DID make it through the day's appointments, and when she was finally able to leave, she heaved a huge sigh of relief.

The drive to Toronto had never seemed so long. But finally she was in the lobby of Sam's building, giving her name to the concierge. The man, whose old-world presence never failed to intimidate her, rang Sam, and Beth could have sworn there was an exceptionally long period of hesitation on the other end of the line. But after what seemed like ages, the concierge put the receiver down, nodded to Beth and said, "You may go up, madam."

She practically ran to the elevator and paced nervously once inside it, trying not to think about the cool reception she would very likely get from Sam. She formulated a plan: she simply wouldn't let him get a word in edgewise before she'd said her piece. He was sure to accept her apology, wasn't he? Everybody deserved a second chance....

At last she was at the door. She knocked softly. When the door opened she said "Hi" very quietly.

A questioning look had fluttered across his face the first moment he'd seen her, but he'd quickly donned an impassive expression.

"Hi," he returned.

A silent moment followed.

"Can I come in?" she asked tentatively.

He shrugged, then gestured with his arm. "Sure."

After he shut the door, he began walking into the living room. She followed.

"Sit down." He pointed to the couch and sat himself down in an occasional chair. "Would you like a drink?" he asked, none too enthusiastically, she thought. Had this been a huge mistake?

"No. No, thank you," she amended. Then, in a rush, she said, "Look, Sam, so much has happened since we last talked, I don't even know where to begin. Well, yes, I do. I want to tell you that you were right about Mike. Oh, Sam, it was awful. I can't believe we were all so stupid. He was stealing from us right under our noses, and we were all too blind to see it. We—"

"Wait a minute, Beth," Sam said. "You're going too fast. Please, start at the beginning."

So Beth told him the whole sordid tale, including the part Tom played, pacing all the while.

When she was through, Sam whistled. "Wow" was all he said.

Beth sank back onto the couch. "Yeah. Wow."

"So what are you going to do about it?"

"Well, Joel's spent the day trying to figure out what we lost. I think it will take longer than a day, though. We're hoping we still have enough to make a go of things. I think we caught on—" she looked abashed "—or rather, *you* caught on just when things were starting to heat up. Hopefully we'll have enough in the coffers to reinstate the services we cut back on—maybe even more. Then we'll embark on a media campaign to try to counteract the damage done by the article. Tom's promised to help. We've lost clients, but there's hope."

He shook his head. "What a story."

"Sam, I also wanted to say—" she swallowed "—I know I overreacted yesterday. My head's been spinning all day. I can't believe how stupid I've been." She looked straight at him. "All these years, it seems, *I've* put my faith in the wrong people."

Sam shook his head again, vigorously this time. "No, Beth. I've been doing some thinking, too. I didn't present my supposition too carefully yesterday. I knew even at the time I was saying it that I could have told you in a more tactful way. I think it was a way of testing you—I've been doing that since I met you again. I wanted to regain your trust and faith so badly, I went a little further than I should have to see if you trusted me, but of course you didn't. I expected too much too soon. I've always expected too much too soon. My sister pointed that out to me this morning, and if anyone knows me, she does. Why should you have trusted me over someone who had never hurt you in the past? It was definitely me who hung out with the wrong people."

She walked over to where he was sitting, put her hand on his shoulder and said, "You know, Sam, I had a long talk with Selma yesterday, and she really helped me gain some insight into our situation. We've been acting like a couple of high school kids." She took a deep breath. "We should either commit to each other or we should leave each other."

She snuck a glance at him, but he appeared to be waiting for her to continue. So she did. "I know now that part of the reason I've been acting that way is that I've been afraid of committing, of making myself vulnerable. But this thing with Mike had such a huge impact on me. I can't tell you how it feels to have someone you thought you could trust betray you that way. What you did in high school was kid's stuff in comparison. That kind of thing isn't behavior that sticks to a person. The important thing is, I know who to trust now. We don't have to play games anymore."

He pulled her down onto his lap. "Does that mean I'm forgiven?"

"It sure does," she said affectionately, wrapping her arms around his neck.

"Beth, I really need you to trust me, trust that I'm acting in your best interests. This up-and-down stuff has been driving me right up the wall."

"I'm sure going to try, Sam," she said. "But I'm not perfect. I'm going to make mistakes. If I slip, you can't flip out and leave me. You're guilty of having done that, same as me.''

"You're right," he said slowly. "I guess it was an ego thing with me. I couldn't bear to know you didn't trust me. Like I said, I expected too much, too soon."

"And like I said, I know who to trust now." She placed a soft kiss on his cheek.

"Does that mean you believe in my abilities and trust me to be honest and straightforward in all my business dealings as well as in my personal life?"

"Uh-huh," she answered, nuzzling his cheek, wondering vaguely why he'd mentioned business dealings.

The answer came with his response. "Does that mean you'll consider hiring me on as the new business manager of the spa, providing everyone else approves?"

"Wh-what?" Beth gasped.

"Beth, listen," he said excitedly. "It just came to me today after breakfast with my sister. It's ideal! I've been in such a rut with work and the rat race. I used to love my business, love the city, but I've known for a while now that I needed to make some pretty big changes in my life. Living and working at the spa would be perfect. If you liked the idea, I was going to suggest to Mike that I work alongside him, but doing it on my own is a lot more appealing. We'd be together—that would be the best part. Well, what do you think?''

"I...I," she sputtered, "I don't know what to say! It sounds too good to be true! Maybe you should take some more time to think about it, make sure that's what you really want to do. And what about your business? What would you do? Sell it?"

"I don't have to sell it. I have the perfect manager in mind—my sister, Evelyn!"

"Your sister, Evelyn?" Beth repeated, dazed.

"Yes! It's unbelievable! She's dying to get back into the work force, she's bright and wants to learn, and I can trust her implicitly." He hugged her. "You were so right. I've let the business consume me, and I know my folks wouldn't have wanted that. Still, I couldn't help but worry about what would happen. But with Evelyn at the helm, it'll be all in the family. I know I can count on her." He touched her chin. "Of course, if I do come to the spa, I'll want to live in your bungalow."

"Oh! Well, it's probably big enough for two, and I don't think the guests will particularly care if we live together without benefit of clergy...."

Beth's tone was light, but Sam's was dead serious when he said, "I have no intention of living together without benefit of clergy."

"Oh," she said again, very softly this time. She was afraid to jump to conclusions.

"Beth," he said tenderly, "will you marry me?"

"Oh, Sam," she cried, "I would love to marry you."

And then they kissed—a long, passionate kiss that left them both breathless. When Sam put his hands on her shoulders, pushed her off his lap gently and said, "Wait here just one minute," she was too dazed to reply. And when he came back with a small velvet case in his hand, she could only sit there speechless. Slowly he took a sparkling diamond ring out of the box and said quietly, "This was my mother's ring. I know she'd want the woman I love to wear it. Will you, Beth?"

"Oh, Sam, it's beautiful," she whispered. "I would be honored to wear it."

Slipping it on her finger, Sam said, "My mom didn't actually wear this ring until quite late in life. Until then, she wore a simple gold band and nothing else. My father didn't care about material things at all, but he'd always wanted her to have a proper engagement ring and a proper wedding ring. So when he finally had some money to spare, he splurged. My mother told him he was crazy, but I think she loved him even more after that, if that's possible. He could have bought anything with that money, but he bought those rings. You'll wear the wedding ring after we're properly married—if you want to, that is."

"Of course I want to. What a wonderful story," she said, fingering the emerald-cut solitaire diamond.

"I was going to give it to you yesterday, but, well, you know how things turned out...." His eyes glittered. "It's sure not going to end that way today!"

She laughed when he picked her up and carried her to his bedroom.

At the threshold, Beth said, "Aren't we supposed to do this *after* we're married?"

Sam shook his head and continued walking, dumping her unceremoniously on the bed. She stretched out languorously, and with a mock leer, he bent to unbutton her blouse. "The problem with most newly married couples," he said in a pseudoserious tone, "is that they haven't practiced doing things together. As far as I'm concerned, the more things you do with your spouse before marriage, the better prepared you'll be for the rigors of married life."

"And you wanted to practice carrying me over the threshold," she said innocently.

"And doing this," he said in a voice that wasn't at all mocking now. And with those words he proceeded to kiss her again—starting on the cheek and working his way down to her neck, then her shoulders, and then her arms and stomach as he slipped off her blouse. His lips were tender, yet insistent, and Beth could feel the desire behind the heartfelt kisses, as well as the deep love he had for her. It was as if each kiss was a promise of things to come and a tribute to their feelings for each other. Beth realized that their newfound mutual trust and their pledges to each other would add yet another dimension to their lovemaking. They were inextricably bonded now—in every way. She was utterly and blissfully content.

When his loving trail turned upward again and reached her breasts, she placed her hands on either side of his head and lifted it gently. Looking into his eyes, she said, "I've never loved anyone as much as I love you. I love you so much it hurts."

"Don't be afraid of that love, darling, please," he whispered, stroking her arms. "I swear I'd never do anything to hurt you. I cherish you with all my heart."

"I know." Her eyes filled, and she said, "I never knew I could be this happy."

"We've only just begun," he said, continuing his loving exploration, arousing her so much that she soon joined in. When she had reached the peak of her desire, they united in a loving meeting of body, heart and soul that left each of them feeling as if they'd reached paradise.

Indeed, they had.

CHAPTER FIFTEEN

THE REST OF THE SUMMER, and the fall, floated by in a golden haze. Beth had never felt so surrounded by love and affection. In August, Jill, Selma and Joel hosted a "Jack-and-Jill" shower for her and Sam, and it was there that the gang finally got to spend time with Nora, Joel's companion. They had met her briefly when Joel had brought her to the spa to show her around, but because she'd wanted things to progress slowly, Joel hadn't pushed her to mix with his friends. Now she was feeling more comfortable about the relationship and was glad to get the chance to talk to his partners. The shy, gentle woman stole their hearts instantly.

It was a real treat for them to see jokester Joel being so tender with a woman and so quiet himself! They played off each other beautifully. Beth could tell by the combination of wisdom and weariness in Nora's face that she had seen some hard times, but she, too, obviously benefited from the romance. When she smiled at Joel, her whole face lit up, and her eyes reflected a kind of wonder and thankfulness that this very special man could love her and treasure her the way he did.

Beth was also getting to know Sam's sister, Evelyn, and her husband, John. They were warm, fun-loving people, and Beth was coming to consider them good friends. At the shower that day, Beth felt a special warmth envelop her, and she thought that with a man like Sam and good friends like these loving and honoring her for the rest of her life, she couldn't possibly lose....

September 20, the day of the wedding, proved to be beautiful. The sky was a gorgeous shade of blue, the grass was lush and green, the birds were chirping and the waves off the lake lapped quietly against the sandy shoreline. Beth had fantasized about an outdoor wedding for years, and since Sam had moved in with her in the middle of August, holding the wedding on the spa grounds had become practical as well as desirable. Like everything else these days, it was almost too good to be true!

It was 11:00 a.m., and Beth was finally dressed in her lovely cotton sateen gown, complete with a daisy garland headpiece. Yvonne, the spa's ace cosmetician, was putting the final touches on the bride's makeup. Barb was Beth's maid of honor, and she was chatting merrily with Beth's bridesmaids—Jill, Selma and Evelyn. All four women looked equally wonderful in pale peach-toned dresses that were styled similarly to Beth's. And Evelyn's daughter Gillian, the flower girl, looked good enough to eat, dressed in a frilly peach confection and carrying a small basket of fragrant flower petals.

As Beth quietly studied the people around her, she noted that Barb looked particularly radiant. Beth was extremely proud of her sister. She'd come through a very difficult experience with flying colors. The few weeks she'd spent moping around seemed inconsequential now. She'd moved into a lovely apartment that she'd found with Beth's help and had even looked into taking some science courses at the University of Toronto so she could apply to dental school the following year. Beth wondered if in times of adversity, she'd reveal half the strength her sister had during that difficult period. Her admiration for Barb was boundless, and she called her sister over and told her so. Barb hugged her gratefully—earning a scolding from Yvonne—and said she couldn't have done it without her example and support. The two had never been closer.

Mrs. Finlayson announced her arrival at Beth's house with a cry of delight. "Oh, darling, you look *splendid.*" She promptly misted up and wiped her eyes. "Look, Albert, isn't she the most beautiful bride you've ever seen?"

"She sure is," Albert, standing slightly behind his wife, pronounced. Beth thought he'd never sounded so sure of anything in his life.

"And the setup at the shore—well, darling, it all looks fabulous."

"Thanks, Mom," Beth said, truly touched.

Mrs. Finlayson turned her attention to the other women. "Evelyn, lovely to see you again. Barb, you're a vision! Selma and Jill, you look marvelous. You girls will have to try this sometime, hmm?''

Jill and Selma glanced at each other, and then Jill said with a perfectly straight face, ''Selma's not really my type, Mrs. Finlayson.''

Beth hooted, and her mother wagged a finger at Jill. ''Oh, you were always a kidder, Jill! Some young man will be lucky to have you!''

Just then, Sam came through the door and Mrs. Finlayson cried, ''Sam, you're not supposed to see the bride yet!''

''Mother, believe me,'' Beth piped up, ''we've done lots of things we weren't supposed to do yet.'' She stared at her husband-to-be appreciatively. He was nervously fingering his bow tie. Beth thought she'd never seen a more impressive-looking groom in her entire life.

''Hi, handsome,'' she said softly.

''Hi, beautiful,'' he returned, glancing up and down the length of her body and whistling. ''You are truly beautiful,'' he announced. ''I'm a very lucky man.''

She scooped up her skirt, ran over to him and gave him a great big bear hug, at which her mother exclaimed, ''Beth, dear, your dress will get all wrinkled!''

''I don't care, Mother. This day is for Sam and me to celebrate our love with those near and dear to us, and I'm going to hug as many people as I can.'' On cue, Barb, Evelyn, Selma and Jill stood, and each hugged Beth tightly.

"Well, everyone," Sam said when all the hugging was done, "I came in to tell you all we're ready to start. If you'll come with me, we'll line up outside and get this show on the road."

Everyone began shuffling out, and Beth's mother pulled her back.

"What is it, Mom?"

Mrs. Finlayson toyed with a tissue, lowered her eyes and said, "Darling, I just wanted to tell you something..."

"You're not going to tell me about the birds and the bees, are you?" Beth said jokingly.

Her mother laughed nervously. "Heavens, no." She lowered her eyes again. "I'm sure you could teach me a few things in that department. Darling, I just want you to know that...I know I haven't always been— supportive of you, and I'm going to try to be better. You're an adult, and you're perfectly capable of making your own decisions, and they certainly don't always have to be the ones I would make—"

"Mom, stop. That's wonderful to hear. It means a lot to me—really. But our problems weren't all your fault. I've always expected human beings to act superhuman—Sam taught me that. You're only human, after all. You have a right to be imperfect."

"Thank goodness for that," Mrs. Finlayson stated, wiping tears from her cheeks. "But the fact is, I've been making your life miserable with my constant disapproval and selfishness. We would have had such a wonderful relationship if I had only forced myself to let you go years ago, trusted you to make decisions that were right for you. The experience with Barb taught me a valuable lesson. I love you both equally, but I always thought she'd chosen the 'right' path. There is no right path. I know that now. What's right for one person may be completely wrong for another. Besides, the world has changed so very much, and I suppose I really haven't kept up with all the changes...."

Beth looked at her mother curiously. "Mom, I'm surprised. You've never spoken like this before."

"Well, I've been having some lengthy telephone conversations with Selma...."

Now Beth really was shocked. "Really? She never told me."

Mrs. Finlayson waved a hand. "Oh, well, client confidentiality, I suppose. She's a lovely woman and very clever."

"Yes, she is. And so are you." Beth held out her arm. "Come on, Mom. Let's get the ball rolling so that Sam and I can get to work on creating a third generation of Finlayson women."

"Oh, darling, I'd love a granddaughter." She sighed. "It's hard being a parent, Beth."

"I can't wait to find out just how hard, Mom...."

"SHE'S LOVELY, isn't she?" Nora whispered to Joel when Beth came out of the bungalow arm in arm with her mother. Joel, an usher, was lining up with the rest in the wedding party, and Nora was getting ready to dash off to her seat. "I'd better go." She placed a quick kiss on his cheek. "Good luck, darling."

She turned to leave, but Joel grabbed her arm. She turned and looked at him questioningly. "What?"

Joel's eyes were bright. "What do you say we try this someday?"

Nora just stared at him, then a huge grin broke out on her face and she cried, "Oh, yes, Joel, yes!"

Applause and whistles erupted in the small crowd surrounding them, and when the noise had died down, Jill said, "Uh, I have a little announcement to make, too, folks—it seems to be the right time." She grabbed on to Tom's hand—he'd been waiting with her, also—and said tremulously, "Tom is moving to Orillia! He's decided to work on his fiction writing full-time, and maybe get a part-time job in town. We're going to be living together."

More hoopla, and then the sound of a single flute was heard. Everyone moved quietly into their places. In the mild confusion, Bob, Sam's best man, bumped into Selma. "Oh, Selma," he said contritely, "I'm awfully sorry." Their eyes met, and his softened. "I certainly wouldn't want to muss up such a beautiful bridesmaid."

"Why, thank you, Bob. You look very handsome yourself." Her eyes lowered. "Well, I guess it's time to do our thing. We'll talk after the ceremony."

"We certainly will, Selma. We certainly will...."

ONCE SHE AND SAM were alone—they would be leaving for Quebec City in the morning—Beth kicked off her shoes and sank onto the couch.

"It was a beautiful wedding, wasn't it?" she said, sighing dreamily.

"It certainly was—complete with a beautiful bride," her new husband replied, throwing his jacket off, then walking over to her to plant a kiss on her forehead.

As he walked to the kitchen to get a glass of water, Beth mused aloud, "There were virtually no hitches. That's truly incredible."

"Unless you consider some of Jane's unidentifiable dishes hitches," he called.

Beth laughed. "Well, yes, there were a few of those, but at least she did the basics well. The steak tartare was exceptional, and the pasta with smoked salmon made my mouth water just looking at it. I wish I'd had time to eat some of it...."

"And then there was the anonymous good-luck telegram," Sam reminded her, coming back into the living room with two glasses of water. "Not a hitch, exactly—just a little strange."

Beth looked at him. "You think it was from Mike, don't you?"

"What do you think?"

"The same as you." She leaned back. "I wonder where he is, what he's been doing."

"I get the feeling he's not far from here," Sam said, putting the glasses down on the new coffee table and settling on the couch beside Beth. "He seems to be keeping close tabs on us."

"Sam, do you think he would ever come back? After all, there wasn't too much financial damage done...."

"Don't even think about Mike, darling. And if he does come back into our lives one day in the future, I would certainly hope we would all have the good sense not to become professionally involved with him ever again."

She sighed. "Of course you're right. I'm such a sucker."

Sam nuzzled her neck. "Not a sucker—just an incurable optimist and a sloppy romantic underneath that sophisticated professional veneer. You never fooled me a bit."

"I didn't, did I?"

"Oh, I almost forgot. I have a present for you...."

"Sam! I thought we agreed no gifts."

"It isn't anything big. In fact, I think I stuffed it in my jacket pocket." He retrieved his jacket from where he'd tossed it and rummaged in his pockets. "Got it! Close your eyes, honey."

"Okay, they're closed. Sam, you really didn't have to—hey, what the heck is this?"

"Open your eyes."

She did, and a moment later, squealed delightedly. In her hand was a small jar of—mock mustard!

"Oh, Sam," she said, "did you develop this just for me? It must have cost you a fortune!"

"Relax," he said, sitting back down beside her, "We made thousands of them. Evelyn and I did some research—she's everything I could have hoped for in a manager—and it turns out that a whole lot of people are allergic to mustard. What do you think?"

Eagerly she opened the jar, and took a bit on the tip of her baby finger. After tasting it, she pronounced, "Sam, it's *fabulous!* I'm in mustard heaven! Darling, that was so sweet of you." She kissed his cheek. "I'm pretty lucky to have such a thoughtful and creative husband." She snuggled up to him.

"Well, I'm certainly glad you're so appreciative," he said, gathering her in his arms.

"Indeed?" she asked, and was answered with a kiss—a wonderful kiss that sealed their new identities as husband and wife. When their lips separated, finally, Sam scooped his bride into his arms and carried her off to the bedroom.

She giggled. "I seem to recall we did this once before."

"Ahh, yes. Well, like I said, practice makes perfect. And I have no doubt that this night will be absolutely perfect, as will all other nights to come...."

IT WAS NICE to be back, although he had to take great care that no one saw him. What a brilliant stroke that had been: returning to the spa grounds when the authorities his ex-partners had, in every likelihood, sent after him, were probably combing the country for him. But he'd had little choice. He was far too tired to run. He much preferred to live out his destiny in familiar surroundings, and if they caught up with him sooner or later, well, so be it. Everyone had to go sometime....

Beth's wedding had been lovely, if a little too maudlin and middle-class for his taste. Poor, naive Beth. She persisted in denying the facts: that more often than not, dreams died before they were even born, happiness was illusory and people were dark and deceptive under their pleasant exteriors. Soon enough, hubby would grow tired of her and wander, and she'd be saddled with the kids and bored out of her mind. Maybe then she'd know what it meant to reach the end of one's rope, as he had....

But despite his mixed feelings toward his former partners, today he felt a remarkable kinship with them—so much so that he'd even sent a message to the newlyweds. He hoped they knew it was from him. A kind of peace had settled over him, at last. There was nothing more for him to do, no new position to aspire to, nothing else to acquire.

He wondered vaguely what would happen to the others—to Jill and Tom, Joel and Nora, and Selma. He found it hard to believe that he'd ever wanted Jill. When he looked at her now he felt only a dim recognition and a mild affection. He was actually happy that she'd found someone she could live out the rest of her life with.

Joel, too, deserved happiness. He was an all-right guy. He just needed some life experience. Nora would give him that.

And he had few worries about Selma. Smart woman, she, for a psychologist. He hoped that in time, she'd find someone to love, someone worthy of her.

He was tired now—so tired, and his stomach ached. He couldn't remember when he'd last eaten, and he was too drained of energy to worry about it.

Suddenly he knew exactly what it was he had to do. Slowly and methodically, as if measuring every step, he wandered toward the woods and didn't stop until he had reached a patch of moss next to a babbling brook. He stared at the luxurious-looking bed of grass for a few moments, then tentatively sank onto it.

This place was the only real home he'd ever known, after all. Here he could be comfortable for all eternity. Expelling a breath, he shut his eyes. He felt a kind of dizziness overcome him, and then he saw, in his mind's eye, a series of exploding graphic images, in all colors of the rainbow and all the patterns in the universe.

This was what he'd been waiting for. His time had come. He felt his lips curve up in a smile.

Destiny.

EPILOGUE

"SO EVERYTHING IS GOING great guns. That's terrific. I'm really happy for you guys," Bob commented as he toured the grounds of the spa with Beth and Sam in late November.

"Mmm." Beth looked away suddenly, as if distracted.

Sam put his arm around her. "Thinking of Mike?" he asked softly.

"Uh-huh." She held on tightly to Sam. "Sometimes I can't believe he's gone. It was all so surreal."

"I was real sorry to hear about your friend, Beth," Bob said. He shook his head. "What a way to go. It was almost as if he just let himself die."

"He was a very troubled man," Sam said simply. "He seemed to have lost it in the end—he wasn't in his right mind. According to the coroner, he hadn't eaten in days before he died."

"I believe he repented at the end," Beth said quietly, "and he's in a better place now, where there's no dishonesty and no crime—only good things and lots of love."

"Some people believe in a heaven on earth," Sam commented.

Beth looked up at him. "Are you one of them?" she asked.

He pulled her even closer to him and kissed the top of her head. "I sure am. I have a beautiful and loving wife, terrific friends, a great job and a lovely home. What more could a guy want?"

"Stop it, you guys! You're making me blush. I'm going to have to change the subject."

Sam laughed. "So change it."

"I can't believe what you two have done with the place. It's amazing. And in so little time—just a few months."

Beth crooked her arm through her husband's. "Thanks to Sam. You'll learn all about how he did it in the December issue of *Financial Post*...."

"They're doing an article on you? Fantastic!"

"Tom had a contact there. That helped a lot," Sam said modestly. "And I suppose I have a pretty good reputation in the business world...."

"That's the understatement of the year!" Bob quipped.

"Well, however it came about, it's a real blessing for us. Think about who reads the *Post*—frenzied businessmen and businesswomen, people like the person I used to be. Who knows? We could be overrun."

"We're really doing some great things," Beth added excitedly, "things no other spas are doing—like special honeymoon packages and the cooking school. Oh—did Sam tell you about the new line of low-calorie dressings he developed in collaboration with

Jane? It was his last big project at the Condiment Company. We're selling them right here at the spa. And the preliminary numbers look really good. Oh, Bob, you have to see the new stables. You'll love Greg, the head of the horseback riding program—"

"Whoa! Information overload. I promise I'll see it all later. Right now I have to go get Selma or we'll be late for the play."

"At the opera house?" Sam asked.

"Uh-huh."

"Orillia growing on you, my friend?"

"Let's just say the town holds some very special charms."

"Our resident psychologist is obviously one of them."

"Most definitely."

"Keep our honeymoon package in mind, Bob," Beth said mischievously. "Joel and Nora loved it."

"You guys!" Bob said in mock exasperation. "Your wedding was like an old movie—all those news flashes! This is real life we're talking about. Give me a break!" He smiled sheepishly. "But now that we're on the subject, tell me how you like living in Orillia, Sam."

Sam's hold on his wife tightened. "I've never been happier."

"That's good to hear. I'll keep it in mind just in case any friends of mine feel the urge to settle down here...." He smiled and winked at Beth but turned back to Sam. "And you're feeling good—eating right, exercising? You're not getting all caught up in the business again, are you?"

Sam held up a hand. "Scout's honor. Evelyn's doing a great job with the mustard business—I hardly think about that now. I've even made her a full partner, so she's really motivated to see the business do well and grow even more. As for my life here—" he smiled at his wife "—well, it's just about perfect. I love the challenge of running the place, but there are far too many health professionals around me to risk becoming obsessed! And Beth and I have been especially careful not to overexert ourselves since—" he looked at Beth questioningly and she nodded shyly "—Beth became pregnant."

"Pregnant!" Bob yelped. "Omigosh! Congratulations! That's wonderful news!"

After lots of hugging and kissing, Bob said, "You guys make a terrific team."

Sam looked at his wife, his eyes shining, and she gazed back adoringly at him. "We sure do," he said softly. "And I have you to thank for everything, buddy. You sent me to Couchiching Spa in the first place."

Bob grinned and put his arms around two of the few people he truly admired. "Hey, what are friends for?"

HARLEQUIN®
OFFICIAL SWEEPSTAKES
RULES

NO PURCHASE NECESSARY

1. To enter, complete an Official Entry Form or 3"× 5" index card by hand-printing, in plain block letters, your complete name, address, phone number and age, and mailing it to: Harlequin Fashion A Whole New You Sweepstakes, P.O. Box 9056, Buffalo, NY 14269-9056.

   No responsibility is assumed for lost, late or misdirected mail. Entries must be sent separately with first class postage affixed, and be received no later than December 31, 1991 for eligibility.

2. Winners will be selected by D.L. Blair, Inc., an independent judging organization whose decisions are final, in random drawings to be held on January 30, 1992 in Blair, NE at 10:00 a.m. from among all eligible entries received.

3. The prizes to be awarded and their approximate retail values are as follows: Grand Prize — A brand-new Mercury Sable LS plus a trip for two (2) to Paris, including round-trip air transportation, six (6) nights hotel accommodation, a $1,400 meal/spending money stipend and $2,000 cash toward a new fashion wardrobe (approximate value: $28,000) or $15,000 cash; two (2) Second Prizes — A trip to Paris, including round-trip air transportation, six (6) nights hotel accommodation, a $1,400 meal/spending money stipend and $2,000 cash toward a new fashion wardrobe (approximate value: $11,000) or $5,000 cash; three (3) Third Prizes — $2,000 cash toward a new fashion wardrobe. All prizes are valued in U.S. currency. Travel award air transportation is from the commercial airport- nearest winner's home. Travel is subject to space and accommodation availability, and must be completed by June 30, 1993. Sweepstakes offer is open to residents of the U.S. and Canada who are 21 years of age or older as of December 31, 1991, except residents of Puerto Rico, employees and immediate family members of Torstar Corp., its affiliates, subsidiaries, and all agencies, entities and persons connected with the use, marketing, or conduct of this sweepstakes. All federal, state, provincial, municipal and local laws apply. Offer void wherever prohibited by law. Taxes and/or duties, applicable registration and licensing fees, are the sole responsibility of the winners. Any litigation within the province of Quebec respecting the conduct and awarding of a prize may be submitted to the Régie des loteries et courses du Québec. All prizes will be awarded; winners will be notified by mail. No substitution of prizes is permitted.

4. Potential winners must sign and return any required Affidavit of Eligibility/Release of Liability within 30 days of notification. In the event of noncompliance within this time period, the prize may be awarded to an alternate winner. Any prize or prize notification returned as undeliverable may result in the awarding of that prize to an alternate winner. By acceptance of their prize, winners consent to use of their names, photographs or their likenesses for purposes of advertising, trade and promotion on behalf of Torstar Corp. without further compensation. Canadian winners must correctly answer a time-limited arithmetical question in order to be awarded a prize.

5. For a list of winners (available after 3/31/92), send a separate stamped, self-addressed envelope to: Harlequin Fashion A Whole New You Sweepstakes, P.O. Box 4694, Blair, NE 68009.

PREMIUM OFFER TERMS

To receive your gift, complete the Offer Certificate according to directions. Be certain to enclose the required number of "Fashion A Whole New You" proofs of product purchase (which are found on the last page of every specially marked "Fashion A Whole New You" Harlequin or Silhouette romance novel). Requests must be received no later than December 31, 1991. Limit: four (4) gifts per name, family, group, organization or address. Items depicted are for illustrative purposes only and may not be exactly as shown. Please allow 6 to 8 weeks for receipt of order. Offer good while quantities of gifts last. In the event an ordered gift is no longer available, you will receive a free, previously unpublished Harlequin or Silhouette book for every proof of purchase you have submitted with your request, plus a refund of the postage and handling charge you have included. Offer good in the U.S. and Canada only.

HQFW · SWPR

HARLEQUIN® OFFICIAL SWEEPSTAKES ENTRY FORM

4-FWHSS-2

Complete and return this Entry Form immediately – the more entries you submit, the better your chances of winning!

- Entries must be received by **December 31, 1991.**
- A Random draw will take place on **January 30, 1992.**
- No purchase necessary.

Yes, I want to win a FASHION A WHOLE NEW YOU Classic and Romantic prize from Harlequin:

Name _____ Telephone _____ Age _____

Address _____

City _____ State _____ Zip _____

Return Entries to: **Harlequin FASHION A WHOLE NEW YOU,**
P.O. Box 9056, Buffalo, NY 14269-9056   © 1991 Harlequin Enterprises Limited

PREMIUM OFFER

To receive your free gift, send us the required number of proofs-of-purchase from any specially marked FASHION A WHOLE NEW YOU Harlequin or Silhouette Book with the Offer Certificate properly completed, plus a check or money order (do not send cash) to cover postage and handling payable to Harlequin FASHION A WHOLE NEW YOU Offer. We will send you the specified gift.

OFFER CERTIFICATE

Item	A. ROMANTIC COLLECTOR'S DOLL	B. CLASSIC PICTURE FRAME
	(Suggested Retail Price $60.00)	(Suggested Retail Price $25.00)
# of proofs-of-purchase	18	12
Postage and Handling	$3.50	$2.95
Check one	☐	☐

Name _____

Address _____

City _____ State _____ Zip _____

Mail this certificate, designated number of proofs-of-purchase and check or money order for postage and handling to: **Harlequin FASHION A WHOLE NEW YOU Gift Offer,** P.O. Box 9057, Buffalo, NY 14269-9057. Requests must be received by December 31, 1991.

ONE PROOF-OF-PURCHASE

4-FWHSP-2

To collect your fabulous free gift you must include the necessary number of proofs-of-purchase with a properly completed Offer Certificate.

© 1991 Harlequin Enterprises Limited

See previous page for details.